NIGHTS ON FIRE

A NIGHTS ON FIRE NOVEL

BY GARY CLIFTON

"Balls, balls, balls," shrieked Dallas Police narcotics cop Muscles Malloy. Then, he morphed into the exact imitation of an electronic siren—for good reason. A midget was trying to bite off his balls.

The flesh was charred black, hair burned away, probably nude before the fire. The remnants of electrical wire circling the remains of wrists and ankles. She had apparently been spread-eagled face down, with each limb tied with the electrical cord to a leg of the bed. Flammable liquid had been poured over her.

...bodies, whole or in various portions, lay on wheeled, stainless-steel carts tumble-parked in every open space in the morgue. Each cadaver, face up and naked, bore a tan identification tag wired to a toe. If the body had no toes, the tag would have been wired to any appendage available.

Juan Morales stared at me wordlessly, a carbon copy of the photo I was carrying in my shirt pocket. Time to walk softly. "What do you want, cop?" In view of reinforcements available to him at arm's length, I withheld any sharp remarks. "I want to talk to you, Juan," I said, "out here in private." He looked me over from head to toe without show of fear and then pointed his bearded chin toward my car. "You got AC in that beat-up mu'fucker?" "Yeah," I said and walked toward the Chevrolet.

...flexible enough to seek solace in the widely separated cultures of biker-land and the Dallas lesbian community. She wouldn't be easy to trace because nobody would care enough to ask where she had gone, except me.

I got my handcuffs out of my belt and began grappling for a wrist. Hooper spat, "That's my wrist, Kobok, dammit!" The suspect was shrieking, "Make the devil turn m

CHAPTER 1: THE LAW OF THE GIVE-A-DAMN FACTOR

The degree of cynicism, pessimism, general distrust of mankind, and a negative view of the future, increases in direct proportion to the number of years a cop works on the streets.

"Balls, balls, balls," shrieked Dallas Police narcotics cop Muscles Malloy. Then, he morphed into the exact imitation of an electronic siren—for good reason. A midget was trying to bite off his balls.

July, 1985. It basically all started that blazing Dallas summer when the midget tried to de-ball Muscles Malloy. Funny thing, the little guy wasn't mad at Muscles Malloy in particular, just doing his job. Really, there aren't too many reasons for a midget to bite off a man's balls, anyway.

From the infliction of this ultimate act of indignity would erupt a sordid tale of debauchery, cruelty, deception, and brutal murder so bizarre, the case almost hit the dead file before I got enough brain around it to put the horrible puzzle into one piece. Even then I never came close to understanding.

I guess I'd better tell the whole story from the get-go, just as I did to Internal Affairs. Well, pretty much the same.

I'm Stephen Kobok. I'd been a Special Agent, Bureau of Alcohol, Tobacco, and Firearms, U. S. Treasury Department for fourteen years at the time. Eliot Ness had held down the same job and all he ever seemed to do was machine gun bad guys and never, ever, write a report. For some of us, things were a tad more complex—sort of like struggling through the Valley of the Shadow of Death naked and blindfolded, dragging a dead mule behind on a rope.

I didn't fit the clean-cut standards of most of the other

agents. I must have slipped in the back door during a year when they were having trouble making their quota. I never felt quite at home amidst the gaggle of Ivy League types on the payroll.

I had gotten into a minor shooting scrape in Kansas City five years before and had been transferred forthwith to Dallas. In those days, things were different. One more screw-up and I was a gimme for the dope detail in Miami.

In the mid-eighties, the cops, particularly the Feds, were in a shooting war with dope traffickers who thought Miami was a free port of entry. We weren't winning, and nothing appeared likely to improve. Violence is easier to handle when you are young, quick, eager, convinced of immortality. I was none of the above. We had lost too many young men and women down there to toss an aging stumblebum like yours truly into the arena.

The Summer had been inordinately long, hot, and unlucky. I had seen a half dozen prime, kick- ass felony investigations dissolve for one reason or another. The rule was simple: no production, off to the war zone. To avoid taking up residence in Miami or someplace with no zip code, I needed to hit the jackpot on a decent case.

The agency had what they called the "No Potential" rule. No Potential was back stab code for "failure to find out who-dunnit." Enough files stamped with the red "no potential" kiss of death stamp and back then an agent would find himself in a place with no zip code…or Miami. Boy, I needed a ground rule single.

Quit, you say. Hey, I was halfway to fifty when I could retire at half pay. That meant finding another job, but not doing what we did.

My squad supervisor, H. D. "Howdy Doody" James was certifiably nuts. In later years he was confined to the Longview State Hospital where he resided, comfortably in a rubber room. But until then, he was my chief tormentor.

I was 36, stood six feet or so, was not the badass some of the boys in the squad room tried to be, and hadn't eaten right in years. Truthfully, I was prone to drink supper far more often that Dr. Feelgood would have preferred. Somebody far wiser than me had once said "A man who doesn't drink has no idea how long the next day can be."

The Feds have agents in several agencies—"several" to preclude the possibility of a national police force. Most, including the ranks of ATF, were represented by a sort of cookie cutter type—clean cut, pretty hair. But we had a special outfit where being shiny was not necessary, the Arson and Bomb Squad. Grubby, bleary eyed guys who spent too much time studying the bottom of a bottle, had no need to look first rate. Digging in burned dreams, shattered hopes, and mangled bodies was an invisible science for which there were no volunteers.

The Muscles Malloy disaster, as it came to be known, developed from an investigation with which he had nearly zero connection.

A good friend, Jackson "Three Hairs" Dorsen, an investigator in the Dallas Police Intelligence Unit asked me for help. He didn't need ATF help in trapping a no-good mope like Willie "Slow Bill" Harris, one of the sorriest mopes ever hatched. Three Hairs needed cash—buy money. The cops had personnel and brains, the Feds had cash. Contrary to the false image of federal-local animosity ginned up by TV cop shows, we had plenty of thugs around to keep everyone supplied and we worked together just fine.

Dorsen had been awarded the nickname "Three Hairs" via the marvelously accurate and imaginative cop squad room banter system. Although he constantly wore a Dallas Cowboy "gimme" cap, it was rumored that he was down to three head hairs, each forty feet long, which he carefully wound 'round and 'round to provide some semblance of hair cover beneath the cap. True? Who knew, but it made a hell of a story over an after-work beer.

Slow Bill Harris operated shot club on Jeffries, off Second Avenue, within eyesight of the Cotton Bowl. A shot club is one of many in Dallas which operates after hours as an unlicensed tavern out of a private residence. The Dallas Police Department, constantly swamped with violence and mayhem, simply didn't have the manpower to snuff every such operation.

Slow Bill pimped whores out of his establishment and

offered a full gambling menu, complete with a pool table converted to shoot craps. He was also known to provide hitters for contract killings and was a suspect in the murders of two rival pimps. He was suspected of, but not charged with, murdering one of his girls with a poker the year before.

Dorsen's snitch, "Grabber" something or other, took my 100 bucks, swore he could buy heroin from Slow, and disappeared into the night. Dorsen and I sat on the darkened street, waiting—hoping to hell, really—Grabber and my hundred were not several blocks away, fleeing at speed.

Grabber slid into the rear seat waving a half pint of Johnny Walker Red like he'd won the lottery.

"New kinda heroin?" asked Three Hairs.

"Naw, mu'fucker said he didn't have no skagg, man. I bought this instead. Sucker also tried to sell me a chrome plated .32, but y'all didn't gimme whut I needed to buy it."

"Tell me this booze didn't cost a hundred, dude," I said back over the seat.

"Naw, man. Cost ten." He lied. The going price was five. Hell, it was 1985.

"Keep the rest, for services rendered," I said. What the hey, nobody else in the federal government gets their whitey tighty's in a wad about handing out taxpayer dollars.

"Christ," declared Dorsen, frustrated.

"Look, a half pint of illegally peddled booze at 2:57 A. M. is probable cause just as good as a kilo of California Brown. Slow will probably still have that shiny .32 pistol. That's an ex-con in possession, another felony. We can get a warrant, come back tomorrow night, and tear Slow a new ass." It was late and judging the exact outcome of that statement was difficult.

So, most of the next day, I spent typing, then re-typing, the typing again, an affidavit for search warrant for Slow's place. The clap trap you see on TV where somebody says, "have a search warrant sent over" is somewhere on the level of Santa. Search Warrants and the Fourth Amendment are tough twins to master. The judge signed off at five P. M.

We clustered up at ten P.M. at the Southeast substation, which was on Bexar (pronounced Bayer) in those days. The warrant was to be served when Slow showed for work around midnight. Sounds easy enough.

All cops throughout the world love to serve search warrants. They sometimes—maybe often is more descriptive—get to break things. Unless you're actually holding the warrant, no officer who assists has to write a report—unless the fructus hits the fan. Declare your intent to serve a search warrant around any police squad room, and the crowd of volunteers will accumulate exponentially.

We ended up with enough hired help to quell a small riot, which was good, because that was what was about to happen. Included in the mob was a squad of guys from the Tactical Unit, commonly called "Swat", Homicide Detective Bull Hooper, and a guy from Vice, Muscles Malloy. Tac was known for being tough. Hooper was known for being very tough. Malloy was known for being six feet six and so skinny he could stand under a clothesline to avoid rain.

A word about Hooper. Thirty years with the DPD, eighteen in Homicide, he was recognizable at 200 paces by the thin rim of red hair that surrounded the rear of his head just above the ears. Husky and sometimes short on patience, a wide circle of the Dallas area crime crowd knew him as an extremely poor choice to piss off. He was only a year or so from mandatory retirement.

With four ATF agents, and half the DPD, we caravanned to Slow's joint. The deal was for Dorsen, Hooper, me, and four Tac guys to take the front door. Four Tac officers were assigned to the rear door. The rest were to remain on standby until needed. Listen, I explained all that to IAD several times.

As we sat in a string of cop cars in the humid night air a block down, Slow pulled his Lincoln Continental Mark V into the front yard at 12:12 A. M. We attacked in force at 12:15.

His dive was a more or less public facility and the door should have been unlocked. But somebody hadn't read the rule book. Dorsen hit the door with his best pee wee football shoulder block. Tom Landry might have been impressed, but the door was not. The locked and immovable door failed to cooperate. Dorsen's head collided with the doorframe, opening a nasty cut which would eventually cost him all three of his head hairs.

Forty feet of carefully cultivated, treasured top-cover gone in a heartbeat.

The four TAC guys, not known for hesitating when adrenaline was at max, and close behind Dorsen, hit and drove him into door at full bore. All plunged through, knocking the entire doorframe into the room behind, which just happened to be surrounded by a group of men shooting craps on the pool table. The glut of cops, including Dorsen, plus two or three gamblers and Slow Bill himself, slid under the table in a jumble of arms and a philharmonic caliber symphony of profanity.

Of critical significance at this juncture was that that damned snitch had neglected to tell us that Slow had a broken jaw—laid low with a muscatel bottle by an irate customer. The jaw was wired shut. Slow could talk, sort of, but had been on a liquid diet for the past week. The upshot, he could not open his mouth more than a half inch.

Now, a small army of backups, deciding that help was needed, piled into the room, led by none other than Muscles Malloy. As TAC guys tried to restore order, Malloy managed to be swept under the table, already occupied by ten or so people.

Slow Bill, struggling to extricate himself, showed his head, doing his dead level best to talk. But the jaw wouldn't cooperate. Muscles Malloy, last man in, emerged beside Slow.

Muscles took one look at Slow's clinched jaw and shouted the universal dope cops' mantra, "He's eatin' the damned dope!"

Muscles and three TAC guys pounced on Slow and began a full assault on his disabled jaw. One of the Tac officers managed to insert a baton between his front dentures. The score: Two lost front teeth. A baton blow to the head and Slow fell, limp and semi-conscious. Someway, Muscles Malloy ended up on the bottom.

Enter Thomas Ray Jones, Jr., commonly called "Short T", three feet six inches tall, seventy-six pounds, forty years old, a long record of arrests, and mad as hell. A fixture in the place as a sweeper and general flunky, Short T had long since learned that to try to strike a blow against another man invariably resulted in a severe ass-kicking. But he had acquired a method of attack that seldom failed.

Seeing his boss and benefactor, Slow, in the clutches of the law, with Muscles Malloy's lower half turned upward, Short T, being about half Malloy's length, attacked. He fell upon Muscles and took a giant, little person bite of his scrotal area, to wit, Muscles Malloy's balls.

At first, Muscles began the aforementioned "Balls" alarm, a reasonable reaction considering the situation. His shrieks quickly blurred into the electronic siren imitation. Although ten or twelve cops extricated Short T from his bite-hold, Malloy continued to make electronic siren noises until a real ambulance with a real siren took him off to Parkland Hospital. After the fifteen-minute brawl, two cops and five patrons, including Short T, were also ambulanced to Parkland.

We learned of Slow's impairment, but only after an officer named Hancock, joining the fray late, spotted the clenched jaw and—you got it—shouted, "He's eatin' the damned dope." Hancock grabbed Slow in a choke hold. Slow was unconscious again before we drug Hancock off.

I wrote a note, "This man is not eating the dope. He has a broken jaw which is wired shut." I signed the TAC sergeant's name to it and taped it on his back. I should have taped one on his forehead, too.

When they rolled Slow into Parkland emergency, the officer on duty, seeing Slow regaining consciousness and grinding his jaw, shouted, "He's eatin' the damned dope." Two nuns, doing benevolent work at the hospital and trained in karate, piled on the gurney with the officer and began clawing at Slow's now mangled mouth. They managed to break two fingers on Slow's left hand and his left femur before knocking over the gurney. Slow was out cold again.

Slow's lawyer showed up. Slow agreed to allow the Doc's to re-wire his jaw and set the broken bones in his left arm and hand only if a male nurse was posted outside his door in the event the cops returned to finish him off and Short T wasn't around to protect him.

Slow sued the City of Dallas and the Federal government for several million. However, we had enough dope, guns, illegal gambling, and general negatives, that a trade was negotiated.

Eventually, he got thirty days in the county jail and I would get three days off without pay. But I bet his lawyer cost more.

After several days with Internal Affairs Ghouls in squeaky chairs and shrinks in even squeakier ones, I was cautioned, whispered to be partially insane, and sent back to the street. How that caper avoided a move to Miami was heavier than I ever let myself consider.

The next couple of weeks, I caught a couple of bar fire bombings in the July swelter, both of which had a transfer to Butte, Montana or Miami engraved on the assignment sheet. Damn, I needed a case with a live defendant sewed on the end of it.

One quiet Tuesday evening, I stopped by Adair's, a cop and cop groupie hangout on East Commerce for a quick beer. I had eight. I met, then mixed with a 2:00 A. M. Queen who said she worked in records—I forget which records. We ended up in my apartment and the evening lasted until just past 4:00 A. M. Damn, was I drunk on a seemingly normal Wednesday morning?

Yeah, I was the duty agent that week. That meant any calls of any significance were routed to a beeper I carried in those days before cellular phones. Nothing important had happened all week. What harm could come from a wee hour of the morning orgy?

When the beeper I carried screeched, chickens, then the chicken coop began coming home to roost. If there was ever a night I ever should have bedded down at a reasonable hour.

CHAPTER 2: THE LAW OF CHANCE

One who lives by the luck of the draw long enough will eventually draw a loser, ending the game.

The dream was intense. Somebody had firebombed the backyard rose garden of the mayor of Highland Park. The mayor had showed up in my office wearing a dinner jacket and pink tennis shoes, and I was taking a statement from him. Every time he tried to talk, his voice rang.

"How many rose bushes did you have, Your Honor?"

Blurb... ring... ring... ring. "What a strange thing for a mayor to say." Ring... ring... ring.

"This rings of No Potential." Ring. ... Ring. ... Ring.

On or around the eighty-ninth ring, I answsered the telephone beside my bed. It was Bull Hooper, the Homicide detective who'd been a willing destroyer in the Slow Bill search warrant.

"Asleep?" he asked.

"Oh, good God," I managed. I couldn't do any better.

"What were you doing? The phone's been ringing for five minutes."

"Studying my Sunday School lesson, hoping you'd call."

"Are you awake enough to understand me?"

"Yeah," I gasped.

"Kobok, wake up and get down here? We've got a homicide by arson fire bombing. White female, tied to bed, telephone up her ass."

"Oh, good God," I groaned.

"Wake up and get over here," he said. "And say something besides, 'Oh, good God.'"

"Ooohhh," I said.

Hooper gave me an address on Lemmon Avenue. "Are you coming right away?" he growled.

"Yeah, yeah, I'm code three," I managed and hung up.

Code Three meant "blow the siren." I couldn't actually blow the siren on my "take home" car since it had been inoperable for the last six months. I would hurry, though, and just pretend the siren was on. Siren noise would have been more than I could handle anyway.

As I struggled to my feet, the pain was close to terminal. I couldn't tell exactly what hurt. I felt my way down the hall, into the bathroom. Lying face up next to the commode was a skinny woman who was what my mother would have termed buck nekked. Hooper had just called me about a woman with a telephone up her major area. Lost in the distant brain-fog of sin and degeneracy I tried to concentrate on Hooper's call. Had he said she was in my bathroom?

John Wayne style, I hooked my toe under her back to flip her over. An inspection of the proper area showed she was telephone-free. It was the 2:00 A. M. queen I had brought home the night before. She opened one semi-uncomprehending eye and tried to focus on me.

She rose to a half-sitting position and hugged the commode, retching about twenty-five dollars' worth of vodka Collins into the sewage system. I shaved in the shower and let my mind refocus on the phone call that had awakened me. It had been Hooper all right, but the girl with the phone problem was at Lemmon Avenue, not in my bathroom.

When I stepped out of the shower, the girl without the phone was still frozen in an embrace with the plumbing. She vomited and heaved until she appeared to be out of ammunition.

"Top of the morning," I greeted.

She dry-heaved some more and was still death-locked to the stool when I left for Lemmon Avenue. I didn't have anything worth stealing, and she appeared healthy enough to eventually survive. She and the commode made a handsome couple. Funny how bar-room queens always look better at 2:00 A.M.

Armed with a cup of 7-Eleven's finest caffeinated, I found

the crime scene in a nearly new, fairly expensive, two-bedroom apartment facing the pool. The apartment and the complex that housed it were clones to hundreds of others in the Dallas "Uptown area" just north of Downtown and not far off Central and running several blocks along Lemmon Avenue.

Among the glut of emergency vehicles parked around the complex were the Dallas Police Department crime scene search van and a car from the Dallas County Medical Examiner. The fire appeared to have been largely confined to the one unit, which was now occupied by about twelve police officers, four firefighter's residual from the fire, a police photographer, and a fire department photographer, flanked on the outside behind the yellow tape by a glut of newsies and spectators. I could smell gasoline when I climbed out of the Chevrolet.

I badged past the uniform on the door and worked my way to the rear bedroom. Bull Hooper, plus a field agent from the medical examiner's office and about ten other assorted cops and fire department personnel were standing around a pile of burned debris that had once been a human being. Inside the room, the smell of gasoline and burned flesh was overpowering.

"Hot damn, the Feds are here. We can all go home," somebody chided from the group. No offense was intended. None would have been taken, even if I wasn't near death.

The Field Agent, Herman Jones, looked up at me soberly. He and his peers managed to provide a measure of stability in these situations. They were dead-level serious toward matters that most police officers would tend to pooh-pooh, but they offered shocking dry-humor quips about bloody matters of gore when least expected.

They also tended to overplay their casual disregard for blood, mayhem, or misery by having regular gross-out and smartass contests. They were just as revolted by things like the mess on the bed as anyone else, but they compensated by affecting a nonchalant attitude that was only a facade. Either that or they were all nuts.

"Had breakfast, Kobok?" Herman Jones asked.

"Yeah," I said, the room spinning.

The thing on the bed was only barely identifiable as human.

The flesh was charred black, hair burned away, probably nude before the fire. The remnants of electrical wire circling the remains of wrists and ankles. She had apparently been spread-eagle face down, with each limb tied with the electrical cord to a leg of the bed. Flammable liquid had been poured over her upper body and head, then a Molotov thrown atop the heap. Broken bits of a wine bottle were strewn about the bed and floor. The results were horrifying.

The scene was ghastlier than anything Hollywood could ever concoct. Jones rolled the thing on the bed onto its back. The mattress had partially shielded the chest from the fire, and from the front she was vaguely recognizable as female. Teeth marks on the chest were vivid evidence that the nipple area had been bitten or partially eaten off.

I doubted I'd ever have another sexual thought. Why the hell hadn't I found a job in a bank? Unbelievably, an image of Short T darting out of a shadow and biting Herman Jones in the balls tickled the back of my mind. A continuation of a dead-end summer of dead-end cases loomed.

But the shadows remained stationary as the group ginned up the crude jokes—the defense mechanism which were nearly always a part of such crime scenes. Leaning slightly on a soot coated wall, I braced against fainting in the middle of the carnage.

"Maybe it was the Wolfman," said one of the crime scene search officers, entering the smartass contest.

"Or my supervisor," added Jones, warming up.

"The apartment manager says her name is Katherine Mae Pritchard, early twenties, single, and employed by the Texas Bell Telephone Company," Hooper said, to no one in particular.

"Texas Bell!" said the fire department photographer. "Y'all always thought all operators had their heads up their asses. Now you know the rest of the story."

"Oh, good God," I said. "I need to step outside for a breath of fresh pollution."

I found a cup of coffee from the American Red Cross coach that frequently appeared at major fires that had been mentioned on the early morning news.

"Are you sick?" asked the old man who dispensed the coffee.
"Yeah. Touch of flu."

I re-entered the devastated bedroom in time to see Herman Jones probing at the end of a yellow telephone receiver that had been forced into the victim's vagina. Don't confuse the sensitive instruments used by your family physician with the burglar tools used by medical examiners, pathologists, or field representatives of the local medical examiner's office during examinations of a possible homicide. Jones was digging at her private parts with a chrome plated number six tire iron—or a reasonable facsimile.

Herman Jones drew a plastic body bag, technically called a "disaster pouch" from his satchel, and I knew that I was through with that phase of the torture.

Hooper and I retreated to the parking lot and began the "It ain't our damned deal" contest, a regular feature of crimes like the atrocity we were witnessing.

"Kobok, it's as clear as the mole on my secretary's nose, this is a fire bombing. The Feds always have primary jurisdiction."

"Bull, dammit, this was a murder. The vic was tied, then the Molotov tossed in. The DPD owns this one."

"Yeah, dude, but a Molotov was tossed in. We both know that's a federal offense."

"We didn't see any gas can either."

"Perp took it with him."

A second homicide officer called Hooper over to an unmarked squad car. He leaned in, picked up the radio microphone and spoke for less than a minute. He strolled back, poker-faced, sweat forming on his brow in the early morning humidity.

"My lieutenant has been in touch with your idiot supervisor, whatsie's name. We work the case jointly."

Working double with a hoss like Hooper beat going it alone. But I wasn't about to admit that. Howdy Doody James. Hard to believe he'd gotten up in the middle of the night.

"Have you got enough stroke with Texas Bell security to get her file?" Hooper asked.

"Yeah," I replied, adding that Texas Bell would probably like to be notified that their employee, Ms. Pritchard, had been converted to a crispy critter.

Then, like an apparition from the gloom, Bruce McClain, pudgy director of security for Texas Bell walked up, a folder in hand. McClain had been a Fed, but habitually unable to push away from the table before dessert, he'd grown tired of the struggle to maintain a weight standard. Lured to greener salary pastures of private industry, he now carried around fifty extra pounds.

"DPD Alarm Office called me." He handed me the thin folder. "They're digging out her master file, guys," McClain said in his fat man's wheeze. "She's worked for us two years as an operator, native of Brown County, Oklahoma, good work record, no record of having been married. She seems to be the all-American girl your mothers wanted y'all to catch. Next of kin is her mother back in Oklahoma." He concluded his synopsis in about ten percent of the words that would have been required if he was still writing government reports.

I asked Bruce, "What the hell do you pay telephone operators? Her apartment is furnished like the Taj Mahal." The burned remains of her apartment indicated that Katherine Mae Pritchard may have been receiving a little financial assistance in maintaining her lifestyle. I asked Bruce if his file would have the victim's photograph. He opened the folder and tapped a head shot of an attractive blonde.

It was past 8:00 A. M. I said, "Gents, earlier, I was sick enough, I was afraid I'd die. Now I'm afraid I'm not. I've got to puke, take something for this headache, and call the office."

I walked over to the management office of the apartment complex, and made the calls. The office was at the far end of the complex and service had not been busted. I also performed the other two chores, both in the office restroom.

It would take several hours to make proper inquiry throughout the apartment complex. From a side window, I saw Herman Jones supervising two paramedics as they loaded the black-bagged body into the M. E. dead-wagon. An autopsy would follow shortly.

I tried to figure out which would cause the least agony: Witnessing the inevitable autopsy at the county forensic lab or spending the day in and out of the man killing summer heat, interviewing the assortment of uncooperative people in and around the Rose Garden apartment complex. Hooper must have been reading my mind.

"Kobok, if you'll cover the autopsy, I'll do the neighborhood inquiries," Hooper said.

I nodded, too sick to care.

Hooper said, "Manager and a couple of tenants confirmed she had lots of male visitors."

A hooker's income would explain the upscale furnishings in Ms. Pritchard's apartment. "Prostitute, you think?"

"Could be. Or maybe she picked up a cannibal," he added somberly.

I walked out into the humid heat to the Chevrolet and started out toward the Southwest Institute of Forensic Sciences, tucked behind Parkland Hospital, near the south end of Harry Hines Boulevard. The institute was housed in a four-story building that contained a marvelous assortment of scientific types vital to law enforcement—firearms experts, handwriting specialists, and the like.

Tucked in the basement was the end of the world, literally, for some. The morgue was sort of a dark secret that society tends to ignore. Fifty thousand people passed the Parkland complex daily. Very few ever realized a glimpse of hell was secreted in the rear of the sprawling facility. Even fewer could imagine the horrors there. And they sure as hell didn't give tourist tours.

CHAPTER 3: THE LAW OF WORK ETHIC

Most labor at what they must; a few at what they choose. Then there's that fortunate few who manage to labor at something they actually enjoy.

Texas law required that, when possible, an investigating police officer was to be present during the mandatory autopsy when homicide was a factor. It supposedly facilitated proving that a crime actually had been committed. The autopsy was scheduled for 8:30 A.M. I made a point not to be early. I had another cup of 7-Eleven caffeinated en route. I also threw it back up, beside the Chevrolet, before I went inside.

That morning, as always, naked bodies, whole or in various portions, lay on wheeled, stainless-steel carts that were tumble-parked in every open space in the morgue. Each cadaver, face up and naked, bore a tan identification tag wired to a toe. If the body had no toes, the tag would have been wired to any appendage that was available.

Portions of human bodies of various shapes and sizes, sealed in plastic bags, were stacked in heaps on and around several shining, stainless-steel sinks against the outer walls. Visible on shelves everywhere were clear-glass crocks of about five-gallon capacity filled with assorted body parts sealed in those little plastic containers with formaldehyde. I never did understand how the hell they ever found the proper remnant when it was needed. The overwhelming stench of burned, rotted, mutilated flesh mingled with the odor of formaldehyde, alcohol, and other necessary chemicals. The smells tended to stay with the visitor's nostrils for days.

On a stainless cart near the center of the room lay the

unblemished, nude body of an elderly white man, watery blue eyes fixed steadily on the glaring overhead light. His genitals were pathetically shriveled as if attempting to evade the final indignity of the examination by the glaring light. He appeared to be able to sit upright at any moment and demand a blanket against the chill.

I asked an attendant, "What happened to the old man?" You'd think I would have known better.

"He died, man," giggled the skinny tattooed youth on duty, ecstatic at his opportunity to play the morbid-in-the-morgue game on a member of the police establishment. I fantasized slapping him off the stool but didn't have the energy.

Dr. Paul Westra strode into the room. A textbook pompous ass, he was shadowed by his faithful sidekick, Jesus, a scrawny Hispanic wiseass. Westra always managed to enter with the bearing of General George Patton. Jesus always followed with the bearing of Patton's mule. Like all of us, Westra was only doing what he had to do, but he loved it. Jesus, having achieved the highest status of his life, also relished his bloody occupation.

I had hoped for one of the female pathologists on the chance of enduring a minimum of morgue jokes on a raging hangover. But lately, the women had become almost equal to the men in gross-out remarks directed to test the fiber of any outside observers to that ghastly scene. I had witnessed an autopsy the week before where the female pathologist had actually eaten a jelly roll while directing the procedure. Any veteran will tell you that the jelly roll deal is designed solely for introducing rookie cops to the morgue. Chances are good that every morgue in the world keeps a supply of the things on hand.

Pathologists and their assistants wear rubber aprons over their traditional green surgical gowns. In general, most pathologists tend to be gentle people, who attend their patients with respectful sympathy. It is difficult, however, to face thirty examples daily of the injuries people inflict on each other, without becoming at least surface-tough. Stop to shed tears for every sad scene in the morgue and they'd dissolve like a pop cycle on a July Dallas sidewalk.

The pathologist has very little actual contact with the

cadaver. He or she directs the operation, which is carried out by one or more enthusiastic assistants called dieners. Jesus was Westra's Number One diener. The process generally involved the diener doing the cutting, chopping, tearing, and overall removal of the pieces, while the pathologist examined and dissected extracted parts.

"Kobok," Westra nodded to me in greeting. Jesus looked sullenly in my direction without speaking.

"Good morning," I said in the abstract. If I said much to Westra, I'd barf again.

In a corner of the spacious room, the skinny, goateed attendant on duty, who had made the crack about the dead elderly man, was eating a cream-filled pastry and reading a Spiderman comic book. A dedicated professional.

The charred remains of Katherine Mae Pritchard, late of Brown County, Oklahoma, had been dumped from the black body bag onto one of the stainless carts. The charred remains were a stark contrast to the steel table under the powerful overhead lights. As I had already observed in the apartment, she had burned while face down. The mattress had partially shielded her face and upper chest.

Her fingers had burned away, leaving the hands as blackened stubs. Portions of the flesh bore lesions and ruptures that allowed blood, grease, and other body fluids to spread onto the table. The smell of burned flesh, flammable liquid, and discharging body fluids was overpowering. Amid all this was the outrage that only a few hours earlier, the terribly violated form on the table had been a young woman.

Westra pulled down a built-in microphone from overhead and spoke into a recorder. He gave the victim's name and other vital statistics, as known, including that the "exterior of the cadaver bore evidence of exposure to an open flame, fueled by flammable liquid, at temperatures in excess of one thousand degrees for approximately five to fifteen minutes."

After a thorough look at the charred exterior of the body, Westra said, "You may begin, Jesus." He pronounced his helper's name as "Hey-soos."

The diener picked up a saw that was similar to, but smaller

than the saw commonly used by carpenters. In his other hand he held a clear plastic shield, which he held in front of him to keep off the gore. The ceiling above had no such shield and was mottled brown from the splattering of a thousand previous autopsies.

Jesus began the procedure, as is usual, by sawing a circle from the top of the cadaver's head. Using a pointed spatula and large forceps, he cut through the dura-matter, the tough, clear plastic-appearing wrapper of most body parts beneath the skin. He pried the brain out into his hands with a swoosh and handed it to Westra.

Westra turned it in his hands as if examining a head of lettuce in the supermarket. He described the brain in lengthy terms, concluding by saying that it was not remarkable. I wondered, what in the hell did he expect the thing to be? It looked remarkable as all get-out to me, a gray, mass of substance that, until about six hours ago, had been called upon to perform a wide range of tasks.

I looked at the thing in Westra's hands. Which part of that glob of matter had functioned when a lunatic was stuffing that telephone up her private parts? What would Westra have said if the brain had been remarkable? "This kid did well in arithmetic," perhaps?

Westra handed the thing back to Jesus, pointing his chin toward a circular spare parts bowl at the head of the cart. The brain of Katherine Mae Pritchard had received its last examination. How remarkable.

Jesus stepped partially around the table and tossed the brain at the steel bowl, missing by a foot. The brain hit the floor with a sound like a wet towel striking concrete.

"Headache," Westra said out of the side of his mouth, Al Capone like.

Jesus snickered obediently. My vision spun momentarily. I stole a quick glance at the old man on the next cart. He remained quite dead and uncomplaining.

The procedure passed slowly. Also passing was any similarity between something human and the body of Katherine Mae Pritchard, who would never see Brown County, Oklahoma again except perhaps in a box.

Jesus methodically attacked the body from head to foot with a combination of axe, tree-pruning shears, meat-cleaver, hog ring pliers, and other tools. Various body parts would be numbered, bagged, and retained in one of those glass urns that adorned the walls for use and evidence at some future time.

Westra looked at me over his bifocals and said, "Tits chewed partly off."

I looked at him through bloodshot eyes and said nothing. Chest quickly became chest cavity. Jesus ripped out a large section and handed it to Westra. Westra turned it in his hands, droned into the microphone, and handed it back to Jesus, who sliced it through with a knife like homemade bread. Westra took it back and exclaimed, "Okay, Kobok, take a look at this."

Having no idea what that portion of the body could have been, I waited.

Westra gave a detailed anatomy lecture on lungs. I concluded that Jesus had dissected a lung. He made a statement about internal trauma and other words that didn't register. I guess my expression gave away my ignorance.

"She breathed fire into her lungs, Kobok," he said paternally. "She was alive when torched."

Jesus carved out a piece of throat that had occupied the space between the base of the tongue and the lungs. To get a better angle, he twisted the head sharply toward me. The distorted mouth gaped partially open, showing a mouthful of gleaming ivory teeth, undamaged by the fire. He handed the foot-long section of throat to Westra, who slit it lengthwise.

"Trachea," Westra said, turning toward me. "Look, the entire length is seared and clogged with soot. She took three or four breaths after the fire started."

As he handed the piece back to his diener, he said, "Bag it and tag it, Jesus, and make sure it's photographed."

Jesus received the piece in sullen silence.

Next, Jesus opened her pelvic area with the meat cleaver and a tire tool. The noise of snapping bones and tissue was surprisingly loud in the still chamber. Then he invaded her crotch with the meat cleaver, splitting her most private areas in three strokes. Indignity does not abide in the morgue.

The telephone receiver was now fully exposed in pastel yellow. Jesus removed it with chrome-plated channel lock pliers, dropped it into a plastic bag, and tossed it under the cart.

"Did you get a dial tone, Jesus?," Westra asked.

Jesus giggled. He then cut and chopped several parts out of her pelvic and crotch area and handed them to Westra. I don't recall if those parts were remarkable or unremarkable.

"Alive when the telephone went up her snatch," Westra said. He dropped several parts directly into plastic bags without handing them back to Jesus first. Then he said, "Let's get out, Jesus."

Jesus collected numerous body parts, including the brain from the spare-parts bowl next to the table. He also picked up a Salem cigarette pack that had fallen from his pocket and threw it, along with the body parts, into her gaping body cavity. He then began sewing the opening with a very large needle threaded with catgut. I wondered if I puked on the table, and nobody saw me do it, if anyone could tell that it was different from the mess already there. The cigarette pack was over the line.

"If you don't want my foot in your ass, remove that damned cigarette pack," I said.

Jesus looked up at me, then reached in and tossed the cigarette pack into a large trashcan.

Westra discarded his rubber gloves into a garbage can next to one of the stainless steel sinks.

"Okay, Kobok," he said, "some evidence of strangulation. Breasts bitten partially off. Severely beaten about the head. Six shallow, torture-like stab wounds to the area of the chest. Wounds probably inflicted while the vic was alive before the perp rolled her on her face and tossed in the match. COD is traumatic injury as a result of the fire. I'll send y'all a report with photos and diagrams."

"Any sign of venereal disease, Doctor?" I asked, thinking of her frequent male visitors.

"Only toxicology will tell, Kobok. You should know that. The lab tests usually take several days, but I'll try to hurry these through."

Westra wheeled and strutted out, leaving Jesus sack-stitching the horribly violated body cavity of Katherine Pritchard.

When he finished, He threw his equipment into a case and slithered out, leaving the attendant, rows of corpses, and me. I wondered who was better off.

On the way out of the building, I caught a glimpse of myself in the mirror. Graying hair and sunken eyes that looked worse than most of the occupants of the stainless steel tables that I had just left. I made a mental note to do more sleeping and less boozing.

CHAPTER 4: THE LAW OF SUPERVISORS AND DISTANCE

Criminal Investigation becomes increasingly easier for police supervisors in direct proportion to the amount of time they have spent away from the street not conducting those investigations.

Harry Hines Boulevard, beginning in suburban Carrollton, many miles to the north and ending just short of downtown Dallas, is a four-lane thoroughfare, glutted with traffic, and flanked with every possible vestige of humanity. Dotted with industry, used car lots, coffee shops, pawnshops, a television station, numerous topless and regular bars, several motels, and many liquor stores.

In those days, it was also a multi mile long showcase for the sex on the hoof industry. From the area around Parkland running several blocks south, hookers worked the street like fire ants. Was it remotely possible Katherine Mae Pritchard, sparkling cheerleader and athlete from Logan County, Oklahoma, had sold herself along this street? Was the telephone company just a day job?

The whores, the pimps, the johns, and the law all knew the southern mile or so of Hines as the "Hose Line," or the "Line." The source of the name is fairly obvious.

Street-walkers worked quietly or brazenly, depending upon the number of Vice officers available at a given time. The prostitutes came out at noon and stayed until business diminishes around dawn. They walked in twos and alone.

Their uniforms were always similar, differing only in the amount of clothing necessary or not necessary for the day's weather. Each girl invariably wore enough makeup to grow a crop and dressed—or undressed—in various combinations of shorts, halter tops, blouses, skirts, dresses, and scarves in a daz-zling array of color and bare skin.

Each always carried a standard-issue American prostitute shoulder bag. Not every woman who carries a shoulder bag is a prostitute, but every prostitute usually carried a shoulder bag. A street girl can carry enough provisions and makeup in one of those bags to stay on field maneuvers all night. The filled bag, a formidable weapon in itself, could also carry a pistol, knife, or other weapon. Ask any officer who has arrested prostitutes.

A streetwalker who got out early in the day and stayed late was practicing a very profitable enterprise. A girl who was good at her trade, who worked hard, and who was fortunate enough to avoid misfortune, could gross more than the President of the Drover's and Merchant's Bank of Omaha.

But streetwalking is a dangerous business with no retire-ment system and no benefits. Girls who worked south Harry Hines were mostly young and usually averaged about forty percent African American, forty percent white, twenty percent Hispanic. They ran the spectrum of looking fairly attractive to looking like death warmed over. I never saw one who was actu-ally pretty up close. The street digests them.

Girls who worked the street in this area were known by an endless variety of assumed names from Alice to Zelda. They all too often end up with one label—dead.

I turned off the Hose Line, threaded through downtown traffic, and found a parking spot in the GSA Garage. My sec-retary, Tootie, greeted me as I walked into the outer office. She was African American, young, attractive, intelligent, and pleas-ant. And she always typed reports reasonably promptly. I had always figured she was a plant for Internal Affairs, because she had too many good qualities to be another government secretary.

"The fat guy from the telephone company left you this enve-lope, and Bull Hooper has called you three times," she said. When she finished with the business of the messages and really looked at me, she added, "Jesus Christ, are you sick?"

"Yeah, I think I have acute alcohol poisoning. Where did Hooper call from?"

She handed me a slip of paper with a telephone number I didn't recognize. As I dialed the number, I sat at my desk and opened the file that Bruce McClain had left.

"Rose Garden apartments," a tired female voice answered. Hooper was still canvassing Katherine's apartment.

I asked for Hooper.

"Hooper," he answered after two minutes.

"You called?"

"Boy, either our victim was a hooker or she screwed half of North Dallas for recreational purposes. She sure did have a lot of male visitors. She also didn't mix with the neighbors and apparently didn't give away any lovin' to any of the guys in her immediate neighborhood. Gotta be a hooker."

"How do we know she didn't screw any neighbors?" I asked, envious that Hooper had gotten to ask sex questions while I had watched a massacre.

"This apartment complex has some pretty loose parties. You know the kind-first they grab-ass, then everybody plays turnabout. It doesn't make for many secrets. She didn't participate."

"Has the city notified her family in Oklahoma?"

"Yeah, it's mama only. Father hasn't been around for years."

"Divorce?"

"Abandonment, I think. Departed...lemme see...1973, according to the Records Unit who called the mother," he said.

"Brothers or sisters?"

"An older brother killed in Vietnam in 1972."

"Pretty efficient, my boy," I told him. "If the federal government had notified her, it would be three weeks before you could find out the results. Do you need me out there?"

"Not unless you just want to come out. I think I've pretty much got a handle on her activities here."

"Bull, where the hell did she go at night? Do we know if she bar-hopped? If so, did she go to a bar last night?"

"Well, before you got there this morning, I picked up a book of matches in her kitchen. It is from the Rooster Club on Harry Hines. You were so hung over that I didn't try to cut that up with you."

"Look," I said, "I've got her photograph here in the file the telephone company gave us. I'll show it around the Rooster Club this evening after the night crew comes to work. What's the street number?"

"Five-three-seven-five."

I wrote it in my notebook. " Did she have lady friends-or boyfriends? Was there a trick book or at least a telephone book in the apartment?"

"Not a thing."

"Her purse?"

"Nothing. Texas driver's license, a few bucks..."

"Well, listen, I'm feeling like death warmed over. I gotta make a preliminary report and try to eat something. Then, I'm gonna show the photo from the phone company around that bar and then go home for some sleep."

"Okay," he said." Call me first thing in the morning."

"Will do," I said and hung up.

I opened the Texas Bell file on Katherine Mae Pritchard.

Graduated Brown County Consolidated High School. Forty-eight hours credit University of Oklahoma. Employed Farmers State Bank of Wilby, Oklahoma, from 1979 until 1983. Mother: Mrs. Thelma Pritchard, Route 6, Wilby, Oklahoma. Father: Willard Pritchard, last known address unknown. Hobbies: Tennis, basketball, reading.

A very average file from a very average appearing young lady from a very average place like Wilby, Oklahoma. It even included her dental chart and a physician's statement from the physical exam given when she had first gone to work. I studied the photograph. Westra would probably have found the face unremarkable. Very pretty, but not Miss America. But at least a six or seven by Dallas standards, in a system where there was an abundance of nines and better.

She would have been accepted but lost in the pack of attractive young women warehoused in the "Singles Only" apartments along Greenville Avenue, or Lemmon Avenue, or in the Uptown area. A "beautiful people" syndrome frantically directed the lives of thousands of young women who lived there. Dallas was a mecca for young, unattached females. They came from Oklahoma and Ohio, from New York and New

Hampshire. They came in droves, in some indistinct quest for perfection among others of similar age and ambition. They were not exactly driven by career ambitions, but they strove to be at the center of a hollow sub-culture that was dominated by bad dope and a fast life. Their collective aim in life was too often to develop a suntan, work out at the spa, and party at all costs. The tragic, violent end of this kid was no more or no less shocking than numerous others to which I'd seen. Even the occupation was not a surprise.

The smiling face in the photo stared steadily out at me. There was no resemblance to the carnage I had seen heaped on the stainless-steel cart, now at least, minus the Salem pack in the body cavity.

I asked Tootie to get me the number of the Brown County, Oklahoma, sheriff's office.

I dialed the number and, on the second ring, got a disinterested female dispatcher.

I asked for the sheriff, and she placed me on hold. "Sheriff Decker," growled the distant contact.

I explained who I was. I then detailed facts known to me relative to the murder of Ms. Katherine Mae Pritchard. The Dallas Police Records officer had routinely called his office earlier to verify the address of the victim's mother. The sheriff had apparently made some inquiry into the girl's background. I explained that I could arrange for an Agent to drive out from Oklahoma City, or Muskogee, but pointed out how much he could help by telephone.

Dallas Records had already called him. "No, no, hell no, Kobok," he answered. "I know your Agent up in Paul's Valley, D. A. Taylor. He's good people. Fact of business is, he was in here two or three days ago. I'll give you all we got here on the phone and follow with FAX copies."

"Good. Is there anything that you know or can find out that would tell us anything at all about this girl?"

"Well, I called out to the high school. The superintendent remembered her. I'm not sure I do. I remember when her brother was killed in 'Nam."

"Good thing the super has to work in the summer."

"She played basketball and was a cheerleader at the same time. He said she was a pretty little thing."

I thought of the burned carcass I had witnessed being butchered earlier in the day. "Any criminal record?" I asked.

"No, nothing at all that we can find."

"What about her father?"

"Now that's another story," he said reflectively. "Willard, I remember well—a sorry rascal. Went wacky out there at the house back in nineteen seventy-three and took some potshots at passing cars. No injuries, though. He was using a damn twenty-two! We brought him in on a mental warrant and then carried him over to the funny farm in Muskogee."

"What kind of work did he do?" I asked.

"Small farmer, over-the-road truck driver, part time thief. It's in the file. Worked for Bradly Motor Freight out of Muskogee, hauling general freight."

"Do you have any idea of his whereabouts?"

"Naw, hell no. Just another trucker who found better pickin's elsewhere."

"What about the mother, anything negative?"

"No, she cooks at the elementary school. Lives out there alone. I know the place. Run down as hell. Kobok, I drove out there a while ago and broke the news to her about Katherine Mae. The place looks like she ain't had a man there since Willard left several years ago".

I scribbled on a note pad.

"She told me all about how good Katherine had done down there in Dallas, being a telephone company executive and all, at her age, no less. Thelma showed me a couple of checks she had received from Katherine that she hadn't cashed yet. Each one was four hundred dollars and dated three weeks apart. I wish I could send my boy down there, and he could land a job half as good."

Katherine had a good job all right-in an old profession. The sheriff's son might have a problem fitting in. I thanked the sheriff and gave him my telephone number with the request that he call me if he heard or thought of anything else important.

I sat there, still inundated by a world class headache and

reflected on Katherine. Broken home, all-American girl, pretty, chaste, high expectations from the folks at home, fancy Dallas apartment, possible prostitution, cash to mom, and violent death. All pointed ominously to another No Potential and a one-way ticket to Miami.

I told Tootie that I was going by the Rooster Club on Harry Hines and then home.

"You look like you ought to check into Parkland instead of going to another damn bar," she said.

I didn't elaborate and started out of the office. I was intercepted by Group Supervisor Howdy Doody James, as I tried to sneak by his office. Howdy was a new man in the chain of management. He met the standard in spades: Stupid, overweight, insecure, inept, and vindictive. Most of the supervisors I had seen had been screened more efficiently. Howdy was an idiot and an insufferable asshole.

"What's your deal look like?" he asked.

"Crispy critter, white female, telephone operator, murdered, tied to bed, telephone stuck up her private parts," I summarized.

"Damn, long distance on the fly," he quipped.

I ignored the comment and anticipated his next question. "I'm going to show a photo to some employees in a bar where she might have gone last night. Then I'm going home. I think I have a touch of flu."

He looked me over from head to toe and back. "Kobok, you look like a damn reprobate."

I adopted my courtroom face of no expression. "Oh no, Mr. James. Actually, I'm a Capricorn."

The quip, not surprisingly, passed over his head. "You look like a corpse."

"Thank you," I replied. "In that case, I know a good place to go where I'll have plenty of quiet company and a stainless steel cart of my own."

"Huh?" he asked, as I ducked out the door.

I knew he was in the process of building a case for sending me to another place, one with no zip code if he could arrange it. I never quite understood what he had against me. I guess I just didn't fit his expectations. Maybe my clothes weren't exactly

Fifth Avenue, but Howdy didn't look so hot either. He probably saw his own failings in me. I decided to send the sport coat I was wearing to the cleaners—or to the Salvation Army.

CHAPTER 5: THE LAW OF NORMAL

So called "Normal" lifestyle is only another word for rule by majority, a passing condition at best, subject to change to fit the needs of the next majority.

I drove out Harry Hines in the gathering rush traffic. From the super-heated asphalt parking lot, I pushed through the front door of the Rooster Club at 4:10 P. M. The place was basically a straight bar catering to the primarily redneck crowd in a busy, mixed race neighborhood just south of the intersection with Mockingbird Lane. The skeletons of two burned-out bars where I had investigated fires in the past year were a block away. We sent two ex-convicts to the joint (that means prison in human-speak) for one offense and wrote off the other as No Potential.

The place was empty, except for a skinny, rat-faced white man with a flowing mustache who greeted me from behind the bar. "It's the damn Feds," he said in a nasal, markedly redneck Texas voice.

"Hello," I said. I was good with greetings.

"You don't remember me do you, Mr. Fed?" he intoned.

"Sure, I remember you," I lied.

"You and the big Afro pig-cop threatened to break my fingers over the Stud Rail fire, remember? He was a total asshole."

I recalled the Stud Rail fire, a three-alarm flammable liquid fire in a bar on Gaston Avenue two years earlier and the bartender who was busy trying to break some balls. The wimp behind the bar had been our best suspect. As a matter of fact, Jim East, a huge, African American agent I was partnered with at the time, had mentioned breaking the dirtbag's fingers. Only it was a promise, not a threat. That investigation died as another no potential. Agent East, incidentally, got assigned the Miami dope detail.

"How's your love life, Shark?" I asked, suddenly recalling his name. "Small world."

"My love life is written on the wall of the john, Kobok," he replied. "And the world isn't nearly as damn small as a pig policeman's rape-tool."

"I'm glad you're glad to see me, Shark. Pig? Damn, dude, you're way behind the call-the-cop a name trend. Pig?"

"If this is a bust, Kobok, I got to call Ralphie up from the back to cover the bar," he whined. "I wanna lawyer."

I bluffed. "Sharkie, I only want to talk. However, my boy, I can find a reason to haul your ass downtown if you insist on talkin' trash.."

"I don't want no more trouble, Kobok," he appeared to surrender. I showed him the Texas Bell photo of Katherine Mae Pritchard.

"Who is she?" Shark asked.

"Was she in here last night?" I ignored the question.

"Never saw her before." Slack-jawed, he shouted for Ralphie to come up front.

A defeated, tired-looking white man about thirty-five with greasy, shoulder length curly hair shuffled out of the back. He studied the photo I showed him.

"Hooker," he said matter-of-factly.

"You asking me or telling me?" I asked.

"Tellin'. She in trouble? The dykes from up the street at Boobs send her in here to turn a trick or two. I tossed her out. We don't allow no whores in here."

"Ralphie, I'm not from Vice. I'm not into your business... yet." I wanted his answer.

"Well, no matter," Ralphie answered suspiciously. "She's a les anyway."

"Lesbian?" I probably let my surprise show.

Ralphie nodded, smirking.

"Well, Kobok," babbled Shark. "If she was a whore, she couldn't have been too bad."

"Gimme a draft beer, Shark," I said. Shards of pain passed

through my head from front to back. Was a stroke painful?

"One dollar," Shark chirped.

As I dug in my pocket, Ralphie waved him off with a look of boss-to-flunkie and a slight head shake.

"Have one on me, partner," he said.

I removed my hand from my pocket. "By the way, Ralphie, who are you?"

"Ralphie Mahone, I own this dive," he answered. "Well, I own the debts. C and C Vending owns the bar fixtures and other stuff. Look, I know a hooker or two slips in here through the cracks no matter how we try to run a straight joint. I try to keep the bitches out."

I thought he might cry. An ideal time to exploit his fear of cops. I took a pull on the beer and motioned Ralphie to the side for private consultation.

"From where I sit, Ralph, guy like you in a joint like this needs a friend," I started with a line I had used a thousand times. It worked for picking up women, for telling high grade lawyers that they didn't know crap, or for leaning on human backwash like Ralph. His existence, like my own, depended on pure circumstance and luck anyway—Players in a game who were both fully and equally expendable. Either of us bought the farm—not a ripple on the pond.

I explained, "You know, Ralph, I need to screw with a certain number of people just like you all the time. I also need friends in many places, including this area. Since I don't need to screw with you right now, and you can't handle being screwed with, then we could do okay by being friends. You run into police or prosecution problems…a rival shouldering into your business. You know?"

"I ain't no damned snitch," he stepped backwards like I'd barfed on his foot.

"Oh, hell, man. Snitch is a dirty word. You probably don't like your lawyer or your bookkeeper, but you do okay by being close with them. Think it over. Besides, all I cost is a free beer once in a while." I gave him my card and said, "Think it over and call me at that number, day or night."

He took the card like it was a wet diaper and quickly put it in the pocket of his greasy shirt. I'd probably never hear from him again. However, like a lot of people in his situation—stuck in the mud and blood and beer, he was willing to gamble on a deal to make his sorry life less complicated. He motioned for Shark to refill my glass.

"No thanks, Shark," I said." I've got a Boy Scout meeting and then church."

"Well, screw me," Shark said.

"Shark, I only like girls."

Ralphie disappeared in the back room, grinning. He probably didn't like Shark, either. "What'd you tell him about me, dammit?" Shark asked.

"Who me?" I said. I leaned over the bar and said in James Bond fashion, "Well, frankly, Shark, I told him you were my best snitch."

"Prick," he spat. I could feel him looking a hole through my back as I walked out of the bar.

The blazing afternoon temperature was slanting from its apex and the air burned my lungs. The discomfort drew up visions of Katherine's seared throat. Dallas at five P. M. on a July afternoon was not meant for human habitation. My head kept repeating it was later than I could stand.

But, Boobs was only a couple of blocks up the street. The owner/manager, Chris Rochambeau was an old friend. Chris was a big, usually affable, sometimes meaner than a junkyard-dog, about six feet tall and weighing at least 240. Four years or so earlier, I had investigated a major arson fire at a bar over on Fitzhugh where Chris had been the manager.

That fire had been set by somebody pouring several gallons of gasoline down a kitchen ceiling vent. The oxidizing gasoline fumes had ignited when the arsonist dropped the match, and the resulting explosion had blown the front of the bar through the front of the building across the street. It had also propelled the arsonist into low orbit. We identified his body from fingerprints. An image of Jesus lopping off his remaining fingers with hedge pruning shears and dropping them into plastic bags circulated in my aching head.

We traced the motive to a vending company who wanted

the business closed so their own nearby bar could survive. But that was as far as we got. I eventually wrote that case off with another, 'No Potential,' red stamp decorating the folder. I beat the No Potential cycle that year with a lucky break on an arson bombing in Garland, Texas, a Dallas suburb. But this was another year, and another cycle.

Sociologists identify female transgender women as lesbian, whereas police tend to refer to them as dykes, both terms inaccurate and offensive. To my knowledge, no handbook on "how to be a successful member of the female, same-sex culture" exists. As a general rule, transgender women keep their intimate lives to themselves, as do most of the rest of society.

As I saw it in those days, a sizable portion of lesbian women often dressed in men's clothes and adopted a male persona. Some did not. It was apparent that a small faction retained feminine personas, dressing and conducting themselves as what society might term "normal" ladies. The latter were sometimes referred to as "femes", but that was not a rule etched in granite. A contributing factor was that the women who acted as "femes" and who played the female role in transgender relationships were normally more likely to have sex with men. That is not to imply that any transgender woman could not enjoy relationships with men. Often feme types were married to men or at least interacted sexually with men while in one form of relationship or another, while continuing to balance intimate contact with other members of the so-called lesbian community.

It appeared to me "Butches" as they often referred to themselves, outnumbered the femes ten or so to one. Women engaged in same sex relationships tended to be a society of love. Where male transgenders appeared to function as more of a macho-bitch relationship, female on female relations were inclined to be gentler and softer.

Most female relationships—most because I doubt statistics are reliable—involved women who had no part of the feme/ butch hang up. Many female, same-sex couples are only that: a pair of ladies who prefer female partners, and who enjoy a same sex relationship with no regard for nightclub life or titles which attempt, feebly, to describe their lifestyle. Some were masculine as hell; some were not.

All that is probably distant propaganda today, but that was the language of the mid 1980's.

The fact remained that some transgender women resorted to prostitution as surely as did many females from the so-call "straight world." If Katherine had been into the butch/feme world, she could well have used her so called, feme tendencies to more easily reach out to paying, male prostitution customers.

Ralphie's accusation that Katherine Pritchard had been sent into his joint to solicit sex was probably crap. But in view of the lack of leads and the lack of case production I'd managed that summer, I opted to brave a little more afternoon swelter and visit Boobs.

Chris Rochambeau had bought Boobs when thrown out of work by the fire that sent the arsonist into orbit. Chris had been living with the same woman for several years, a strikingly beautiful blonde with classic Hollywood knockers. So, the bar was named Boobs for Chris's lady. Only butches and accommodating females were welcome. Men could come in for a beer, but they'd soon learn there was no men's restroom.

By the way, did I mention that Chris was a woman? A woman who would have pulled the head off the arsonist on Fitzhugh if he hadn't been fatally inept.

The darkened bar held four or five women in men's attire sitting around a table near the bar and two more playing pool near the back by the restroom. The bartender, a fortyish woman with the traditional man cut hair, appeared to be a retired linebacker for the Dallas Cowboys. I recalled her name to be Frankie. On second look, I decided that she might have been a defensive tackle. She looked at me and said, "Yeah?" The customers around the tables eyed me menacingly. I was wondering why the hell I hadn't gone home.

I walked to the end of the bar and ignored the crowd at the table. "Is Chris around?" I asked the linebacker.

"What do you want Chris for?"

"Because I want to cash my relief check," I said as I leaned over the end of the bar and showed her my badge.

The linebacker edged backwards, and the table of masculine women went back to their conversation.

Chris Rochambeau walked out of the office behind the bar. The bartender had summoned her by alarm button when I walked in. I assumed that ol' Chris had been back there entertaining a friend, and the bartender was only watching out for the boss. I marked the bartender's protective move in my head file of people who could be dependable when the shit hit the fan.

"Kobok, what you doin', robbin' the damned place?" she roared in her baritone, grinning like a long-lost cousin. I had a vaguely erotic vision of her engaging in wild sex in her little office behind the back bar. I wondered if I was going completely nuts.

"How's your love life?" I asked Chris, still eyeing the bartender.

"Slow, son," she roared, laughing. She walked around the bar and slapped me across the back. "Have a beer, boy," she ordered. Frankie, the linebacker, now slightly de-fanged, drew a large schooner and slid it across to me.

I took a hit on the beer and said, "I need to talk to you, Chris. Can we use your office?"

"Yeah, come on back," she said.

I followed Chris into the little office monitored by the gaze of several patrons. I thought of the nude feme I imagined was in Chris's office waiting for her return. Then, voila. A gorgeous girl was there, apparently serving no function beyond that already envisioned by my lustful imagination. She wasn't nude, but was wearing too-small shorts and a little tie-on top. She was cute—-about a eight or better. I thought of Ms. Katherine Mae Pritchard of Brown County, Oklahoma, and wondered if she had been in this office.

"My secretary," Chris said calmly.

"Can she type a letter for me?" I asked.

"Shit, I dunno," Chris said thoughtfully. "We don't have much need to type here."

"Excuse us, Shelly," Chris dismissed the girl.

"What's up?" Chris asked as the girl wiggled her way out

of the office. "You were about to screw over Frankie behind the bar out there."

"No, no, no," I said, "Only establishing rules of conduct."

She roared with a throaty, masculine laugh again. "Well, boy, if you shoot that one, you better use two bullets."

"Chris, I don't need a quarrel with your linebacker out there. I want to show you a picture." I threw the photo of Katherine Pritchard on her desk.

"Yessir-by-god-eeree," she said in an imitation of the night foreman at the Fort Worth stockyards. "Bring her to me, and I'll teach that little teat not to violate society's laws. I'll use her little twitchy ass-right here on this genuine imitation leather sofa." She stood and made hunching motions, manlike. "What you got the bitch locked up for, whoring?"

"Worse. Tell me about her."

"I never got any of her, but I'm goin' to." She made humping motions again.

I wondered how her ardor would be affected by photos of the remains of Ms. Pritchard on the stainless table after she had been gutted from crotch to shoulders.

"Dead," I said. "Somebody killed her. It's bad, bad, bad."

"Good God!" she exclaimed. "She's been in here within the past two, three days. What happened, I mean how, where?"

"It's bound to be in the evening papers. Murdered in her apartment. Apparently, a sex thing. Tied to a bed and set afire. Molotov cocktail involved."

"Jesus H. Christ," she said. "Well, you can't tell what some of these goddam goofy half-stud bitches are going to do. Some of them are really into the S and M scene, man. I know a couple of apartments that are fixed up with more straps and chains than Dracula's castle."

"Women don't have a corner on that market, Chris. I've seen plenty of male occupied set ups decorated the same. But I'm not certain if this a voluntary S&M scene or just a sadistic nutball."

She nodded, unconvinced.

"Chris, I didn't say we suspected one of your people. I heard she was turning tricks with guys off the streets. It could have been some looney she picked up. She was bi-sexual, I suppose you'd say. Do you know if any of your crowd put her to selling sex on the street? Or which one she might have been true-lovin' with?"

"Damn, I don't know exactly who she was shackin' with, if anyone," she said, "but I can find out."

"Do you know much about her at all, Chris? I mean her personality, what perfume she wore, anything?"

"Well, I'd describe her as kind of sad or melancholy. We get all kinds out here, Kobok, but she didn't seem, well, basically into our lifestyle. Most of our girls are tickled shitless to become part of the culture. You know, sort of finding themselves. Don't laugh, asshole."

I hadn't. "Go on, Chris."

"She was the type who seemed to have been pushed away from where the hell ever she started. Maybe as if she came to us for some reason other than attraction to those ugly-assed dykes sitting out there. But, they'd show her love which she seemed not to have from where ever she came from. Kind of like the guy running from the law who lives with hobos, so nobody would know where to look. I mean, Kobok, if she was some kind of fugitive or runaway, the law would look in hippie dope dens and such. Nobody looks for their lost one among us."

I wrote my home telephone number on the bottom of my card and handed it to her. "Call me when you hear something. She was wired to a bed. See if you can learn if she was into the S and M scene. And, Chris, it's important that you don't tell any more around here than you have to."

"I don't really know crap, son, so I can't tell much. But I'm goin' to find out."

"Don't kill any suspects till I get a chance to talk to them." I got up to leave. "I've got to go to a PTA meeting, Chris."

She laughed the infectious laugh.

"Call me. It's important. By the way, is that secretary of yours a virgin?"

She laughed again, "You Goddamned pervert. She definitely ain't had much contact with men."

I walked out through the bar area, ignoring the stares. The non-virgin in the halter top was not in sight.

CHAPTER 6: THE GOLDEN LAW OF POLICE BEHAVIOR

Record all that you see or hear. Believe no one. Tell no one any-
thing. Seek friendship only among your own kind.

At 5:20 P. M., traffic would be stationary. I started north in
the Chevrolet. I bought a single 7-Eleven beer to sip on
the way home. Breathing was optional in the afternoon heat. I
drove across Mockingbird and started up Central Expressway,
which, if fairness was ever achieved, should be renamed the
"Central Parking Lot."

By 6:45, I made the Spring Valley Rd. exit. Having permitted
myself the luxury of belonging to a health spa, complete with
all kinds of cable-operated weight machines, a whirlpool, and
a steam room, I stopped in. It was right across the street from
my not-so-luxurious apartment. The steam room might make
me feel better.

The attendant, a tall slender African American kid, was a
regular who greeted me with the customary: "How many innocent folks you screw over today, Mr. Po-lice?" He was only half
kidding.

"Two, my man," I said soberly, looking him in the eyes.
"One, I had to beat with a club. Put one eye out. He's down at
Parkland fixin' to croak."

He eyed me evenly for several seconds. He would have
liked to continue his attempt to give me a little needle, and he
was reasonably certain that I was jiving him about the story.
However, he shied away from overcrowding the police in general for his imagined fear I'd climb the counter and kick his
ass. He'd talked trash for so long about police brutality that he
believed it, a common malady of the time. He shoved a towel,

lock, and shorts across the counter and took my plastic membership card without further comment.

I worked out on the machines for about forty-two seconds and melted into the steam room. I didn't want to get too strong with that damn weight lifting, you know—always yanking off door handles and stuff.

I showered, left the club, and walked into my apartment at 7:30. I put a Mexican food TV dinner into the oven, opened another beer, and called the answering service. The government was too poor to maintain a night switchboard. The voice that answered was dripping with southern sexuality. I recognized her as a regular who I knew well. When men called to leave information, it was likely that her voice often made them forget why they called.

"Mr. Kobok," she emphasized the Mister.

"No, ma'am," I answered. "This here is the Green Hornet."

She giggled. "You need to call Detective Hooper at five-five-five- four-three-two-one. Also, a Doctor Westron called and said for you to call him at home at five-five-five-one-two-three-four."

"Westra," I corrected.

"Oh, sorry, Mr. Kobok," she purred seductively. "I get off at ten o'clock tonight, and I'd love to inspect the art collection in your apartment again."

"I've got to attend a YMCA fund-raising dinner tonight, kid," I answered. "But I want a rain check-soon."

"Ohh," she said. "Well, okay."

I wondered if I shouldn't have turned her down. She wasn't bad, as I recalled.

A polished female voice answered Westra's number on the first ring and summoned him on my request. Westra sounded as if he was on his third martini.

"What's up, Doc?," I asked. I figured if I had to absorb the morgue jokes, he could take a little Bugs Bunny. Besides, it must have been important to him if he asked me to call him at home.

"Herpes," he exclaimed, "and heroin addict."

"Penicillin and methadone, Doc," I said. "Then take two aspirin and call me in three days, after you get my bill." I was making a doctor joke.

He surprised me by laughing. "I guess I asked for that," he said. "What I mean is that your burn victim today was in an advanced stage of herpes and was also shot up on heroin, according to preliminary laboratory findings. I thought y'all might need that information tonight, so I went ahead and called."

"I'm glad you did, Doctor. Herpes, Christ, I don't think that's exactly an epidemic among lesbians."

"Lesbians?" he asked.

"Yeah, I think the girl might have been a lesbian. She apparently was turning tricks out of a ladies' gay bar on Harry Hines."

"Tricks-gay bar?" he stumbled with the inconsistency.

"Possibly some, uh... friends were sending her up on the street to sell a little tail to some dirtbags who hung around the Rooster Club on Harry Hines," I explained. "I guess she got herpes from the tricks and heroin from God knows where. Can you check if Herpes is the only disease she was carrying?"

"Sounds like she won't be missed," he said. "But the lab will run a full screen for further diseases."

"If she isn't missed, we may never figure out who cooked her for breakfast. Our first order of business is to see if she had a butch."

"Butch?" He sounded confused again. Westra needed to get out more.

I considered an explanation of my mini-view of the relationships among sub-cultural divisions and the pecking order of lesbians but reconsidered. "I mean her lover."

"Oh, boy, how damn obnoxious," he answered.

Westra calling somebody obnoxious was like the King of England criticizing welfare. "Yeah, pretty kinky sometimes," I added to the hypocrisy. "Listen, thank you, Doctor. I'll get back to you."

"Say, Kobok," he interrupted, "we called Texas Bell and asked them to send us her dental chart and other medical records. They said they'd already gave you copies. As soon as you give me the records, I'll send y'all a copy of our report." He had worked overtime, a good sign.

"Two root canals, one herpes, one heroin habit," I quipped. "Maybe so."

"Say what?"

"Thank you, Doctor," I dismissed the conversation. It sounded like Westra was Howdy's cousin.

"Good evening, Kobok," he said formally, probably feeling his martinis.

In the bathroom, I found a note from the commode-hugger taped to the mirror with a Band-Aid: "Had a marvelous time. Call me. I demand a rematch."

I wondered if the rematch related to drinking, fornicating, or vomiting, because frankly, I had finished second in all three categories. I thought how difficult it was going to be to call her because I had no idea who the hell she was. As a matter of fact, I couldn't recall what she looked like. A rematch would probably kill me, anyway.

I called Hooper. He answered with an officious, "Hello." Hooper was reputed to be the son of a Baptist minister. That he swore like a profanity aficionado, was another one of those things that doesn't fit the world plan.

"Got some news on our murder."

"Workin' late, huh?"

"Naw, right in the middle of a Methodist Youth Fellowship meeting."

He smirked politely at my temporary transgression into the normal world and said, "Finished the neighborhood canvass. Already filled you in. Katherine was not a big social mixer but had lots of male visitors."

"You hinted at that earlier."

"I interviewed everybody that Texas Bell would let me get at today. Only verified this chick was kind of a loner. Didn't seem to date anyone from work. I got the impression that she was kind of goofy, you know, distant and troubled."

I explained the herpes, heroin, lesbianism, and probable prostitution.

"Well then, she had a full plate," he answered. "Several good reasons to be troubled." I then told him in detail about the interviews with Shark and Ralphie at the Rooster Club and with Chris at Boobs. He recalled Shark from the Stud Rail fire on Gaston Avenue, although he had not actually been assigned to the investigation. He also knew Chris because we had both been assigned to investigate the arson homicide in the bar on Fitzhugh.

"A lesbian prostitute with herpes and a heroin habit! Man, that's a file for the sociology textbook. If she screwed both men and women at random from that neighborhood, we already have three to four thousand suspects."

"Yeah, and that doesn't count the chance of a random crazy breaking into her apartment."

"The only evidence of forced entry was where the firefighters kicked in the front door. The first units reported all windows and doors locked."

"Does that mean the killer let him…or herself out and locked the door behind with a key. Or that she let him in?"

"Entirely possible."

"What did the scene search turn up?" I asked.

"Nothing remarkable," he said.

I wondered if he had borrowed that term from Westra. "Letters from her mother. One letter from her father. Fancy furnishings, a closet full of women's clothes. And some men's clothing, including cowboy boots. Not surprising if she was gay, I reckon."

"Were the clothes her size?"

"No, man's size clothes, and the boots were ten and a half."

"Don't forget that she was bi-sexual. They could have belonged to either a boyfriend or a big footed butch."

"Yeah, either," he reflected.

"What was the father's address?"

"Kansas City was the postmark on the letter we found."

"Did she have a car?"

"Yeah, the title was in her dresser. It's financed with Farm and Home, a nineteen seventy-nine Malibu. But we couldn't find the damn car."

"Which probably means that she rode home with the looney who killed her and left her car somewhere else," I said. "If we can find the car, we might find where she met the killer. Did you find the keys?"

"Yes, but that doesn't mean we found the only set. I've

already put the license number and description out to all districts. I asked for a concentration on the Hose Line."

"Good. I need to get some sleep. Can I meet you at your office at seven-thirty in the morning?"

"Okay," he said.

I hung up and took my overdone TV Mexican dinner out of the oven. I got most of it down with the help of two more beers. Funny what a little health food will do for the system. Feeling fed, half drunk, and definitely better, I tried to recall the face of the chick I left in close embrace with my commode that morning. Blank. Crap.

Over another beer, I sat down at the kitchen table to rearrange notes on the day's activities. I wanted to get a head start on the lengthy, detailed report the federal system required of investigative activity. The system was carnivorous. It had an insatiable appetite for paperwork, often totally unnecessary paperwork. I had also learned long ago I could never feed it enough paper fast enough to choke the monster.

I reflected on what we knew. Farm girl comes to big city. Enters the complex society that too often devours the moral fiber of its inhabitants. Apparently becomes a welcome part of the lesbian community although apparently not naturally attracted to a so called alternate lifestyle. Also, learns to accept sex from strange men and sells her body to the low-life customers of the bars around Harry Hines Boulevard.

But she was young and attractive enough that she should have been able to sell her favors to a wealthier clientele. Why turn tricks on the Hose Line? Why no arrest record? The Dallas PD Vice Squad rounded up hookers by the bus loads, literally. I made a mental note to check with Vice first thing in the morning. Maybe she used another name.

We hadn't found her car or her purse.

Her father had split, brother had died in Vietnam. Both events tragedies, but bearable. The kid was distant. Were there other factors to pursue? I hand wrote eight pages for Tootie and looked at my watch. It was 10:15, too early for humans to go to bed solely for the purpose of sleeping. I went to bed any way.

I attempted to lie in bed and fantasize about the nameless

lady from the night before, but my mind refused to unload the events of the day. The face of Katherine Mae Pritchard smiled at my imagination from the darkened room. The scene from Westra's table was indelible.

Prostitutes worked the streets in several areas of Dallas. We needed to find her favorite street or other base for turning tricks if she didn't work Harry Hines. A sweep of Dallas PD vice files and of records of similar murder was in order.

I needed to find Katherine's butch or boyfriend or what the hell ever arrangement she had. Who treated her herpes?

CHAPTER 7: THE LAW OF SOCIAL BALANCE

To pursue the myth of social harmony, society must send someone to deal with the dirtballs responsible for the problem.

Beat to hell, still half-hungover, physically spent, I was still wide awake when the telephone shrilled at 10:52 P. M. Go figure.

"Asleep?" I had heard that line earlier in the day. It was Chris Rochambeau's deep voice.

"Gettin' any?" I asked.

"Some," she answered. Then, "Sherlock, I found the dude of whom you seek."

"Dude?" I asked lamely.

"Her butch, dammit. That little sweetheart Katherine who you say got fried. Her ugly assed butch uses the name Charlie, real name Doris Johnson. Hell, Kobock, she's probably as old as you 'n me."

"How can I find her, Chris?"

"She works as the bouncer at the Club Twenty-Six on Maple."

"Is that the place with the blue front, just south of Inwood?" I asked.

"Yeah."

"Did you tell anyone that Katherine was murdered?"

"Goddam, it's on the afternoon news."

"Chris, I'll drive down and talk to her. I'll keep your name out of it."

"Well, Kobok, I don't give a damn if you tell that punk assed bitch my name or not. Send ol' Charlie over, and I'll break his fucking arm." She emphasized the masculine reference to Doris.

I didn't mention herpes or heroin. "You reckon she's, I mean, he's working now?" I asked.

She was Chris again with a laugh right out of a coal mine. "She, dammit, she. And yeah she's working. I know the manager of that dive. Just hung up from talking. Go for it. And by the way, Charlie is plenty mean. Real likely to kick you in your little nuts."

Bars had three hours till closing time at 1:30 A.M. I dressed and peddled the Chevrolet down to Maple Avenue. I parked a block away and walked to the Club Twenty-Six. It was still stifling hot. I entered at 11:40. The walk had caused me to ooze sweat. Ol' Doris, sometimes Charlie, was on the door. Or at least, I assumed it was Charlie the bouncer. Chris was right—ugly, squat, about forty, wearing a black Members Only, with a cut scar across the bridge of her nose.

"Charlie?"

"Who wants to know?" she growled.

"Federal officer." I flashed my badge. "I need to talk to you."

"Piss off," she said and pushed me one-handed in the chest. Bad idea.

I looked around. Only two or three inside near the door and none looking our way. I grabbed ol' Charlie/Doris by the lapels of her Members Only and threw her through the open door down the three stairs onto the concrete sidewalk. She hit face up, and her head took a pretty good lick against the concrete. I single-stepped the stairs as she tried to turn over to raise herself and kicked her in the ribs. Yeah, yeah, I know all about the rule about not hitting girls. Somehow, this was a tad different. A little gut kick certainly put her out of the fighting mood.

"Careful, partner, you'll make me really angry," I said.

She tried to get to all fours. Two fat women in men's clothes came down the stairs. More filled the doorway.

"What's the deal, man?" one said, a little hesitantly, I thought. They smelled police on me.

I pulled up my shirt and showed them my trusty government issue. .357 Magnum. "Who wants to come out here first?" I asked. The two nearest retreated. "I want to talk to my old lady here, and I can't decide whether to kill somebody first or not." I made a little gesture for the pistol, and all scrambled back around the doorway. I expected the Dallas police momentarily.

I took Doris by the nape of the neck and back of the pants and walked her around the corner into the alley.

"You're an ill-mannered little darlin'."

"Whatchu want, man?" she spat. She could still fight.

I considered several one-liners about cultural communication gaps but said, "I want to know about Katherine Mae Pritchard of Brown County, Oklahoma."

"Why didn't you say so, dammit? Now you probably got me fired from my job."

"Mostly because you were intent on seeing if I'd kick your ass. I know somebody who knows the owner of the Twenty-Six. I'll make her an offer she can't refuse," I said. "Now tell me about your deal with Katherine." I yanked her to her feet by her torn Members Only.

"Hey, damn. Okay! I only been with Katy three or four weeks. Come on, man. I heard she was dead. I didn't do it. I'm gonna kill whoever did."

I think I saw a glisten of tears in the dark of the alley. But remember the old saying, "The greater the oath, the greater the lie."

"I think you caught her wrong with another lover and treated her to a high-octane bath," I said.

"No, no, no, hell no, man," she pleaded. Suddenly a woman again, she had lost her masculine veneer. "I only heard a couple of hours ago," she allowed a sob to slip out. "Lemme go, or I'll scream for help," she further reverted to the feminine. She then attempted a vicious, heavy weight man-kick to my groin.

I drove my fist into her midsection, far enough for her to know I meant business. She went to her knees, but I caught her before she went all the way down. "Scream over that," I said. "Now Doris, you and I are going to walk a block down to my car where we can talk in poorly air-conditioned comfort."

I jerked her back to her feet. She tried to argue but only managed a gasp as she vomited on the alley floor.

Then, there they were. Three of them were blocking my exit from the alley. Two were white, and one was African American. The African American and one white must have each been 240 pounds.

"Where the hell you goin'?" the biggest white said, brandishing a club. The smaller white temporarily blinded me with one of those flashlights that is also a club.

I showed my badge and credential case and said, "Me and my girlfriend here are having a social conversation. Ain't that right, sweetheart?" I shoved Charlie in front of me as a sort of shield. She made no answer.

"Do you need company?" the African American grinned. I could see white teeth in the dim light of the alley from the glare of the flashlight. A good place to get killed, I thought.

"Only to turn the natives back into that damn club," I said.

The alley behind them was glutted with civilians.

As the three turned toward the crowd, I could see their badges shine in contrast against the dark blue uniforms in the dark of the alley. "Police business. Get back inside, ladies," the smaller white officer said.

The patrons of Club Twenty-Six were used to violence. Unless I missed my guess, the bouncer was probably a bully and not popular with the regular clientele anyway.

"Do you want us to stick around, Kobok?" the big African American officer asked. He looked to be about twenty-three. I wondered why he wasn't playing defensive tackle for the Cowboys—or at least for a weaker team like the Redskins. Maybe he had knee trouble.

The bigger white officer looked like a twenty-year-old giant Robert Redford. What the hell was I doing in this business? All three of these kids looked not only fit and mean enough to stuff me into a bushel basket but spoke with the diction of Southern Methodist University professors. The quality of the young people coming up in the business was clearly passing me by.

"No, men. Thanks for saving me from these bad-ass ladies."

I still had a grip on ol' Doris' Members Only.

"How does a guy get on with ATF?" The smaller white cop asked a popular question.

"First, you got to be nuts." They laughed in unison at the regular answer. "Let's walk down the street," I said, "and I'll give you my card. If you'll call me sometime, I'll buy the beer."

They followed the chubby bouncer and me in two white

patrol cars down the block to my white Chevrolet. I put Doris in the front passenger seat and stood outside, passing the time with the three young cops.

Patrol officers are the soul of law enforcement. They're usually the youngest and most enthusiastic members, anxious to make some impact on the law enforcement community. They often feel isolated from investigators and almost always are glad to be taken into the so-called confidence of older investigative types. And, boy, was I older than those guys.

I recounted the details of the Katherine Pritchard case. I mentioned the burned wire on the stubs of wrists, her employment with Texas Bell, the yellow telephone receiver forced into her private parts, her Oklahoma origin, and everything else that I felt pertinent to a dark street, in-house police discussion.

There was only a remote chance that these young men could help, but they made numerous service calls into homes and bars in the area, and that they were willing to assist in any way.

"Hey, aren't you the ATF guy who worked the deal where the midget bit Muscles Malloy, the vice guy, in the crotch?" the larger white officer asked.

"In the balls, to be more specific," I replied.

"We heard that Malloy has taken to wearing a plastic nut cup," laughed the big white officer. He was just a kid himself.

Doris opened the door of my old Chevrolet and said, "I gotta puke, man. I think you broke one of my guts." She wretched on the concrete.

"Somebody she ate didn't agree with her," quipped the smaller white officer. Everybody laughed.

They worked for Central Patrol and finished their shift at midnight. I promised that if I could get rid of Doris before 2:00 A.M., bar closing time, I would meet them at the Shouldn't Do for a beer. I watched them drive off in opposite directions in two cars.

I settled into the driver's side of my Chevrolet. Doris had regained sufficient composure to qualify at least partly as Charlie again.

"Man, what you dickin' with me for? I think you broke my gut or a rib. I'm trying to puke blood. Goddam you," she said.

"Look, dipshit, you shouldn't have come on me like King Kong."

"Damned ape. You half killed me and got my ass fired," she complained.

"Look, I already said that I'd make the owner an offer she couldn't turn down. Besides, think. You're still alive, which is more than I can say for your girlfriend, Katherine Mae Pritchard."

She sobbed, again female. "I didn't hurt her, and I swear I'm gonna kill whoever did," she hissed. A look came over her craggy, flaxen face that told me she meant it. An angry butch like an angry anybody else, could be violent enough to mutilate her lover, properly motivated.

"Okay, Charlie, let's talk by the numbers. Gimme a driver's license."

She obediently handed me a license from her hip pocket. It read: Doris Marie Johnson, 6300 Rio Bravo, Dallas. She was born January 31, 1946, and was five-feet, nine-inches tall. She looked about 180. I wondered why she hadn't whipped my ass.

"Is this the correct address?" I asked.

"Yeah."

"Got a telephone?"

"Yeah, five-five-five-four-three-seven-two."

"Where are you from?"

"Amarillo."

"When did you last see Katherine?"

"Last night around ten. She came by the club here where I work—used to work before you stuck your ass in." I declined to repeat my relationship with the owner.

"Came by here? How?" "In her car, the blue Malibu."

If Doris was telling the truth and Katherine Mae Pritchard had, in fact, been at the club at 10:00 P. M., then she was in route to her doom, based on the time of the fire. Of course, the wretched heap of humanity on my car seat could have very well taken time out to murder Katherine—but why?

"Sure you didn't take her home?"

"No, she was with a friend. She said that she'd be back at closing," she said.

"Friend?" I smelled a rival girlfriend.

"Yeah, a guy."

"A trick?"

"Look, I didn't like her turning tricks. I sure as hell didn't know who he was."

"Bullshit. It looks like you were pimping her right out the front door of the Club Twenty-Six."

"No, no!," she exclaimed. I saw tears glisten in the darkened car again. "She had two or three regulars that she knew before I met her. I think it was one of them. I didn't see him. She was driving and got out across the street. He stayed in the car."

"Did she say he was a trick?," I asked.

"No, but I knew. She was also all upset."

"Upset?"

"She was excited or something. Just upset mostly."

"But she did say that she would be right back?"

"Yes," she sobbed again.

"How did you get home?"

"I gotta car. I drove, I got off here at two and waited until two-thirty. I got to thinking that she might have gone on to my apartment, and I went there. I waited up. Kobok, it wasn't the first time she didn't come home. She had her own place, but I didn't go over there. I went to bed at maybe four o'clock. I got a call from a dude at Boobs this afternoon who told me Katy had been murdered. Now you're accusing me." More tears.

"Charlie, I want you to take a polygraph examination first thing in the morning," I said.

"I didn't do it," she became more agitated. "You're gonna frame me with a machine."

I gave her the standard speech that we used to induce someone to take a polygraph before they conferred with a lawyer who would invariably advise them not to take the exam.

"Charlie, we want to clear you, first, before we go onto other leads," I lied. I intended to use the polygraph as a wedge to drive her fat ass straight to death row in downtown Huntsville, Texas, USA, if she was guilty.

"Okay," she said, finally. "What if I flunk?"

"It can't be used against you in court," I said, glossing over the fact that a polygraph certainly could be used to secure an indictment, and it certainly was a good tool of interrogation to use against a suspect who had "flunked." The results could not, however, be used as evidence in a courtroom trial. But that's what I had just said.

I had heard all I needed for the time being. "I'll drop you at your car," I said.

"I'll walk," she said, looking at me questioningly with her hand on the door. Her red eyes and look of total hopelessness was convincing. I probably had the wrong perp, but I wasn't about to drop her this early in the case.

"Okay, I'll pick you up at this address on Rio Bravo at eight in the morning. If you're not there, Charlie, you had better find a steel box in Australia to hide in." I leaned over and looked into her face. "Understand?"

"Yeah, yeah, I'll be there. Don't hit me no more."

I watched her fat backside sway a few steps under the dim street lights. I started the Chevrolet and drove down a block before I turned into a darkened parking lot and looked back. She had turned a corner and was out of my line of sight. I turned around and slow-trailed her. She walked back past the Club Twenty-Six and a block down, got into the old green Ford pickup with a tan fender parked on the lot of an all-male gay bar. What the hell was that?

She drove the pickup directly down Maple to Lemmon and turned off to the burned apartment of Katherine Mae Pritchard. She got out of the old pickup and stood in front of the burned-out hulk for several minutes. She then abruptly re-entered the truck and drove directly to the 6300 block of Rio Bravo, the address shown on her driver's license. Again, I watched as she got out of the truck and waddled into a ground floor apartment.

Inside, a light came on. I found a mailbox for apartment 112. On the leaf was the name "Johnson", and I made a brilliant James Bondish deduction that it must be her apartment. I waited in the car nearby to see if she was going to split. I was now uncertain if she might have actually murdered and roasted her lover, Katherine.

Doris was a low-class, unattractive, aging loser, trapped in a culture where the mates available to her were in a minority. The really attractive ones out of reach. Sweet, vivacious Katherine was far and above anything old Charlie/Doris had gotten a hold of in years. Maybe she had caught Katherine wrong with another mate, possibly the man she spoke of from the night before. Had Doris, the lover, become Charlie, the maniac. Or perhaps, Charlie, the lover, had become...?

The gender doesn't matter. Sometime, kinky sex went down, even when murder wasn't in the picture. The leap to what should have been a lovers' spat developing into a bizarre mutilation murder, complete with a $300,000 four-alarm fire, would not really be that unusual. In fact, it was probably right out of chapter thirteen of a first-year sociology textbook. The gay community, like the so-called "straight community" had all types.

I waited ten minutes until the light switched off. I expected her to come out the front door on a trot. Five more minutes. Could she have gone to bed? Maybe a couple of downers and crash. Come on, Doris, don't destroy my theory. Run.

I gave up. It was ten minutes past one. The Shouldn't Do was only seven minutes away and was open until 2:00. I rationalized that Doris was probably asleep, so I headed downtown.

I drove and tried to gather my thoughts. Where the hell was Katherine's blue Malibu? I was beginning to see her more personally. I envisioned the vaguely smiling face in the photograph. Boy, what I'd give to find that trick Charlie had spoken of. I was hopeful that if I could get ol' Doris on the box, the polygraph, she would flunk. Kobok's brilliant interrogation breaks down perpetrator, perpetrator gets ninety-nine years, case closed. Let Howdy stuff his No Potential stamp someplace uncomfortable. I was beginning to hallucinate again, I think.

I made The Shouldn't Do in five minutes by running four red lights on the way.

CHAPTER 8: THE LAW OF INFORMERS

Citizens who come forward with information are not really inform-ers in cop-speak. True informers, snitches if you would, cooperate with the law for one of three reasons: money or other gain (like a get out of jail card), revenge, or mental instability. Most are motivated by a com-bination of all three.

The place was about half full. The big, African American officer, easily recognizable even in his civvies, waved to me from a table in the rear. He was wearing a black T-shirt that said EARTH, WIND, AND FIRE in all capitals across the front. I wondered what the hell that meant. Later, I heard on the radio that it was a rock musical group. You learn something new every day.

The Shouldn't Do was a "safe" bar, patronized primarily by law enforcement officers and a few police groupies. It was safe in that the proprietor, Donald "Two Jumps" Preston, a living and wrinkled copy of the ancient mariner, catered to cops only. He also was a professional snitch.

The place was on East Commerce, three blocks from the Police and Courts Building where the world had seen Jack Ruby put one into Lee Harvey Oswald's guts on live world-wide TV. Various law enforcement agencies' badges adorned the walls in blown-up logo versions, each in violation of the individual agency's ethics code. Hung over the main bar was a visi-bar, the thing with dual red revolving lights designed to be mounted on the roof of a marked squad car.

Two Jumps used the light for several things, but its main purpose was to signal free rounds of drinks to different combinations of the house at odd times. That didn't happen often, by the way.

I don't know if he made a dime on the joint, but he had a hell of a lot better life than most people I ever met. Two Jumps had started this life as a burglar. He did his rookie training on residence burglaries and graduated to larger, more profitable commercial break-ins. He developed an MO whereby he would take off an entire appliance warehouse with a crew of illegal aliens using rented trucks.

Old-time burglary officers described Two Jumps as a "pretty damn good burglar." Translated into normal-people talk, that means not good enough to avoid getting caught. A Dallas police officer interrupted Two Jumps and his crew of thieves loading television sets into trucks on Irving Boulevard. A TAC officer relieved Two Jumps of his left foot with a riot shotgun.

Thereafter, in the twisted jargon of the dirtbag world, one-legged Texas Department of Corrections inmate #Cl24F25, Preston, Donald, became "Two Jumps." The name evolved from the limp with his artificial foot, for which the citizens of Texas graciously purchased and fitted to the stump of his left ankle.

Two Jumps eventually got paroled back to Dallas County. A long story simply stated, he fell on his ass again. He got himself involved with a group of high-rolling burglars and managed to get re-arrested by the Dallas Tactical Unit during a burglary in progress. Through some skillful manipulation by Dallas cops, Two Jumps snitched his way out of the case, sending all his fall-partners away for a free vacation.

He eventually married the widow Hortense Fay Shetland, of Waxahachie, Texas, formerly a street whore of downtown Dallas, Texas. Hortense had received a sizable inheritance from her late husband, a furniture tycoon. She purchased the Shouldn't Do and established Two Jumps in one of his lifelong vocations.

His other vocation was maintaining criminal contacts and systematically snitching to nearly every law enforcement agency in the Dallas area. He jumped on the opportunity—no pun intended—to do all he could to encourage and promote his relationship with his former tormentors, the police. On the whole, he was probably a better barkeeper than burglar.

He was leaning on the back bar when I walked in, grinning like he had won yesterday's Irish Sweepstakes. His hairline now six inches north of his eyebrows, he kept what hair he had left in an elaborate comb over. But he was nowhere in Three Hair's Dorsen's league.

The crowd at the table started out with three young Dallas patrol officers and one fading ATF hack. In a half hour the crowd had grown considerable, all cops. Around 1:00 A. M., Muscles Malloy limped in and good naturedly endured a round of "don't let the midget bite off your package" jokes. By enduring the banter, he managed to avoid paying for any drinks.

By the time Two Jumps activated his visi-bar to signify last call at 1:20 A. M., I had managed to get down four cold beers. We continued the gathering on the parking lot behind the place with two quarts of scotch that Two Jumps had obligingly bootlegged to us out the back door. We consumed the scotch amid a morass of police war stories that grew increasingly ludicrous in direct proportion to the declining level of the booze. We passed the bottles around hand-to-hand until the last drop disappeared down the gullet of a City of Richardson officer who appeared too drunk to work for the next three days.

The party ended with Malloy dropping his trousers to allow several drunk cops to make a flashlight inspection of the damage done by the midget. Actually, he displayed no sutures, only about five pounds of swollen, purplish flesh.

How time flies when you're doing something important. I looked at my watch, and it was 4:50 A. M. and I hadn't slept in 24 hours. Why break a successful run, now?

CHAPTER 9: THE LAW OF A COP'S DUTY

In the cop trade it's not difficult to rationalize that, in the name of the good of society, you do what you have to do.

I drove out to Spring Valley, showered, shaved, and found some cleaner clothes. I called Bull Hooper at home before I started back downtown. He said he'd meet me in the 6300 block of Rio Bravo at 6:00 A.M. the next morning..

He was waiting down the block in his Dodge pickup. City officers didn't have take home cars like ATF agents. He jumped in with me, grinning, unlit cigar stub clenched in his teeth. I ran down last night's activity. Well, I omitted the trip to the Shouldn't Do and the extension of festivities on the parking lot.

"You look like you got an hour to live," he observed gravely.

I drove down the block to a greasy spoon that afforded a view of Charlie's green pickup parked in front of her apartment. Hooper and I went inside for breakfast. After we both shoveled down a ration of grease, carbohydrates, and stale coffee, we only had to wait until 7:20 before she fled. Charlie suddenly popped out, entered the pickup, and sped away toward Greenville Avenue. We left in a rush, following north on Greenville in the Chevrolet.

Morning traffic outbound was not heavy enough to impede her, and she passed under LBJ Freeway in minutes. She entered the city of Richardson, turning east on Main. Without hesitation, she turned into a low-rate apartment complex on Bower just off Belt Line. We watched as she drove to the rear of the complex, just out of our view.

"You better pull round to the back," Hooper said. He could smell the significance in her actions.

"I don't want her to burn us just yet. It's a small complex. If she gets inside an apartment, we can find her easily enough." I waited four more minutes.

Charlie spun the wheels of a blue Malibu out of the apartment complex back west on Belt Line in the direction she had just come from. The Malibu bore Texas license HPS 2134. Katherine's lost car was found—in Charlie's possession.

We followed her west on Belt Line. She apparently saw us just past Greenville Avenue. She gunned up the Malibu, and I put my foot to the old Chevrolet, which had too many miles but lots of engine. We went through the red light under Central, and by the time she passed Richardson High School she was crowding ninety. The front end on the old Chevrolet wanted to shimmy, but I knew the Malibu couldn't do any better for long. Parts literally flew all over the street when her engine blew, with steam and smoke enveloping the speeding blue car. She nearly lost it at ninety, but by the time she spun out in the intersection of Belt Line and Coit Road, she had lost enough speed to keep the old Malibu upright.

Just like on TV, she bailed out and tried to run. I caught her as she side straddle hopped across a Safeway parking lot. I resumed my hold on her Members Only. I was getting a feel for that coat. I sort of dragged her off her feet backwards, and she hit sitting down with a medium grunt. Like most fools, I figured the fight was over. Wrong.

She came up with a good right—well, pretty good for a girl - at my crotch and caught me with a lick in the right inside thigh that would raise one hell of a strawberry later.

She sprang to her feet and reversed her field with the grace of Tony Dorsett, right back in the direction of Hooper, who was ten feet behind. She bowled over the husky Hooper in her panic, and they dog-piled on the asphalt.

Hooper came up on top, but only temporarily. Doris boosted him over with more flair than Saturday night wrestling, partly tearing the arm off his shirt in the process. She almost broke free as she regained her feet a second time and waddled across the parking lot. Hooper caught her by an ankle, dumping her a third time. She sprawled on the hard surface with a resolute "Bastard!"

Hooper sort of straddled her and looked back at me with an expression less than loving. He half laughed. "Lemme kill this piece of shit."

"Hell, Bull I was here in reserve, son. Keep it up. I think you can whip her eventually." He pulled his handcuffs from the back of his belt and snapped her wrists behind her.

"Doris, we really do need to stop meeting this way," I said.

Some well-intended citizen must have called the police. A Dallas squad rolled up. The two uniformed officers surveyed the situation and inspected the Richardson/Dallas city limit markers nearby. They concluded that nothing but grief could come from a collar like this and quickly advised the Dallas dispatcher that the roadside brawl was, happily for them, in the city of Richardson by about ten feet.

Not surprisingly, Richardson police cars began arriving in numbers. A sergeant was dispatched to the scene, and he strode up with a grave expression. I explained the situation, and he agreed to arrange to have the car towed to the Richardson city pound. Hooper, ol' Charlie/Doris, and I headed downtown in the Chevrolet.

We'd gone about a mile when I stopped and changed places with Hooper. I slipped into the back seat with Charlie. Hooper was a journeyman, taking a circuitous route and play straight man in the old game of "Cops Screw the Maggot."

We passed Rosemont Cemetery. Doris had decided to dummy up. "Pull in here," I growled." I'm gonna' have to do what needs to be done."

"No dammit, come on," Hooper pleaded. "Not this one, too." He herded the old Chevrolet into the cemetery. He drove through the nurtured rows until he observed an open grave, halting prudently near the neatly squared abyss.

He shut off the engine and leaned back over the seat. "Listen, Kobok," he started, "They damn near got us for that Russian guy you did. Look, I got grandkids. If you blow this, I could go to the damn joint. Please, don't do it."

He might win an Academy Award, given time to develop his lines.

"No, by God," I said harshly. "We got pressure to clear this damn case, and this mope isn't telling us all she knows, like how the blue Malibu got to Richardson."

Charlie had now become Doris again, complete with sobbing. She appeared to be genuinely terrified. I didn't think anyone would be fooled by our charade. The hard eyes had blended to wild animal fright.

"Hell, man, if you're going to do another one, please give me a chance to get out and not be a witness." Hooper opened the driver's side door and got out on the gravel drive. He leaned back in and said, "Here's an open grave. Just give me a chance to walk off somewhere first." He looked like he was going to cry. Hell of a performance.

He slammed the door, and Doris went snot-blowing berserk. "Crazy bastards! Lemme go. Lemme go! Damn you. Lemme go." She tried to kick at me within the constraint of hands cuffed behind.

"How did the Malibu get to Richardson?"

"I already told you I don't know, man."

I opened the rear door and called to Hooper, waiting nearby, a freshly lit stogie in place. "Get that shovel outta the trunk." That did it. Shovels always play well in the graveyard.

"Awright, awright, good God awright," she blurted., wild-eyed. "I'll run the deal down for you. But, first, please… please… get me the hell outta here."

I motioned Hooper back to the car, and we drove toward downtown. I suggested we go to DPD. I wasn't sure the Federal Building was ready for Charlie.

"Gimme …gimme a cigarette," she said, finally.

"I don't smoke and you can see Hooper's tobacco habit isn't cigarettes."

We stopped at a convenience store. "What brand, Charlie?" I asked.

"Winston, in a hard pack," she specified.

I delivered the smokes, lit her a Winston, and put the pack in the pocket of her shirt. She was still not fully collected, and she sobbed sporadically. I cut her some slack and didn't ask any questions for a few minutes. Within eyeshot of the skyline, I told Hooper to pull to the curb. He complied, wordlessly.

"Well?" I looked to the bad assed bouncer of the Club Twenty- Six.

"There's two more people," she sighed apprehensively.

"Yeah?"

"Okay," she said. "Yeah, two.. A chick and some goddamn dude."

"Tell us about it," Hooper looked back.

"The dude first," I said, speculating that the man, if he existed, could be our murderer.

"Him, I don't know," she said, again hesitant. "He had been with Katy before I ever met her. He's the dude I mentioned she was with the first time you kicked my ass. She never brought him around me. I think he might have been older. A trick from way back."

"What'd he look like?" I asked.

"Gray, grayish hair, white man, maybe fifty or more."

"Tall or short?" I asked.

"I don't know. I only saw him in cars, you know."

"Slender, fat, medium, or what?," I continued.

"Average," she answered. "Never seen him in daylight."

"Would you know him if you saw him again?," Hooper asked.

"I don't think so," she replied. I believed she was telling the truth, so far.

"Was he a boyfriend?" I used the forbidden term.

"No, that's the funny thing. I even asked her. She never really gave me a straight answer. I just assumed he was a regular trick."

"And you wouldn't know him if you saw him?" Hooper asked.

"No, he had silver-gray hair, combed straight back. I don't really know nothin' else about the way he looks," she asserted. "Drove a dark blue Ford pickup."

"Texas tags?" Hooper asked.

"Dunno."

"The story you told us about the trick in the car with Katherine at the Club Twenty-Six? Was that the truth?," I asked.

"Yeah, it was the guy I'm talking about. Do you think he killed Katy?"

"He's as good suspect as any. The chick? Tell us about the other girl you just mentioned, Charlie," I tried to ask gently. Her countenance changed at the thought of another woman. She tossed out a bomb.

"I know her name. Sharon Jaco," she said authoritatively.

"And?" Hooper asked.

"And what?" she asked.

"What was her relationship to Katherine?" I said. I figured Hooper and I could handle one busted down female. I leaned her forward in the back seat and removed the handcuffs.

Grateful, she took the Winston from her lips. "I...I'm not sure. Probably an old lover. You know."

"Your rival?" I said.

"No, dammit," she glared at me. "Katy and I had a thing, and there was no rival. Whatever or whoever she done was business only. Moisture was forming in the corner of her tired eyes.

I retreated from the rival lover theory." Then what was she?," I asked, "A pen pal?"

"A friend. Maybe they had made it, but Sharon was a feme, all girl, uh, totally bi-sexual. I guess you understand our ways. If they made it, you know, if they slept together, it was a passing deal. I really don't think they did," she answered. "Katy needed a dude like me to keep 'er happy."

"Yeah, I could tell she was very well adjusted," Hooper looked at her in the rear-view mirror.

"How old is Sharon Jaco, Charlie?" I interrupted.

"Maybe twenty-five, I dunno, really."

"Where did she live? Where did she work? Where did she go?" I asked.

"Uh, she lived in Richardson, I think. She worked around. Tended bar some. Mostly slept around. That's another reason she couldn't have been permanent with Katy. She was too promising."

"Promiscuous?"

"Yeah. Uh, what was the other question?"

"Where did she go...hang out, this Sharon Jaco?" I repeated.

"She turned tricks. I've seen her around for a year or so."

"Seen? Where?" I leaned toward her. She instinctively shrieked. I figured I wasn't going to have to wrestle her anymore. Good. I was due to lose the third fall.

"At the Twenty-Six. At Boobs. I heard she had syphilis, Christ. Or something."

"Syphilis?" I asked. "How do you know?"

"Word gets around the bars," she said. "Nobody wants a disease for Christ's sake."

They weren't alone, I thought. Jesus, if Sharon Jaco had syphilis, then probably, so did Katherine. Westra had said Katherine had herpes when he called me on the telephone. Maybe both had herpes, the "or something" Charlie had just mentioned, and not syphilis at all?

"You sure it was syphilis, Charlie, and not herpes?"

"Hell, I don't know, man."

Hooper swung through McDonald's. I bought Charlie a Big Mac and chocolate shake, which she devoured with a fervor. She had another Winston. As she talked, she gradually described the evolution of her relationship between Sharon Jaco and Katherine. Charlie admitted she'd known Jaco for some time and had even been intimate with her several times.

She had met Katherine, she explained, after the pretty young Oklahoma native had watched her ass-kick two men who had become rowdy in front of the Club Twenty-Six. She soon "made it" with Katherine, and they had discussed sharing an apartment.

Sharon Jaco had only been a common thread. Sharon appeared to be no more than a gay or bi-sexual groupie prostitute who had engaged in casual sex with both men and women as circumstances provided. I figured Katherine Pritchard might have followed a similar path.

Charlie steadfastly contended that she had last seen Katherine on the night before her murder at about 10:00 P. M., accompanied by the gray-haired man she had just described as an old trick. She tearfully maintained that her entire story was the truth.

As we drove downtown, Tootie called me on the radio.

"Three-three-two-three," I answered into the microphone, leaning over the front seat.

"Call Detective J. E. Jones of the Richardson Police

Department, right away," she instructed. "He said it was important."

"Thank you." I handed the mic back to Hooper.

Hooper found a gas station where I could pay-phone Jones.

Jones, a good friend of mine, followed the standard police practice of using initials of name not only for the usual reasons. He worked for the relatively small suburban Richardson police department that only employed about 125 officers. He had been partnered with the only other officer in the department with the same name, James Jones. J. E. Jones was in-house code to differentiate J. E. from the other James Jones, commonly called "Jim" Jones.

"Jones," he answered.

"Eliot Ness here," I said.

"Hey, where the hell you been?" he asked.

"Stopped at the First Church for services," I answered.

"Oh, a funeral," he laughed. "Who'd you kill this time?"

"My former supervisor," I retorted quickly.

"Which one?" he laughed again. "Lotta sergeants and super-visors who need killing."

"What's up?" I asked the subject.

"I helped our people inventory that Malibu before placing it in the pound. Among other crap, we found a woman's purse that belonged to a Sharon Jaco. I thought it might help in your case. Is she anybody you want to ask about?"

"Yeah, I think so," I said, wondering how Sharon Jaco's purse was in Katherine Mae Pritchard's Malibu, which shouldn't have been in the Bowser Street apartments in Richardson. I had a headache. It must have already been over a hundred degrees.

I got back in the back seat of the Chevrolet with Charlie. The air-conditioned interior of the car must have been twenty-five degrees cooler than outside the car.

"Charlie, you were telling us about Sharon Jaco," I said. "Where exactly did she live?"

"I-I'm not sure," she said. "Like I said, maybe Richardson."

"Bullshit," I shouted into her face. "Charlie, I'm gettin' tired of kickin' your ass, but I got enough energy for one more go at it."

She tried like hell to get smaller. "Don't hit me, Kobok. You already hurt me." I had no intention of hitting her.

"Okay, okay. I knew the car was parked at her apartment on Bowser."

"The Malibu? Katherine's car?" Hooper asked.

"Yeah," she answered.

"How did it get there?" I asked.

"Katy took it there."

"Why?" Hooper asked.

"I'm not sure," she said. "Okay, look. Katy called me at the club after I had seen her at ten o'clock. She said that she was leaving the car at Sharon's apartment. That's how I found it. I figured they were out there screwing around. Maybe she was cheatin' on me, the bitch. I should have driven to both apartments...Jaco and Katherine's." Her lower lip began quivering again. "Maybe she'd still be alive."

"When did she call?" I asked.

"I was drunk. About one-thirty, I think," she said.

"How did you get the keys?" I asked.

"I had a set of my own."

"Why did you split?" Hooper asked.

"I figured you were going to frame me or something. The Malibu was a better car than my old truck." Her explanation sounded sincere.

"Where were you going?" I asked.

"West. Maybe Amarillo. Maybe China or hell. Who knows?"

"Where is Sharon now?" Hooper asked.

"I don't have the slightest damned idea," she answered, looking apprehensive. She looked beat. I wondered how I looked.

We sweated Charlie—literally in the rising heat. I calculated that she had told us all she was going to. Sharon Jaco did not appear to be a rival lover, only a passing fling.

I wanted to let her go, but she was a definite flight risk and we might need her later. We transported her to the Dallas County jail and explained that we were going to give her a big break. We would only file charges for assault on a police officer and not auto theft. We would ask the judge—a Justice of the Peace in this case, to grant a reasonable bail.

We didn't explain that the particular Justice of the Peace that we had in mind was, as the phrase goes, about two notches to the right of Gengis Khan. He eventually set bond at $25,000, easily attainable by certain dope dealers but way out of Charlie's reach. I doubted that Charlie could raise twenty-five dollars. She would ride a cell for a while, at least until we had room to develop more background in this mess the legal system called a case.

CHAPTER 10: THE LAW OF FOOLS

Proverbs 26:16 observes that a sluggard is wiser in his own conceit than seven men who can render a reason. And to think they had that figured out before modern police supervisory promotion policies were invented.

Hooper said he needed to drop by Homicide, then interview Texas Bell employees and any additional sources in Katherine's neighborhood he could find. I dropped him back on the street where he had left his pickup. We agreed to meet back at his office the next morning.

I told him I needed to go by my office and then go back to Richardson to examine the contents of Katherine's Malibu. He got out of the car into the simmering afternoon sun. He leaned back in and suggested that I get some sleep. I maneuvered back down Central Parking Lot to the Federal Building.

I walked into the building through the rear loading dock. The GSA maintenance crew was busy at the incinerator, disposing of stacks of paper that were too sensitive to trust to the many small office shredders throughout the building. The supervisor, a bald, effervescent African American man named Chadsey, grinned and waved through the heat of the incinerator.

"Hey, Kobok," he laughed. He looked big enough to stuff me in that incinerator if the notion pleased him. "Get over here and help us do some honest work."

"No, thanks," I answered. "That thing looks too close to hell."

"You got that right," he roared.

He was still laughing when I rounded the corner of the

loading dock into the cool caverns of the Federal Building.

I slipped into the office, trying to ease by Howdy's desk without being noticed. I should live so long.

"Kobok," he rasped, "See you a minute?" I wondered why people who always managed to talk for two hours invariably used the phrase, "Got a minute?"

"Yes sir," I said.

"Jesus Christ," he looked into my face. "You sick?"

"Yes sir," I said. "You remember, yesterday I told you I thought I had a touch of flu."

"If it's fatal, can I have your shoes?" He heehawed at a well-worn joke.

"Yes sir," I continued.

"Say," he sobered, "Where you been?"

"Working on the Katherine Pritchard murder. I called Tootie several times," I lied. I wondered if those kind of lies counted on the "go straight to Hell" tally. I opened a case jacket file and started typing a preliminary report.

"Can you clear it?" he asked. Clear was cop talk for solve.

"I hope we can. I'm working a joint investigation with Bull Hooper from DPD Homicide."

"Hooper," he answered reflectively. "A crude, but capable man, I hear."

I hoped I didn't appear surprised at his rare compliment of anyone or anything remotely associated with me.

"Yes sir," I said, "As good as you can find." I could have bitten my tongue at the slip. A favorable comment from me about Hooper could have the inverse psychological effect of having Howdy on the telephone to Hooper's chief in minutes.

He changed the subject to the one topic that aggravated me even more.

"Your case files look like they have been swabbed with mercurochrome, Kobok. Your ratio of 'No Potential' sucks."

I had "sired" enough. "Well, I'll tell you what, James," I snapped. "You go out and clear a few cases, and I'll set up here on my ass and complain about it, if my damned ratio doesn't suit you."

Easily defeated in low level pissing contests, he could afford to lose a battle since the system was rigged so he couldn't lose the war. "Just don't piddle away too much time on this bunch of lesbians, okay?" he retreated. "Make sure it's all in writing before you evaporate again," he said over his shoulder, disappearing into his little office. Surprisingly, he knew a transgender culture even existed, let along use a buzz word in conversation.

I made my way back to my desk, conscious of being the focal point of every pair of eyes in the office. I was the senior agent in the squad room. That translated to "old." Nobody came to my desk during the hour I spent typing up details of my investigation of the arson murder of Katherine Mae Pritchard. None of them wanted to draw any heat by association.

My head was throbbing. I ate a handful of aspirin from my desk drawer, washed down with machine coffee from out in a hallway. We were on the sixth floor. I wondered if I threw Howdy out the window, how many youthful Agents with staring eyes would be cheering before he hit the pavement. Don't tempt yourself, Kobok.

I finished my report by late afternoon and dropped it into the little basket Howdy left outside his office door for incoming reports when he wanted to hibernate in his hole.

I walked out and headed out the Central Parking Lot. After a nine-mile journey in only one hour and five minutes, I arrived at Richardson Police headquarters. I found J. E. Jones sitting behind a small metal desk in his cubicle puffing on a cigar. A former lineman at a major university, the sight of his great size behind the small desk made a slapstick comical effect. I didn't tell him that.

"Did you hear the one about the guy whose wife was as ugly as fifty assholes tied together?" he began the conversation.

"Yeah, that's my ex," I answered.

He picked up a cardboard box from the floor behind the little desk and dropped it onto the desk top. It contained everything of value from Katherine's Malibu. There were several gasoline tickets for fuel in the Malibu's tank signed by Katherine Pritchard, a letter to Katherine from her mother in Wilby, Oklahoma, and a multi-colored standard prostitute shoulder bag containing personal effects of Sharon Jaco.

We went through the purse. A Texas driver's license showed that Sharon Kay Jaco was a white female, five feet, five inches tall with blue eyes and blonde hair. She lived, at the time the license was issued, on Bowser Street, Richardson, Texas. Charlie had told the truth. There were no credit cards. There was, however, a Dallas Public Library card, number J65D7, issued to Sharon Jaco at the Bowser Street address. We also found a photograph of a smiling blonde girl holding a white kitten. The girl in that photo roughly matched the girl in the driver's license photo. Katherine Pritchard and Sharon Jaco bore a strong resemblance of each other.

Jones and I pondered the unusual circumstance of Sharon Jaco's purse. To cops, a woman separated from her purse is an indication of trouble.

I threw the cardboard box into the trunk of my Chevrolet and drove to my health club. I was greeted by the usual torrent of insults from the attendant.

"Whose life did you screw up, today, Mr. Po-lice," he began.

I calculated answering, "My own," but I gave him a ration of borderline falsehoods, detailing how many poor unfortunates I had ruined on this day. I wondered if I had told him the truth, if he would have believed the charred body, herpes, and two ass-whippings for a broken-down female bouncer. Probably not.

"How's your no potential ratio, brother?" I asked.

"Say whaaat?" he said as I took my towel and walked away. Just as I might have suspected. The standard governmental semi-holy management manual of rules for motivation of rank and file employees was not yet being shared by the great unwashed masses. Some men's losses are some men's gains. What the idiot didn't know wouldn't hurt him.

I worked out lightly-very lightly, and went to the steam room, which was coeducational. I met this babe in, or out of, a shocking flesh-colored bikini. In thirty minutes, we lost two quarts of perspiration and gained a friendship that would have passed for lifelong. I told her that I would marry her if I just knew her a little better. I pledged to carve her telephone number on my wrist if she would only disclose it. She disclosed, and I didn't carve, and we all got along happily ever after. I left her with the promise of an early telephone call for the explicit purpose of a complex social relationship.

I drove across to my apartment and started a TV dinner. The label promised Chinese cuisine in thirty minutes at 400 degrees. It sounded palatable with a few beers. I popped it into the oven to make sure.

I called the answering service and got the same girl from the night before.

"Three twenty-six," I said into the receiver, asking for messages in super-secret code. I often wondered why the hell we didn't just tell who we were.

"Well, my dear Mister Kobok, what a pleasant surprise," she said, interestingly. "Call your supervisor at five-five-five—one-two-seven-five and some guy named Two Dumps at five-five-five-three-two-one-one."

"Okay," I said, not correcting the Dumps to Jumps. One was about as good as the other.

"Kobok, I get off at ten again. Do you suppose we could get together and discuss this new class I'm taking at Westfield College in interpersonal communications?" she honey-dripped into my ear.

Now hell, I thought, if this kid wants to come back over here for some frivolous reason, that's one thing. But by golly, to discuss interpersonal relations is different. A man does what he has to do, sacrifice or not. Inner strength was already erasing my headache.

"Why, yeah, if it's important to you. You know you always have a friend here in time of need. Come on over." God, I was benevolent. I hoped her mother didn't find out.

"Oh, super," she gushed. "I really need companionship to try to relate to this time in my life."

"Well, companionship is my long suit, my dear," I said. "Come by and feel free to release." I felt like a clinical psychologist rather than a dirty old man.

"You're a fine man, Kobok," she sighed. "By the way, can I use your shower? I feel so grungy."

"Why, yes," I said. I felt absolutely angelic, pure, and charitable. Perhaps I could help the poor thing towel off.

"By the way, do you drink beer?" I asked.

"Oh, yes, Mr. Kobok. Got another call," she rushed. "See you at ten-fifteen." She hung up.

I sipped my beer and reflected if they counted having a brew against you in hell, too. I opened my second beer with plenty of hot, late August daylight remaining outside. The doorbell rang. I opened it to find the ten-year-old son of a lady friend, Anne, from two apartments down. He held his baseball glove and a scarred baseball.

"Hello, Tad," I said.

"Wanna play catch, Mr. Kobok?" he asked.

Frankly, I'd have rather taken a bath in liquid dog crap, but his mother had entertained me with numerous spaghetti dinners and all-night desserts. And besides, I liked the kid. His natural dad, a hardware salesman, had split when the kid was smaller. I doubt the kid had seen his father twice in seven years.

I found my glove and went out into the heat to throw a few with the kid. I expended all my energy in the twenty minutes it took me to finish my beer, and we called it a night. Tad was feeling the heat, too. His mother, Anne, in shorts pulled on over her bikini, watched from her second-floor balcony, generating heat of her own. I knew I'd chalked up another spaghetti dinner. I waved to her, thinking how much I liked her spaghetti. As Tad climbed the stairs to her unit, I was sort of relieved she didn't ask me over as she often did. But I had company coming.

I got back into the cool of my apartment in time to save my Chinese cuisine from destruction. I called Two Jumps while the food cooled and while I cooled with a beer. He answered the telephone with his rasp.

"Kobok, here. You called me." I figured I had walked a bar tab.

"Kobok, I heard you was askin' about the whore that got roasted the other night." I assumed that he had heard news of the murder of Katherine on television. I attributed his knowledge that I was working on the case to street talk and to his proximity to half of the law enforcement officers in the Dallas area.

"Yeah."

"Yeah what?"

"Yeah, I'm working on the case. It's no secret." The only secret was the murderer's identity.

"What's it worth if I help you with the case?"

Jumps was a fringe informant, that is, a source who regularly provided information to officers with different police agencies. He was not my own, confidential informant, so I offered him the usual deal: "Give me the information now, and I'll owe you a favor on your next screw-up."

"Come on, Kobok."

"Ten percent discount from the feds on your next fuckup, Jumps. That's it."

"Kobok, a friend of my old lady knows... knowed that hooker, Katherine. She was kind of a regular with a high-powered lawyer. He saw... I mean, he's supposed to have saw her once or twice a week. That much time with fine little honey like that takes big bucks."

"Who is the guy, Jumps?"

"Well, I heard his name is Melvin Higdon."

I knew Higdon, distantly. He was basically an ambulance chasing civil lawyer who specialized in suits against casualty insurance companies. He had, I'd read, received more money in fees in lawsuits in the last two years than I had made in the last twenty. He should be able to afford carnal company. In fact, he should be able to fund a school bus full of girls. He was also fiftyish, graying, average build. He was not a bad description of the trick Charlie claimed she saw in the Malibu with Katherine on the last evening of her life.

"Jumps, I'll ask around about it."

"Yeah, don't forget you owe me, Kobok."

"I won't. You can count on it." I hung up. I finished my Chinese delight with two beers and a syndicated rerun on the television. I fell asleep on the sofa with another beer and awoke to the doorbell at 10:16 P. M. Answering service secretaries are punctual. She was still snoozing when my alarm signaled another day at 6:00 A. M.

CHAPTER 11: THE LAW OF OLD LADIES

"Old women should not seek to be perfumed."—Plutarch, A. D. 44.
That comment is a sure sign that Plutarch didn't know many old ladies.

A little sleep, less beer, and good company added up. I felt better than I had in a week. I left the answering service queen asleep. She worked nights and had a car parked outside anyway.

The Bowser Street address which Charlie had fingered, which was also shown on both Sharon Jaco's driver's license and library card, was in East Richardson, not far from my place. Charlie's old truck was still parked in the rear. I was too early. The manager's office was locked and dark. I found a greasy spoon down the street on Plano Road and tanked up on bad coffee and grease while I perused the daily summary of bad news in the Dallas Morning Courier.

At 8:30, I dropped back by the Bowser address to be greeted by the manager, who said her name was Daisy Thomas. She looked at least 110 years old and was wearing yesterday's makeup... and last week's... and last month's. She also smelled like the Dallas County forensic laboratory morgue.

"Oh my gawd, luv," she purred in a fairly good Marilyn Monroe. "Whatever could I do for y'aaaall?"

I flashed credentials. "My name is Kobok, Miss." I lied again. Calling her Miss missed by about seventy-five years." We're making inquiry here today into a matter of utmost, gravest national security." I tried to affect the same expression that I had seen in old photos of Winston Churchill as he gave grave speeches; like he was facing a hemorrhoid operation without anesthetic.

"Oh my," she answered, losing her cool. "What the hell have I done?"

"We're making inquiry about an international terrorist known as H. Doody James, Miss Thomas," I said soberly. I wondered if old Howdy could get any from this old relic. Probably not even with a hundred-dollar bill.

"We don't have nobody with that name here," she said, regaining her composure.

"We have information that he is in hiding with a woman named Suzanne Douglas-French, also known as Sharon Jaco," I said. If she didn't cough up the office file on Jaco with that story, she never would.

"Holy Balls," she spouted. "We got Sharon Jaco, all right. Good God, a den of spies." She hobbled over to a file cabinet and handed me a manila folder. She went on to explain that Jaco drove an old Dodge or Plymouth, tan in color, with New Mexico plates. Neither Jaco nor the car had been around the apartment for over a week. She pointed out that Jaco was over three weeks late in her rent and would be evicted for non-payment within four days. She promised to call me if and when Jaco returned or if her belongings were seized for nonpayment of rent.

Jaco's work references were a couple of low-class bars. She had lived in the apartment for three months with no prior addresses shown. References: One guy with an address off Maple, which probably would be non-existent. However, her second reference was Sister Maria Shelby of the Garland Avenue Children's Home. That could be productive.

I handed Daisy back the file and casually asked if I could look inside the apartment. Apparently not knowing any more about the 4th Amendment than most people,, she handed me the passkey without comment or expression. I walked around back to the apartment number she had given me as Jaco's. I looked around and, seeing nobody, let myself into the apartment.

It appeared that Jaco had left most of her belongings behind. There were a few clothes in the closet, kitchen utensils in limited numbers, lacy underwear in a drawer of the battered bureau, and a box of letters and other items.

The box held two or three envelopes with personal letters to Jaco, all with a debt-threatening theme and no return address. This kid made friends wherever she went. There were unpaid bills from a gas company and from her dentist. I opened both. The gas bill had a stereotypical demand letter for an unpaid balance of $156.34. The dentist, with an address off Ross Avenue, requested $245.16. The dentist had returned her records, including a folded dental chart, stating that the unpaid bill would bring an end to further treatment. Dental chart? Apparently they'd tossed the baby with the dishwater.

I put the letters, the dental chart, and the two unpaid bills in my coat pocket and let myself out of the musky apartment. I mentally estimated the value of everything in the apartment at less than $300. That's not much to abandon, but why abandon everything you own?

I returned the key and borrowed Daisy's telephone to tell Tootie I would be on the radio. I then telephoned Hooper to tell him we needed to talk with a source who might shed light on Sharon Jaco. He begged off, saying that he had to spend his day on a shooting in West Dallas. I assured Daisy I'd stop by for coffee at my earliest opportunity and started toward the Garland Avenue Children's Home.

I knew squat about the Children's Home. A church-supported orphans' home didn't ordinarily require a lot of contact by someone from my part of the world. Sister Maria greeted me cordially from behind her nun's habit. She was fortyish with kind, blue eyes.

"How can I help you, Mr. Kobok?" She studied my credentials.

"Sharon Kay Jaco might have been a... uh, student here," I stumbled. I had nearly said "inmate."

"Spell the last name for me," she said, walking across the room to a row of gray file cabinets.

"J-a-c-o."

She returned with a thick manila folder. Worn and soiled, it appeared to have been well reviewed. I was not the first inquirer of its contents.

"Yes, now, I recall her," she said. "I thought I did but wanted to make sure. What do you need to know this time, Mr. Kobok?" clearly signaling that my hunch of prior visitors was true. She also held her file close, like she didn't want me to see its entirety. I intended otherwise.

"She is an acquaintance of a girl who was murdered night before last," I explained. "The dead girl's car was found at Ms. Jaco's apartment, and we need to talk to her." I omitted a few lurid items such as sex, arson, prostitution, and other details in which I didn't figure the Sister was interested.

"All right," she sighed. "Sharon came to us as an infant." She thumbed the file. "She was placed in four foster homes and returned each time. Three times for disciplinary reasons. The fourth for reasons not specified in the file."

"Do we know who her parents were?" I included myself in the "we," hoping for additional information.

"No," she looked up." Normally, we answer that question by saying that we can't disclose the information. In this case, however, the record reflects that she was abandoned to Parkland and that the mother was never known."

She turned the file around and handed it to me. "Here," she said, "you might as well read it. Others have. They're noted on the outside of the folder by name and police agency."

In ten minutes while Sister Maria waited with practiced patience, I went over the file sufficiently to learn that there was little to learn. Jaco had been the subject of inquiries by police from several agencies, including Detective Hooper of the Dallas Police Department Homicide Unit, four weeks earlier.

She had no record of ever having been contacted by relatives in the eighteen intermittent years she had spent at the home. She must have been a real sweetheart. This kid had no friends, relatives, next of kin, associates, or what have you.

I borrowed the Sister's telephone and called the Dallas Police Homicide Unit for Bull Hooper. He'd said something about having a homicide to investigate. Instead he answered.

"Hooper."

"Tell me about Sharon Jaco."

"I can't, Kobok."

"Why?" seemed like a logical question.

"Because, I don't know who the hell you're talking about."

"You asked about her at the Garland Avenue Children's Home last month," I said.

"Oh yeah, the Children's Home. I forgot about that," he

recalled. "I called out there trying to get a prior address on a biker's chick. As I recollect, Kobok, the chick didn't have much in her file. Forget her name. Is that girl connected to the Katherine Pritchard case?"

"Yeah," I shot a glance at Sister Maria. "Details later. You got any kinda address on her?"

"Just a minute." He laid down the receiver.

He came back on shortly. "Bowser Street in Richardson," he said expectantly.

"Yeah, I already got that," I said disappointed. "What gang or what dude did she run with?"

"The Esperantos outlaw biker gang. They've drifted up here from El Paso. She was supposed to be with a guy named Juan Morales, who they call 'Asshole.' He was supposed to be living out by Love Field. The Albuquerque Police Department sent us an arrest warrant for check fraud that they wanted served on him. I guess you could figure I never found him."

"Yeah," I said. "Too bad. You got Jaco's record there?"

"Yeah, two arrests and convictions for prostitution, one arrest, case dismissed, for assault."

"Assault?"

"Yeah, barroom brawl at a joint out on Hines…uh, Boobs. Think it's a female gay bar. Typical, complainant wouldn't pursue charges."

"You got a mug photo?"

"Yeah. Blonde, early twenties, not bad lookin', but looks like she's been ridden over some muddy road."

I wrote all the information in my notebook. "Bull, I gotta go."

I extended my credit with Sister Maria on her telephone and called Tootie at my office. I requested a complete printout on the driving record of Sharon Jaco from state records. I also asked her to pull all computer dope on Melvin Higdon, lawyer.

I thanked the good Sister, gave her my card, and walked out into the blazing sunlight. The day was already uncomfortably hot, causing instant perspiration on limited outside exposure. I drove downtown to the office.

I picked up a cold sandwich and Coke from the first-floor

cafeteria for lunch. I eased past Howdy's open cubicle door, but he made no sign of recognition. Maybe he'd forgotten who I was. I reciprocated. Let sleeping dogs lie, you know. Or let lying dogs sleep.

Tootie gave me the computer printout for Sharon Jaco's driving record, which included a small facial shot photo. The last entry reflected a speeding ticket by the City of Dallas less than eight weeks earlier. On a hunch, I telephoned the Traffic Division of the Dallas Police Department and asked the lieutenant in charge to have a clerk pull that ticket from the file.

Street people, like Sharon Jaco, in attempting to keep their correct address from law enforcement officers, often provide the address of acquaintances for a traffic citation. The lieutenant gave me an address in the 6000 block of Lake June as the listed home address of Jaco. He then mentioned she was driving a Dodge with New Mexico license plates that had been registered to an Albuquerque rental agency. I thanked him and hung up.

Tootie tossed a stack of computer printouts on my desk reflecting information as categorized on Melvin Higdon, Attorney at Law. The computer declared that Higdon, Melvin C., 49, resided in a gated community in north Dallas, and held a valid Texas driver's license. His driving record reflected two traffic citations for speeding, both dismissed without disposition. What else could be expected from a high-powered lawyer but to beat speeding tickets? His criminal printout, however, offered a small surprise.

He had been arrested for lewd conduct in Dallas and for public indecency in Fort Worth. Neither case reflected a disposition, which probably meant that his law connection had quashed prosecution.

I telephoned the Department of Public Safety in Austin and requested a photocopy of Higdon's driver's license. I stressed that I needed his photograph that would be displayed on the face of the license and was assured by the clerk that the photo would be on the regular shuttle plane that carried mail from DPS, Austin, to DPS, Dallas, late each afternoon. I guess they didn't trust the U.S. Mail.

I telephoned the Fort Worth ATF office and asked the duty

agent to walk down the street to Fort Worth police headquarters and locate the offense reports and any other data available on Higdon's arrest in that city. I told the agent on duty, a friendly, talkative man with a distinct New England accent, that I needed the information as soon as possible. He promised quick service. I'd believe it when I saw it.

I drove down to the Dallas County Courthouse and went up into the records division in the county jail. I ordered Melvin Higdon's and Sharon Jaco's file jackets. While I waited for them to be located, I reflected on the Lake June address Hooper had given me and the New Mexico license on Sharon Jaco's rental car.

That address in the Pleasant Grove district was the hangout of numerous bikers and associates. Hooper had mentioned that his inquiry at the Garland Avenue Children's Home had been in reference to an arrest warrant from Albuquerque for an outlaw biker. I called Dallas P.D. Vice and learned in two minutes the house on Lake June road was the hangout of the Esperantos outlaw biker gang.

Dallas, while not the mecca to outlaw bikers that other cities had become, still experienced plenty of activity from those people. Narcotics distribution, pimping, and any other combination of crimes imaginable could be attributed to them collectively at any time. Chances were good, Sharon, in attempting to evade giving her Bowser Street address when issued a ticket, had given the address of the biker house Hooper had recently contacted Sister Maria about. I requested any file information on Juan Morales from the clerk when she brought the files on Jaco and Higdon.

Jaco scowled out of the mug photographs, frozen in a mask of hate. If her eyes could have been softened, she could have passed for Katherine Mae Pritchard's cousin. But her eyes bore the expression of many years of degeneration, substance abuse, and pure hatred.

Street women can often preserve their bodies by various means. They can obtain expensive makeup to camouflage their complexions. They can restyle their hair to appear younger. But they cannot hide their eyes. Jaco's eyes had long since hardened beyond any possibility of ever expressing any form of kindness or real love.

Her jacket confirmed information Hooper had provided. A real nice lady. The file gave an old address off Cedar Springs, which I knew to be too old to be of value. There were no further addresses within the past year.

Higdon's file was thin. He had been arrested by a Dallas Patrol Squad at White Rock Lake in July, 1969 for "engaging in sexual relations to wit: Intercourse in a motor vehicle with Wanda Mae Russell, white female, age 26." The report went on to state that Russell, a known prostitute, had told arresting officers that she was the fiancée of Higdon. Each posted $250 and was released. No disposition was shown. That probably meant that Higdon had posted bond for each, and no actual additional court appearance was necessary, because the charges were only misdemeanors.

His photo in the jacket looked out at me with arrogant confidence, contrary to thousands of other mug photos that invariably reflected some degree of despair, drunkenness, or belligerence. His tanned skin, favored with nurtured gray hair, combed slightly back at the sides, beamed at me like a photo prepared by a candidate for the school board. I wondered if he had been such a candidate.

CHAPTER 12: THE LAW OF LOCATIONS

A man who moves from EL Paso to Pleasant Grove, or from any-where else to Pleasant Grove for that matter, has a better reason than the love of change of scenery.

The thin jacket for Juan Ignacio Morales, Latin male, date of birth 7-7-46, Mexico, contained considerable poison. He had been arrested four years earlier in Dallas for fighting at a motor-cycle rally. His FBI rap sheet reflected three prior felony convic-tions. His photograph showed him to have shoulder-length hair and a full facial beard. His eyes glared outward in the usual Dracula fashion, typical of bikers and/or narcotics addicts, of which he was probably both. The file contained a computer printout verifying the Albuquerque arrest warrant Hooper had spoken of. How the hell did the system allow a toad with three felonies and wanted for another to be on the street?

I obtained a copy of the files, including photos of Jaco, Morales, and Higdon and headed toward Pleasant Grove. I had lots of photos of lots of people and still not a damn clue as to who murdered Katherine.

The address on Lake June Road was one of those small frame shotgun houses like thousands more in Dallasof. This dump, like all those up and down the block, had been painted white at one time. It had long since joined its neighbors by blending to a weathered gray.

It was rumored among cops the occupants left refrigerators and the like on their front porches, so, when they came home drunk or stoned, they could find the right house by its distinc-tive landmark. Since most of them couldn't read, they could always invite people with directions like: "Mine's the one with the green refrigerator on the porch and the wrecked Plymouth in the yard."

The occupants of the house were using a swamp cooler for partial air-conditioning, supplementing it by leaving the front door open. A swamp cooler is a water-fed device where air is fan-blown across trickling water to provide some measure of cool air. It is most effective in areas with low humidity and ineffective in swampy, humid terrain. It was very humid that day as I approached the open door and knocked on the door frame.

A very skinny Mexican female, age twenty, going on sixty, answered my knock. She'd been into a killing dope habit for too long. "Yeah?" she said.

"I want to talk to Juan Morales, please," I said. Showing my credentials. The odor from within was sweat and filth. It struck me in the face like a solid wall.

"Nobody here by that name," she said quickly in unaccented English.

"Look," I said. "If I had bad news, I'd have a whole shitload of people out here. Tell him to come out here. I just want to talk a minute."

She looked back into the room. A stocky form materialized from the dark depths of the little house. Juan Morales stared at me wordlessly, a carbon copy of the photo I was carrying in my shirt pocket.

As my eyes grew accustomed to the darkened interior of the room, I became aware of several additional people sitting about. Time to walk softly.

"What do you want, cop?" he asked, obviously unaware of the arrest warrant from Albuquerque.

In view of reinforcements available to him at arm's length, I withheld any sharp remarks. "I want to talk to you, Juan," I said, "out here in private."

He looked me over from head to toe without show of fear and then pointed his bearded chin toward my car. "You got AC in that beat-up mu'fucker?"

"Yeah," I said and walked toward the Chevrolet. He followed, somewhat to my surprise.

He settled into the front passenger seat and stared at me

impassively as I cranked the engine. The rank smell of him quickly permeated the interior. He didn't look as tough as he did worthless and mean. He was giving me the hard look to show his macho. I showed him the mug photo of Sharon Jaco.

"Whatcha' want from me, man?"

"I need to know about this chick," I said, holding up Sharon Jaco's photo.

"Never saw her before," he answered.

Juan was a difficult person to be nice to. He appeared to have already heard most of it anyway. I bit my tongue and proceeded. "We got no beef with you. We got business with this girl."

He tossed me a look of indifference and said nothing.

"Juan, you know the Feds can cause more grief than you can swim with. Don't invite more trouble than you've already had. You don't owe this chick shit. I need to find her."

"Okay, man, what if I did know her?"

"When did you last see her?"

"I didn't say I knew her, man."

"Okay." I shifted gears. "I heard you're from El Paso."

"And?"

"We have ways of hearing a lot about people we're interested in, Juan. Don't make me write down your name and get the entire federal government interested."

He looked across at me, enjoying the game. I realized then that he had intended to tell me what he knew from the first. He wanted to yank my chain a few times first. I showed him the photo again. "When, Juan?"

"When what?"

"When did you last see her?"

"You ain't gonna' bust me?"

"If I'd come to bust you, I would have brought the cavalry, slick. Do you see a bus load of cops around here?" I was visualizing causing the bus load to appear as soon as I could clear the front yard. I held up the photo again.

"The queen of fuckin' Sheeba," he said.

"I need to talk to her, Juan," I began. I repeated my best line of how I didn't want to screw him over. Hiding behind the system, I explained that "they" don't like bikers, particularly ones who don' t answer simple questions.

"She gimme fuckin' herbees," he said flatly.

"Herpes," I corrected, probably wasting the effort.

"Yeah," he said, "looka my face. I shoulda killed the bitch."

His face appeared to be far beyond the reach of the ravage of any disease. He looked bad, but it was probably a long-standing condition. "Yeah," I lied in not totally insincere sympathy. "I can see it now." I couldn't, but he was one ugly mother.

He sat there in his own stink and told me that he had picked up Jaco in a bar on upper Harry Hines about two months ago. Although the connection began as sex for pay, she had been fascinated with the macho-biker lifestyle. Jaco had stayed part time in the house on Lake June with Morales and a constantly changing combination of other bikers and their "old ladies."

"Old lady" loosely translates to live-in girlfriend with the stipulation that she is shared with other biker men as circumstances and need dictate. Jaco had either brought herpes in with her and infected several members of the group living there, or she had contracted the disease from one of the men and spread it. The end result was that Morales had thrown her out about three weeks earlier, after several of the men had taken turns raping her.

They had driven her out in rural Seagoville and tossed her out, naked and bleeding, on the side of the road. He insisted that she wasn't dead and that the beating was limited to a slap in the mouth. He pointed out that they didn't cut off anything or gouge out her eyes. Besides, who did she have to listen to her complaints? It appeared Jaco had managed to reach Katherine who rescued her and hence the recent fling Jaco and Katherine had enjoyed was a result.

I stopped a block down from the Lake June address and dropped a quarter in the pay phone.

"Detective Hooper." When in the hell was he going to his homicide?

"Bull, you got a friend in TAC?"

"Yeah, Mongo Gaulding. Mean as hell, but I'm feedin' him smart pills to help his report writing."

"Is he working today?" I knew Gaulding slightly; big, tough, effective.

"Yeah, in fact, he's working now. He just called me to have a beer after work."

"Well, listen, I've got some good news and some bad."

"Lay some of it on me," he said.

"The bad news is that I haven't got the cuffs on your boy Asshole Morales."

"Yeah."

"The good news is that he's sitting on his ass in the living room of the Esperanto house in Pleasant Grove. I just saw him there." I gave him the address.

"We won't screw up an undercover deal or anything if we run on it?"

"No. Go for it. There were about six people in the house that I could see. All but one men, I think."

"Hot damn, I'll put the call out for Tactical to make the bust. Kobok, I owe you a beer."

"Maybe two." I said and hung up.

I parked where I could see the house on Lake June two blocks down. Shortly, a white Dallas squad car drove by, the youthful officers watching warily. After a few minutes, squad cars began arriving at the rate of about twenty per minute, driving helter-skelter into the yard of the house where I had found Juan Morales. It appeared safe to assume that Asshole Morales would be arrested for the Albuquerque warrant. I left.

CHAPTER 13: THE LAW OF TRUTH, HALF TRUTH, SOME TRUTH, AND DAMN LIES

An incurable affliction common to all cops: skepticism. Officers develop an inability to believe anyone with whom they speak in direct proportion to their time in police service. The trick is to learn to separate fact from fantasy. Ain't always easy.

It was past 4:00 P. M., and I owed myself a trip to the house. Instead, I drove out Interstate 30 to the regional headquarters of the Texas Department of Public Safety. I located the desk of the day-lieutenant in charge and asked about the photocopy I had requested earlier from Austin. He dug around in a large mail sack on the floor and came up with an official-looking envelope bearing my name.

I tore open the envelope for a second view of Melvin Higdon under the photographer's glare. The driver's license photo had caught him in a more somber expression than did the one from the Dallas County sheriff's office. I guess being arrested with a whore is more fun than taking a driver's test. The file and photo added nothing to the case and I started the creep back downtown against outbound rush traffic.

Sharon Jaco was apparently a homeless, itinerant, ill-tempered psychopath with no known relatives, friends, or associates who was flexible enough to seek solace in the widely separated cultures of biker-land and the Dallas lesbian community. She wouldn't be easy to trace because nobody would care enough to ask where she had gone, except me.

It was past 5:00 as I swung the Chevrolet up Harry Hines and drove slowly along the curb lane, making eye contact with as many of the girls working the street as I could get to look back at me. Overall, I eyeballed about twenty-five girls. I had been on the street myself for a long time and had encountered some of these girls before. I spotted a white girl known to me as Bridgett. As I recollected, she did not belong to any pimp. I pulled the Chevrolet into a driveway and motioned her over. She got to the passenger door before she recognized me.

"Did you get demoted to Vice, Kobok?" She grinned in the passenger-side window.

"No, I've come to carry you away and marry you." She was an attractive girl, despite the hardened street eyes that stared steadily at me from the deposits of makeup. She couldn't look too sparkling for long. She was already twenty-three or twenty-four years old. As I've said before, that's fifty-five in the normal world.

Bridgett had snitched off her dope connection to an investigator in Dallas Vice and me about three years before. She was pissed because he had stiffed her on two separate heroin deals, and she agreed to set him up by calling him to make a delivery at a pay phone on Cedar Springs. The Vice man and I grabbed the dealer while he was holding a full two ounces in the pockets of his jacket.

He got five years, and Bridgett checked into a drug abuse rehabilitation program at taxpayer expense. The fact that she was still alive and looking as good as she did, tended to prove that the program was working. Both she and the dealer were back in full business. Checks and balances.

"Kobok, I accept your proposal, but I'm tellin' you now that you're gonna need to bring along three or four friends to keep me serviced." Then she added, "But let's do a quickie over here in the Las Tienda Motel to get acquainted for the honeymoon."

I grinned off her comment and flashed the photographs of Higdon. "Know this guy?"

She studied the photos. "No," she said plainly. "Does this mean I'm not going to get any?"

She never had. I didn't see any sense in changing a satisfied relationship. "Another time Bridge. It's my time of the month, and I have a headache."

"Oh God, Kobok." She laughed and stepped out into the swelter.

I pulled down the street to park the Chevrolet behind a closed down Mexican beer joint. Three Latin youths of about sixteen were lounging behind the building on a rickety trash bin, sharing a joint. They eyed me defiantly. I got out with my pistol showing in my belt. When they simultaneously spotted the pistol, they skulked away as rapidly as their macho would allow. I ignored them and walked around to the street.

I spent two hours on foot, disrupting whore traffic on the Hose Line. Two separate Dallas squad cars stopped to check my ID. I showed officers the photo of Higdon. Both wrote down his name and Dallas sheriff's office identification number with promises to ask their own sources about him. By 8:00, I concluded that I was getting nowhere.

The evening crew of whores provided more potential victims to whom to show Higdon's photo. This was the area that Ralphie, The Rooster joint guy had identified as Katherine's normal working ground.

I had worked my way through several more girls when I confronted a slender, African American girl wearing a wide-brimmed straw hat with flowers in the hatband. I showed her my credentials and handed her Higdon's photos. I used the same story that I had already given to every girlsI had already contacted that evening. Using the best investigative tool available at the time, I lied. I told her that the man in the photo had eaten the teats off seventeen whores in Chicago and Detroit in the past six months. Her reaction was fairly reasonable.

"Sheeit, man. Somebody need to shoot that dude."

"Maybe we will if we find him," I laid it on. "What's your name, honey?"

"Tulip," she replied. "And I ain't turning no tricks here, mister officer."

I looked up and down the street at the eight or ten working girls standing in various provocative poses up and down the street, shoulder bags at their sides. "Do you suppose that some of these other ladies might be engaging in prostitution? I've already asked these other girls. They're all standing in line for the bus to the YMCA for ice cream and cookies. Wonder where that bus could be." I looked up and down the street in mock search. The line may not make national TV, but she liked it.

"Homeboy," she laughed. "I didn't say I didn't turn no tricks. I said I wasn't doin' it right now." She laughed in pure, African American female American. She then called over two nearby girls who were watching out of the sides of their eyes.

Street girls develop a standard, "That cop can't call me over if I ain't looking" countenance. Both were doing it. It is as indigenous to streetwalkers as the characteristic actions of other groups of living creatures. Geese flee danger in one fashion and rabbits in another. The pattern is similar throughout the world, although the groups couldn't possibly learn from one another. Whores demonstrated the same tendency. When confronted with any man who is remotely suspected of being the law, hookers universally avert the eyes and evaporate into the scenery at hand with amazing speed while never appearing to hurry.

Both of the second pair of girls had been in a holding pattern locked into the early stages of this phenomenon, waiting for the signal to evaporate. On Tulip's request, they approached. One was African American, chubby, chesty, toothy, and wore enough cheap cologne to ward off insects, vampires, and smallpox. The other was white, slender, blonde, and flat-chested, with nice legs enhanced by very short, short-shorts. She had a poor complexion, which she had been unable to cover with several coats of makeup. Could the rash be induced by herpes, perhaps? Tulip introduced the two girls. The African American girl called herself Rose, and the white said her name was Flower.

"Christ," I said, "I came looking for a whorehouse and found the botanical garden."

Rose, apprehension in her tone, said "I ain't sold no pussy in no garden."

"I was just joking." I flashed the photo of Higdon.

Rose studied the photo and asked, "What this dude do?"

"Ate up a bunch of whores' teats, the goofy sucker," Tulip interjected.

"How many teats that birch have?" came back Rose.

"It was more than one girl," I explained.

Rose said, "I never seen him. Good thing." She placed a hand under each ample breast, hoisting into the "ready" position. "Dude have a all-day job, chokin' all this down." She gave Tulip a "high-five" and both laughed uproariously.

Flower had not spoken, but when I focused on her I saw from years of watching the reactions of others that she recognized the man in the photo. Finally. She said, "I don't know this dude either." I knew she was lying.

On a whim, I took the photo of Katherine Pritchard out of my pocket and showed it to all three girls. All agreed that they had probably seen her around. The African American ladies stated that they didn't know her name, and Flower gave lip service to the same answer. But I became more convinced that she was evading the truth. I had to talk to her away from the others.

I thanked all three girls and walked back down the block to retrieve the Chevrolet. I got my binoculars from the trunk and drove three blocks down to where I could park in a darkened parking lot. I watched Flower work up and down the block for over an hour without scoring a trick. It had gotten totally dark before she eventually walked to an isolated portion of the cruising area. I drove back down the street. I stopped beside her and popped open the passenger door. "Get in," I ordered with as little edge in my voice as possible. She complied immediately. Whores get used to doing what strange men tell them.

"Look, officer, if this is a freebie...I mean, can I give you head over there in the alley? Let's get it over with."

"No, honey, I don't give it away. I'd have to charge you forty dollars, just like everybody else."

She had to smile a little through her layers of makeup. She looked Emmitt Kelly-sad on close inspection.

Westra and Jesus would have their way with this young body soon. I wondered if her brain would be remarkable or not? Would Westra get to determine death as caused by overdose of drugs or death by trauma of beating by a trick or pimp? Or would death be from being butchered after guessing wrong when obeying one of those stranger's commands to hop into the car?

"Stop staring at my face," she said, turning away. "I know how I look, dammit."

"I was thinking that you have pretty eyes," I lied. Surely that lie didn't count in hell. I made a mental note to ask the priest about that.

"What do you want, Mister...?"

"Kobok," I said. "Tell me when you last tricked with this guy in the photograph." I handed her both of his photos.

"Look, I don't wanna get involved."

"Flower, you're not involved. He is."

"Involved in what?" she demanded.

"Somebody tied one of the girls to a bed night before last, over on Lemmon. It was bad."

"Jesus Christ, Kobok, lots of men are into that crap. I only do it with some choice guys that I know pretty good. You got to be careful in this business."

"This guy stuck a telephone up her twat and set her on fire." I had wanted to avoid telling the whole story. Talking about it to a woman made me queasy.

"Oh, I heard about that." The car seat transmitted her slight shudder.

"And I know that you know the girl who got roasted alive and this guy in the photograph as well."

"Kobok, I don't like to get involved in snitching." Then she dropped an interesting line. "Besides, Slow will piss a bitch if he hears I'm talking to you."

"You're one of Slow's girls?"

"Yeah."

I hate to admit it, but involuntarily, I glanced over my shoulder up and down the dark street. Slow would love to put a bullet behind my ear. Actually, he lacked the backbone to do it, but he would love to arrange for that bullet.

"He's a friend of mine," I said.

"Friend's ass, Kobok. I know you're the one screwin' with him off and on."

More off than on, I thought, but properly motivated, I could become more attentive to Slow. "I've been part of arresting him, but that's only business, Flower. Nothing personal." Another lie on file to consider. I think they keep them all in a book and make some determination when you get to hell. Surely, they don't all count the same.

"Flower, I know that you know this guy in the picture. I don't want to mess in your business, only his. I can guarantee that nobody's going to know that we talked unless you tell them."

"I don't know what to do. Let's drive out of this neighborhood. Can I smoke in your car, Kobok?"

"Sure," I said, pulling the Chevrolet into traffic. I drove to the darkened parking lot of a closed meat packing plant off the south end of Hines. I could see the glint from at least two other vehicles in the distant darkness—girls doing business in the best place available. Nobody inside this fence would complain. By the time I cut the lights, she was on her second Virginia Slim.

"Okay," she said, in control again, "what do you want to know?"

"What you know about this guy and the girl in these pictures."

"His name is Mel," she began, sighing. "I haven't dated him in over six months. He was a regular at one point, but we had this problem with herpes. I was never sure who gave that shit to who, but we both had the symptoms at about the same time. He accused me of givin' it to him but he was seeing other street girls."

"What does he do for a living?"

"Lawyer. Didn't you know that?"

I ignored the question. "Is he Slow's lawyer?"

"I ain't gonna talk about Slow, but I think the answer is no. I don't know about Slow's business, and I don't ask."

"What about Mel's habits?"

"What do you mean?"

She knew what I meant. "I mean was he weird, kinky, brutal, or what?"

She drug on the cigarette, partially illuminating her face with a hint of a smile, "All of the above."

"Whips and chains?"

"In a manner of speaking. He liked handcuffs. Carried them

in the glovebox of his car. He would go down on' me and use his teeth... you know... while I was in the cuffs. Bastard once bit me in the armpit so hard I couldn't put my arm down for a week."

"What did he drive?"

"Uhh, Mercedes, gray or light blue."

"How did you meet him?"

"He was just cruising the Hose Line and I got in with him. He took me to the D'Este Motel. We went there several times. He always had me register while he waited in the car. That's the way most of them do it. I dated him for almost a year."

"Where did you meet for dates?"

"Monday nights, he would pick me up early, always before seven o'clock. I'd meet him over on the street in front of the picture framing place on Harry Hines, across from Parkland. He would stay with me until about ten and then split."

"Did he pay good?"

"Yeah, but I ain't tellin' how much."

I assumed that Lawyer Higdon told his wife that he had to bowl or attend some legal function on Monday nights. I guessed his arrest for fornicating in the park had occurred on a Monday night.

"How about the girl I showed you, kid? How do you know her?"

"I'm not sure that I do, Mister Kobok. I mean, you know. A lot of these working girls look alike. They all wear shorts, and all the whites blonde their hair. I think Mel began running with a chick who looked like the one you showed me. But look, I'm tellin' the truth. I think I've seen the girl in the picture on the street, and I've seen Mel with another working girl around here. I think it's the same girl, but I just don't know."

"Okay, I believe you," I said.

"Look," she said, "I need to get back on the street. I haven't made ten dollars today."

I considered that any trick she turned probably took home herpes. "Okay, Flower, I'll take you back." I drove back to Harry Hines and stopped behind the closed beer joint.

"Keep quiet about talkin' to me, okay?" I handed her a

twenty. She got out and disappeared around the corner. I didn't figure that beating the ground in the midst of the streetwalker traffic all night was going to be any more productive than it had been already. I picked up a 7-Eleven beer and drove out to Spring Valley. I stopped in a private club near my apartment and had a burger and several more beers. I went to bed and dreamed of evil lawyers driving Mercedes.

CHAPTER 14: THE LAW OF INHERITANCE OF THE EARTH

The good and the meek could never inherit the earth, because the vain, the selfish, and the pompous will have already gotten all the good parking spaces.

I got up on Friday morning at 6:00 A. M. and was headed downtown with a cup of 7-Eleven coffee and most of the rest of the people of North Dallas by 6:40. I squeezed off the Central Parking Lot and drove to address shown on Melvin Higdon's driver's license records.

The house itself was a two-story colonial, well-tended, and only worth about half a million dollars in 1985. The rear, which probably hid the household vehicles, was inaccessible because there was no alley. I circled the area and found a copy of the Morning Courier and another Styrofoam cup of life-giving 7-Eleven caffeinated.

At 7:30, Tootie signaled on the radio that she was at her desk, and I called in to tell her that I would be on the radio for a while. I sat a block down from Higdon's palatial household and did what I do best: I waited and did nothing.

At 8:10, a slender, attractive blonde, fortyish woman drove a red El Dorado out of the driveway and came past me on the street. Two scrubbed children were visible in the rear seat. None of the occupants looked in my direction. At 8:40, she returned minus kids, swinging into the driveway and disappearing around to the rear.

At 8:55, a gray Mercedes 450 whizzed out of the driveway and whipped away in the opposite direction. I U-turned and followed. The gray-haired driver maneuvered the car through traffic. When he looked toward the oncoming traffic, I recognized him from the photos as Higdon. I easily followed him to Northwest Highway, where he zipped into one of the many luxury office buildings in the area. He parked under the building in a covered, but unattended parking area. Walking jauntily across the parking garage, he disappeared into an elevator.

I found a parking spot and walked into the deserted garage that housed the Mercedes. The car doors were locked. Hanging on a little chain on a radio dial was an item I had carried in my pocket for many years: a handcuff key.

Handcuff keys are universal. Several manufacturers offer competitive models of handcuffs. They come in different finishes, from blue to chrome to nickel air weights, that are as light as paper. But one key fits all, regardless of model or manufacturer. The key was identical to those carried by the countless law enforcement officers around the world. Higdon, however, carried his handcuffs for another reason.

I jotted down the license number of the Mercedes and walked back to my Chevrolet. I called Tootie on the radio and asked her to obtain the name of the registrant of the Mercedes. By the magic of computer, she returned the name of an automobile dealer: Bobbie Dwyer Mercedes on Greenville Avenue.

The rent on a Mercedes must run $500 per month in those days. I figured Higdon was a big money-maker, but how the hell did even he have any cash left over for hookers after paying his house payment and monthly auto rental fee?

I entered the office building and consulted the directory. Higdon, Melvin, was an attorney on the fourth-floor with the firm of Higdon, Schwartz, and Massoud.

His suite occupied a major portion of the fourth floor. The girl on the front desk was right out of Playboy. The furniture was dark stained oak, rustic and expensive.

"Yes sir?" the girl said.

I handed her my card with my name and title on it. "I'd like to see Mr. Higdon."

"Do you have an appointment, sir?" she asked, as expected. "No, just tell him that I have one of his clients waiting down in the car, and she wants to talk to him about handcuffs. Her name is Flower. Tell him that it's urgent, please."

"She looked at my card. "Well, Mr. Kobok, he's in conference."

"Just give him the message. I'll wait here." She wiggled across the office to a hallway.

In sixty seconds, Higdon angrily burst into the outer office with my card in his hand. "What do you want, Kobok?"

He gave me an up and down that indicated distaste. "How did a bum looking bastard like you get to be a Federal Agent?"

I could see our relationship was going to have limited possibilities. "I used to be a movie star, Higdon," I answered. "I just gradually began to look as shabby as some of the company I have to keep." I returned his head-to-toe inspection. His shoes cost more than all the clothes I owned. I discontinued my inspection.

"What is so important?" he repeated.

Another man had entered the waiting area and taken a seat, waiting. "Do you want to talk here?" I asked.

"Uh, no. Let's step into my office." I followed him into a large, well-furnished office with an extensive wet bar at one end.

"What do you want?" he asked, as he sat behind the large desk.

"Well," I began. "It's a delicate matter. I'm working on a murder of a prostitute. Her name is...was Katherine Mae Pritchard, blonde, twenty-five-ish, pretty, worked off the Line on Harry Hines."

"I'll have the girls check and see if she was one of my clients," he said hesitantly.

"I'm more concerned if you might be her client, Mr. Higdon." I threw kerosene on an open fire. The explosion was even more violent than I had expected.

He jumped to his feet. "What kind of comment is that? You goddamn stupid ass. Do you know that I'm goddamn connected all over this goddamn town? I don't deal with whores, and you get your ass out of my office!" He took half a step around the desk.

"I don't think you can do it, Mr. Higdon."

"Do what?"

"Keep talking with a ratio of that many cuss words to normal words."

He spat a line of invective that actually improved the ratio.

He started around the desk threateningly.

My, my, a mean lawyer. I rose and stared him down. "Higdon, if you come around that desk, I solemnly promise to break your arm and tell the world all about your little handcuffs. Keep coming and learn I'm not some little blonde you can cuff up to play games with."

He froze in mid-stride. Steppping back behind the sanctity of the desk, he reached for the telephone.

"The victim of this murder was a prostitute you knew, Mr. Higdon. And she had a telephone like that one stuck up her vagina."

He moved away from the telephone and sat down glaring across the desk. "You asked about handcuffs, Kobok?" He was struggling for composure. The rough guy fizzled into just another wimp.

"Yes, we know you bought handcuffs and carry them in your car glove compartment. I know you were acquainted with the girl who was murdered Monday night. I want to know your whereabouts after midnight Monday night...Tuesday morning."

"Okay, I got a little thing for hookers who like it rough. I was on the street Monday night. I took a girl to the Capri Two and was home with my wife by eleven."

"Can your wife verify that?" I asked.

"If you tell her about the whore, I'll deny it and make you out to be a liar, and then comes the lawsuit."

"I don't want to tell her, Mr. Higdon," I again lied. I slid the photo of Pritchard across the desk to him. He studied it at length.

He tossed it back. "I've seen her, Kobok, but I've never been in her pants."

"Is she the girl you dated Monday night?"

"No."

"What was your date's name?"

"I don't really know, but it wasn't this girl." He appeared to regain some composure. "If you think I bought some handcuffs, Kobok, tell me where I bought them."

I took that to mean that he hadn't bought the cuffs in an outlet wherein they could be traced. I answered with the standard, "I'll ask the questions, Mr. Higdon."

He gained strength, rising again. "I'm going to report this intrusion, Kobok. You goddamn broken-down, hobo-looking bastard, coming right into my office and threatening me! I'm a friend of Congressman Paullus and Judge John J. Kell. I'll have your job for this." He stood glaring.

I glared back silently.

Finally, he said, "Well, goddammit, say something."

"I'm too frightened to answer," I said, standing up. I started out the door and turned back.

"I'll tell you what, Higdon. If this sorry job is vulnerable to a complaint from a wimpy, perverted little dipshit like you, then get started calling your judges and congressmen. I have a feeling they don't want to hear from dweebs like you, but why don't you get started?"

He slumped in his chair.

"Higdon, I'll produce enough whore and handcuff testimony to make the national evening news. That should interest the Dallas and Texas Bar Associations. Why don't you just trundle down to one of the courts and see if the testimony of an armpit-biting little runt weasel is a more credible witness than a broken-down, bum-looking bastard like me."

His body language showed rage, but he dummied up.

"And, remember, if all else fails and I lose, you'll have to move to Seattle to stay alive. And by the way, does your wife know she has herpes?" I think I had lost my temper.

I walked through the outer office and the Playboy girl said, "Have a nice day."

"Honey, your father, Mr. Higdon, wants you to come in and take a memo to some judge and congressman about whores and handcuffs," I said as I slammed the door. I wondered if he had tried the cuffs on her.

I drove downtown and parked the Chevrolet in a spot reserved for the Department of Labor. It was after 10:00, and I picked up another cup of Styrofoam coffee on the way upstairs. Tootie looked hung over and not in the mood for conversation. I didn't converse as I sat down at my disorderly desk.

CHAPTER 15: THE LAW OF ENEMIES

A man can't be too careful when choosing his enemies.

The records from the Brown County, Oklahoma, sheriff had arrived in a thick envelope. I thumbed through them. The old sheriff had been thorough. He had hustled up Katherine's high school records, the arrest record of her father, photographs of her deceased brother, and numerous other tidbits. I read every word in the file and came away with nothing. The papers relating to her father indicated that he had led a quiet life until his arrest in 1973 for shooting a .22 rifle indiscriminately at passing vehicles. The whole family was withdrawn and reclusive. I put all items back into the brown envelope and slipped the envelope into my file binder.

Westra's promised report was also in my IN box, apparently having arrived in yesterday's mail. I was familiar with forensic reports, and I had no better taste for the written results than for the actual butchery performed in the morgue.

I knew that if they had found anything, they hadn't already told me, Westra would have included a cover letter, drawing my attention to the additional findings. He had a great disdain for the average cop's ability to read and understand his reports, so new information was always included in a simply worded letter stapled to the front of the report. There was no cover letter.

I skimmed the report. It was complete with written narrative, diagrams drawn on paper, silhouette pictures of bodies, and photographs of the remains before the autopsy and after, showing her split from crotch to neck. The camera had invaded her open cranium, her open mouth, and her open other parts that defied description. Her gaping remains of a mouth, grinned two rows of perfect teeth. I put the forensic file in my rapidly expanding binder, along with the other information we had gathered.

I telephoned the high sheriff of Brown County, Oklahoma, and received his assurance of a telephone call if he heard anything not included in the file he had sent.

I called Hooper, and we discussed any possible additional leads we could think of over the telephone.

I spent several hours trying to make my written report of the investigation translate sufficiently into normal-people language so that it wouldn't short-circuit Tootie's reader/printer. At just past 3:00, my telephone buzzed.

"Kobok."

"Kobok, this is Hooper."

"I'm sorry, sir, you want the Marsailis Zoo."

"Kobok, get serious!"

This Pritchard investigation was-serious enough to land me in Cleveland, where the hell ever that was, or in Miami. But I doubted Hooper wanted to hear about it.

"What's up, Bull?" I asked.

"I just wanted to pass on that Slow Bill Harris is out and about today, doin' some serious talkin' about puttin' the hurt on you, boy. He don't like you," he advised in classic understatement.

"Yeah, I met him at a Little League meeting, and we disagreed about team uniforms or something."

"Well, he kicked the shit out of one of his whores last night— a girl named Rachael Cross, white female, twenty. She uses the street name of Flower. We interviewed her at Parkland, and she said that she had talked to you last night. She said you picked her up on Harry Hines and gave her the third degree about Slow's business. Somebody musta seen her get into the car and told Slow. Slow wouldn't believe that you came onto her and that she didn't tell you anything."

"How bad is she hurt?"

"Only a light whore beating. Slow isn't going to permanently disable a money-maker if he could possibly avoid it. She had, uhhh lemme see, a broken rib and sixteen stitches; She'll be back on the Line in a week."

"Can you file charges on Slow?"

"Are you kidding? I don't think in the entire history of whoredom that any girl ever testified against her pimp just for beating her."

"Figures."

"Listen, I only called to tell you not to turn your back on Slow. She hinted around that he might break some of your bones if he had the opportunity."

"I appreciate you calling, Bull. I don't clear this case, it's Miami for me, sure as hell."

"Crap, Kobok, I gotta go."

"See you in Miami." I hung up.

I sat at my desk and thought of Slow. He was quite a talker, and he was mean as hell around women. I took the comments relayed by Hooper to be only street talk by Slow trying to save face.

I returned to banging out my report on my Olivetti. Leaving out Flower's offer to give free head. I included a paragraph about receiving information from Detective Hooper that a source that I had contacted had apparently been assaulted by Willie Harris, also known as Slow Bill, apparently in retaliation for the source having been seen talking to me.

I also stated that I had interviewed Higdon in his office and had left when he declined to be interviewed. That's a reasonably fair summation of what had occurred. I would have bet my pension that Higdon wouldn't complain.

Just before four o'clock, the telephone rang again. It was Jackson Three Hairs Dorsen of the Dallas Police Department, who had had his three head-hairs shaved by a brutal nurse at Parkland after he had collided with Slow's door. The hairs were slowly re-growing. I figured about four years would do it.

"Hey, Kobok, I know you're invincible, but I thought I'd give you a call anyway. A source of mine just called and said Slow Bill is laying in the gap for you. Says next time you roust one of his ladies, he's gonna put out one of your eyes or take off your nuts, if you got any."

I figured that Three Hairs might have added the last four words. The rest sounded like Slow might be talking too much.

"Where is this ambush going to take place?" I asked.

"Along Harry Hines. He's got girls all up and down the Hose Line watchin' for your ass."

I made the usual masculine jokes with Three Hairs and thanked him for saving my life before hanging up.

I dialed the Vice Control Unit of the Dallas Police Department and asked the receptionist to locate Muscles Malloy and have him call me. By some miracle of Polish luck, he was in the office—an extremely rare occurrence.

"Malloy," he came on the line.

"Sir, this is CBS News, and we'd like to sponsor you in the midget joke contest. We've received information that you know several of them."

"Midgets or jokes?"

"How many of each do you know?"

"The answer is one and one million, respectively."

"Hey, my man, how about going through the whore cards in the Vice office and see if you can locate Pritchard, Katherine Mae, white female." I added date of birth, physical description, and last known address. Vice kept intelligence files on prostitutes which might reflect Katherine had been questioned, but not arrested.

"Hold on a minute," he went off the line.

He returned in less than sixty seconds. "Negative in our files, Kobok."

That confirmed that not only had Katherine not been arrested for prostitution, but she had not been the subject of field interrogation or informer information to the Vice unit.

"Kobok?"

"Yeah."

"We been hearing that old Slow Bill has been making threats against you."

"Yeah, I heard. I'm terrified."

"Want to borrow my plastic nut cup in case he brings along the midget?"

"No, I'm gonna start taking an alligator on a leash everywhere I go."

He laughed and hung up. Actually, the midget was probably

more lethal than Slow. He certainly was more bite than bark.

I sat there and reflected on Slow. I had no choice. The only defense in this business was a swift, well-defined offense.

Then, the ultimate motivator drifted in. Hooper called, "Kobok, that clown Slow Bill is now including me in his death threats. I mean to drive up and down the Hose Line tonight until I find his ass and try to give him counseling."

"I sorta had the same thing in mind… eyeball to eyeball counseling."

"Can we take your ride?"

"When and where do I need to pick you up."

The phenomenon here is universal in the cop business. Thugs, criminals, street characters by any name are prone to vent their frustration by threats. "Then cops dick with me, I'm gonna hurt some of them" is the type of generic threat common on the street. Such commentary is to be ignored as clap trap.

But when a specific mope like Slow Bill, makes a specific threat against a specific cop like Hooper or me, that by golly was a different thing entirely. Personal threats required a personal response. Slow needed to be dealt with, specifically.

CHAPTER 16: THE LAW OF THE LION TAMER

The tamer's weapon against the lion is psychology, not strength.
The animal could prevail but seldom has the will.

We began cruising Harry Hines at 7:00. At 96 degrees, the sun was blazing, stifling hot. The street girls working in the early evening stood under whatever shade was available to avoid the slanting sun. Many girls were in sight, but Slow was not. He, like all rodents, was apparently nocturnal, staying in his darkened hole until the sun disappeared for the day.

Hooper and I had some grease and coffee at a drive-in off Stemmons Expressway and waited. By 8:30, the sun had slipped out of view to the west beyond the Trinity River although it was far from dark. We made another pass down the Hose Line.

There he was. Slow had backed his red Lincoln Mark V Continental into a parking spot on a side street near the picture frame store where Flower had said she met Melvin Higdon for Monday night dates. He was sitting alone in the car, air conditioning apparently running against the heat. He had parked perpendicular where he could see traffic passing on the Line.

I stopped in the traffic lane, double parking and blocking the Mark V in. Slow couldn't drive away without going to the sidewalk side, and the clearance wouldn't have fully permitted that. I turned on flashing grill lights and remained behind the wheel. Hooper got out beside Slow's driver's side window.

Hooper leaned back against the passenger door of the Chevrolet, arms crossed, looking steadily at Slow. Slow looked back through the glass. His face first showed contrived macho, but I quickly saw that fade to fear. A concern at that point was that he might be frightened into pulling his pistol from beneath the seat and shooting Hooper with it.

After a minute or so, the glass hydraulically slid down about four inches. "What you want, man?" Speaking freely, he had obviously had the wired jaw released.

Hooper exhaled a load of nasty cigar smoke. "Why nothing, Mr. Harris. I only stopped because I'm so glad to see you."

"I got goddamn rights."

"Not only rights, but goddamn rights," Hooper laughed. "Now there's corruption of the great American dream."

"I ain't done none of that corruption."

I stepped out and walked around beside Hooper's bulky frame. He was gritting his teeth hard enough to bite through the cigar stub.

Slow's paunch rose and fell in increasing tempo of shallow breathing. Perspiration beaded up on his forehead. He had a medium afro that was wilting rapidly. Poor soul, maybe he was in poor health.

"Slow," I asked. "Do you get adequate exercise? Do you eat your veggies? How often do you let your mouth overload your ass."

"Whut...whut the hell. Lemme alone, Kobok, dammit!"

"Give me three reasons why."

"Kobok, shit, man."

"That's not my name, mister Harris." I was trying to look at him without blinking.

"Er, uh, Kobok, I mean."

"No, Willie, that's not quite all of it either." He knew what I meant. You could call it racism, but you'd be wrong. In the steaming turmoil of the street in that crowded nest of trouble, we, the cops retained the exclusive right to be "Mister" to everybody in sight. That's all fallen by the wayside these days and it's open season on cops. Is the world a better place as a result?

"Look, er, uh, Mister Kobok, you gotta quit screwin' with me." Hooper smiled and lit a fresh stogie.

I said, "Slow, we been hearin' all damn day you were gonna put the hurt on us the next time you saw us. Well, dude, we're all here and we got plenty of time for you to climb your ass outta that pimp mobile and get started." He didn't answer.

Slow looked as if he'd panic at any moment. He might jam the Mark V into drive and ram the car in front of him. I kind of wanted to hang around and watch.

"Y'all didn't really think I was dumb enough to try nothin' physical?" He had developed a pleading quality in his voice. He was not, however, pitiful.

"We ask the questions, bad man."

"No, no, c'mon, sheeit."

"Get outta the car," Hooper said.

"Man, I got rights." His dialogue was rather limited.

"You already told us that," Hooper exhaled a cloud.

A mixed-race crowd of assorted whores, homeless, passers-by, and a pimp known as Super Sport had begun gathering on the sidewalk behind Slow's Mark V. Their presence gave Slow a second grip on his courage. He stepped out of the Mark V and began making an impromptu street appeal to the small group. His mouth was swollen from the melee two weeks earlier and his busted arm was secured with only an elastic wrap.

"They screwin' with me. They always messin' with all of us." He expanded the ranks of the oppressed. "We got rights."

His silk, ruffled-collar shirt began showing a circle of tell-tale perspiration at each armpit. The shirt was open to the navel, and an array of gold chains hung at varying lengths, extending over his protruding stomach. He intended to shout up a riot.

A Dallas squad car stopped in the traffic lane behind my Chevrolet, a uniformed officer materializing from each side. It was the same combination of huge African American officer with smaller white driver who had responded to the melee at the Club Twenty-Six three days earlier when I had first met Doris-the-bouncer. Slow immediately began making a fool of himself by attempting to approach the African American officer on a racial basis.

"Brother, these honky mu-fuckers are violating my rights. You gotta help me, bro."

Officer Williams, no virgin in the racial slur department, regarded Slow soberly, without comment. He walked around the Mark V, leaned back against the car, and crossed his tree-trunk arms. His eyes swept the crowd, and he said, "I want this sidewalk vacated... NOW!"

Those folks must have collectively understood quite well, because the entire crowd vacated immediately. Everyone except Super Sport, that is, who only moved slowly to about fifteen feet beyond the hood of the Mark V and sat on the front fender of a parked Camaro.

Williams studied Sport for a long moment before crooking a finger, summoning him back. Sport strutted slowly back, wide brimmed white Panama hat, gold chains, and $400 alligator shoes flashing. The officer leaned over and appeared to whisper into the pimp's ear for several seconds. Sport's face shaded to somber gray, and he hurriedly walked off down the block, turning out of sight at an intersection a block down. I wonder what that officer said.

The officer then walked back to Slow's side of the Mark V. Slow extended one hand face-out, as if preparing for a high five. "Bro," he said.

The big police officer moved his face to within five or six inches of Slow's and said through gritted teeth, "Scumbag, I didn't crawl outta that damned housing project to try to become a white stooge. I did it so I didn't have to consider trash like you my brother. My name is Mister Williams to you, mu'fucker." The two officers got back into their squad car and swung into traffic. Slow slumped like a wilting balloon.

As they drove off, I turned back to Slow and said, "Slow, I don't think he likes you."

"Hey, shit man, lemme go."

I continued, "But I like you, Slow. I think you're a good ol' boy. However, the next time you put out the word that you're going to hurt one of us, you're gonnahave to leave town."

Seemingly from nowhere, a hooker wearing a short wrap-around skirt over a scanty pink gymnast's body suit slinked up. She was African American, leggy, wore huge sunglasses, and was armed with a red shoulder bag. She committed a violation of one of the elementary rules of the relationship between whore and pimp. She identified him by association in the presence of the law.

"Slow, dammit, I been waitin' down there for an hour." Her approach in front of us was such a flagrant offense that Slow must have temporarily forgotten Hooper and me. In blind anger at such an offense, he bounded around the rear of his Mark V and slapped the girl open-handed, knocking her to the pavement. She never really made a complete landing but bounced back to her feet with desperation born of mortal fear. By her fourth step, she had hiked up the wrap-around to the waist, revealing lots of lovely brown skin, kicked off her spiked heels, rounded the corner, and was high-stepping south on Harry Hines, apparently with no intention of stopping before San Antonio.

Slow caught her as she attempted to turn into an alley several doors down and struck her in the back of her head, again partially knocking her to the ground. She broke free, and they disappeared into the darkness of the alley.

I said, "Looks like we're going to have to kick Slow's ass to stop this." I was already moving.

"Yeah," Hooper answered. We headed for the alley.

We hadn't reached the entrance to the alley when Slow came back around the corner in a dead run. His protruding paunch bore a long, shallow stab wound, running at least a foot from side to side. He was losing considerable blood, and the stain spilled down onto his silk trousers. But it was apparent that the wound was not fatal, at least not immediately. He proceeded north on Harry Hines, on foot, as fast as many years of sin and degeneracy would allow his legs to transport his pudgy bulk.

It probably goes without saying that he was being pursued at close range by an African American female, wrap-around skirt hiked over waist, bearing a six-inch switchblade knife in her right hand and demonstrating definite signs of being mad as hell. Slow passed us with his eyes, as they say in books, much larger than silver dollars. The whore's eyes, however, were narrow slits of determination.

Slow verred to the center of Harry Hines amidst screeching rubber and blaring horns, then proceeded north, dead center on the median strip. She had lost about two steps in the turn out of the alley, and Slow appeared to be holding that lead when they passed under the streetlight a block north. Traffic had stopped to watch the spectacle, as Slow cut a circle around a bus and headed back in our direction. The bus turn maneuver added another three or four steps to his lead.

He began twisting and turning in and out of parked and stalled cars, doing an amazing rendition of NFL highlights, with a bleeding gut-wound.

"Hooper, we need Tom Landry's telephone number. He needs to see this."

Hooper was nearly out of control with laughter.

Slow darted around a car and started back north on Hines, passing back beneath the street light a block down with a lead of a good fifty feet. He fooled her with a nifty post pattern around a closed service station and headed back south, still dead on the center stripe. Both were losing the foot race to a third contender, exhaustion.

"I got two dollars says she catches him," Hooper said.

"Depends on whether he makes the next light."

The Chevrolet had an "inter-city" radio frequency, which meant that I could contact the Dallas police Channel 2 dispatcher, in whose district we were standing. After a respectable wait of four or five minutes, I strolled around to the driver's side and reported a possible altercation on Harry Hines Boulevard, providing a street number two blocks to the north.

Two prostitutes walked up. "What happened, man?" asked one.

"He didn't pay his child support," I answered. They walked off, heehawing.

After several more minutes, disruption in the traffic pattern to the north drew our attention to Slow coming toward us, south bound in the northbound lane. He still was making exact motions of running, but exhaustion forced him to go at a pace slower than a normal walk. We could see the whore coming back under the street lights nearly two blocks behind.

"He must have made the light," Hooper said.

"Slow, you're still leading at six furlongs," I called out as he slow-ran at a walk toward us. We still had his car parked in. Poor Slow, trapped on the Hose Line.

Hewasemittingstrangeutterances,like"ARRRRUUUUGH…
UuuuuuRRRRRRRRRMMG."

"Slow, you've got to get hold of yourself."

He reached us, collapsing across the hood of his Mark. He was losing considerable blood from the stomach wound, but unfortunately it still was not life threatening.

The pursuing lady of the night was only a block away and coming on steadily in the same curious slow-walk-with-running-motion.

"Lemme go," said Slow, partially regaining his breath.

"Well, go, and good health be with you," I said.

"Please, Kobok, uh, Mr. Kobok, lemme get my car out. In the name of God, man. Oh God, helllp meee. "

"You'd better call on somebody closer than that, Slow," I said, wondering what Flower had said when he was putting her in Parkland.

The hooker was closing fast. Traffic was stopped for blocks. Suddenly Slow grabbed his keys from the ignition, sprang to the trunk of the Mark V, opened it, and unbelievably jumped in and pulled the lid closed, locking himself in.

When Slow opened the trunk, I had fully expected that midget to pop out, teeth bared.

The whore apparently failed to observe Slow's disappearing act. She slow-ran, with glazed eyes, right past the Mark V, on south on the Line.

Hooper laughed uncontrollably, taking a seat in the Chevrolet to await the next act of the circus.

I pounded on the trunk of the red Mark V. "You can come out now, Mr. Harris. That bad ol' woman is gone."

"Urrmmmff."

"Say again, please."

"URRRRMMLLEME OUT."

"We can't let you out, Mr. Harris, you took the keys in with you."

"Kee-rist."

"Stand clear, Mr. Harris, I'm going to shoot off the lock."

"Aarrrrgh, no, no, no."

Well, hell, maybe he didn't want to be rescued. I got into the

Chevrolet with Hooper, and we drove off toward downtown. I dropped Hooper at DPD and drove out toward Spring Valley. On my way, I swung through the Line. When I passed Slow's Mark, about forty street people, mostly whores, were standing around the trunk. A straight-looking man with a crew cut had parked a pickup behind the Mark and was working on the trunk with a pry-bar. I had a vision of opening Cracker Jacks and finding a booby prize like Slow inside.

I didn't see the offended streetwalker anywhere in the area. If I had seen her, I would have tipped her twenty bucks. It appeared the Great Slow Bill Threat Crisis had been settled.

I drove on up to Spring Valley and had some beer and a pizza at a private club that was filled with drunks and drunk dates. It was after 1:00 A. M. when I arrived at my apartment. My give-a-damn factor was too low to call the answering service. I'd catch them tomorrow.

CHAPTER 17: THE LAW OF NATURAL PROGRESSION

Remember, the seed of the child is to mankind exactly the same as the first glimmer of dawn is to a successful day.

Tad knocked on my door at 7:45 A. M. His innocent little face reflected surprise when he saw my haggard mug. "What the hell happened, Mr. Kobok? I mean, what the heck happened? Are you sick?"

"Yeah, Tad, I was up kind of late, and I don't feel too good. You're up early on a Saturday morning. Something wrong?"

"Are you gonna tell my mama that I said hell, Mr. Kobok?" he said, his earnest eyes wide.

I wondered if such criminal activity should go unpunished. "No, Tad," I said. "Almost everyone does things that they wished later they hadn't. But you've got to learn not to talk that way." It appeared that a probationary sentence might be sufficient. Besides, if he learned not to talk that way, he would be in a very small minority these days.

"Do you cuss, Mr. Kobok?"

"Er, uh, well, Tad, grown-ups sometimes do things that kids can't. But cussing is bad."

"I heard you cuss once, Mr. Kobok." Damn, if once was all this kid had on me, I could coast.

"Yeah, Tad, but I won't do it again."

"Mr. Kobok, why do you bite my mama on the neck?"

"What?"

"I saw you bite her on the neck while she was cooking spaghetti the other night at the kitchen stove."

"I was whispering, Tad, whispering a secret about some grown-up things."

"Mr. Kobok?"

"Yeah, kid?

"I know that's true because I saw Uncle Al whisper to Mamma just like you do, when he used to come over for dinner."

I filed the comment in the creases of my mind." Tad, what are you doin' up so early?"

"Hungry."

"Can you wait until I get dressed, so we can go over to the donut shop and pig out?"

"Yes, sir, I'll go tell Mamma."

"No, Tad, grown-ups already know about that stuff. Better not bother Mamma with it."

"Okay, she's asleep anyway."

I scribbled a note: "Anne, Tad and I are at the donut shop." I got dressed while he ran across to leave it on her night table.

That damn kid ate seven assorted donuts and pastries, including two giant custard-filled, chocolate-covered eclairs, and drank at least a quart of chocolate milk.

We got back to my apartment before 10:00. Tad went home, and I called the answering service. I gave my secret number to the girl who answered.

"Kobok, my boy, my boy," she said. I had apparently reached the ghost of a famous comedian.

"One and the same," I answered.

"You don't remember me, do you, you rotten clown?"

"Yes, of course I do. I just didn't pick up on your voice when you answered," I lied another time. Which one was this? I bought time, trying to recall. I needed an answering service to keep track of my answering service love life.

"How's your love life?"

"I'm glad you asked, Kobok I thought you didn't recognize me. Damn."

"C'mon. You know how it is with you and me." Jesus, how was it? Who the hell was this? She certainly wasn't the girl who made the night earlier in the week.

Providence intervened. "Kobok, I got to answer another telephone. Detective Hooper says to call him at home right away. He's called twice within the last hour. Ta-ta." She hung up. Who was that? I was sure that I knew her. Well, pretty sure.

Surely Hooper had my home number? But he didn't have the donut shop. He answered on the first ring. That sounded ominous. It was.

"You called, sir?" I said.

"Second victim, son. She was carved up. dumped behind a used furniture store, 5100 block of Cole Avenue. Body burned with gasoline. I was going out the door when you called."

"Going where?"

"To forensics. The autopsy is scheduled for eleven this morning. Can you make it?"

I could hardly bear the thought of another autopsy. "I can hardly wait," I said."I'll meet you at eleven. Who was the victim? Another prostitute?"

"Yeah, African American female, twenty-nine. Long list of arrests for prostitution, narcotics, and related stuff."

Wondering why they hadn't called us to the scene, I hung up and found my service revolver and a sport coat. I drove downtown and arrived at the morgue at 10:50. Ten minutes early to an autopsy is bad etiquette. Hooper was already there, standing in the chilly basement talking to two clerks. I wondered how long my stomach could hold last night's booze and this morning's junk food in the putrid air.

She was lying on a stainless-steel cart in the center of the room. She was very dead, torched face up, obviously as an afterthought after she was already dead. The burn damage was much less than that of Katherine Mae Pritchard, but the mutilation took up the slack. The perp apparently only had a small quantity of gasoline.

The killer had stabbed her repeatedly until well after she was dead. She was nude, butchered, bloody, horrible. He had stabbed from thigh to forehead and appeared to have taken fifteen minutes completing the job. The fire had caused considerable trauma to her body, but she would have been recognizable to those who had known her in life.

Westra strolled in like European royalty, Jesus shuffling behind. I'm glad Jesus was there. I would have hated to make the trip and miss him.

"Gentlemen," Westra greeted us in the abstract. Jesus sulked, silently. He carried a suitcase loaded with autobody repair tools that were probably listed in some obscure medical dictionary as "forensic instruments."

"Gentlemen, we meet again," Westra said.

We grumbled a pair of "umerahs."

"Damn, boys," Westra continued, "if y'all don't get that bastard, we'll be out of tables down here before you know it."

Westra brought down the overhead microphone and slipped on rubber gloves and a rubber apron. Jesus put on gloves, too. Examining the tag on the cadaver's toe, Westra spoke into the recorder.

"Shawnda Jackson, African American female, age twenty-nine." He gave the date, time, and case number. "Shall we begin, Jesus?"

Jesus was being paid taxpayer's dollars. He was in no hurry. He drew his miniature circular saw from the tool box and started on the top of the head of the remains of the late Shawnda Jackson.

It occurred to me that the investigation could be best served if Hooper and I moved to the next room to discuss things. I could also witness the autopsy from forty feet away through a closed wall with my back turned. Westra could fill us in on any surprises. We cleared the room to the whine of Jesus's little circular saw.

Hooper flipped out a pocket notebook and said, "Okay, our night guys learned that she was staying a block down from where she was found. Four arrests for prostitution. Apparently, she was murdered at the same spot where the body was found. Her clothes were strewn around the area.

"It could have been a customer she was taking to her apartment or a one she was doing behind the dumpster where she was found. Or somebody could have grabbed her as she walked to or from her apartment.

"We think she lived alone, although one girl said she had had a dude staying with her lately, a white guy. He's described as…lemme see, about twenty-five, six feet five or six, 300 pounds, brown hair, scraggly beard on chin only. We watched her place regularly from four A.M., when she was found, until about an hour ago. Nobody showed up. However, my lieutenant, who is not the regular boss, is all up in my ass to catch somebody. He's a dip."

"Who is the lieutenant, Bull?"

"Sam Allen," replied the big red-headed veteran out of the side of his mouth opposite the cigar stub.

"Oh, for Christ's sake," I said. "Isn't ol' Sheebang only a sergeant?"

"Naw, just made lieutenant, temporarily assigned Homicide."

Allen was one of those officers whose total life was devoted to furthering his own position at any cost. He was an expert at promoting himself. Our own service was full of those types. They never seemed to produce a case, they always avoided unpleasant duties, they seldom worked weekends, and never got out in the rain. In short, they never did anything except sit on the fence, usually within earshot of a supervisor, waiting to kiss any ass necessary to move forward.

At promotion time, these types never have any complaints from citizens or lawsuits received because of trying to make a case. This is because they never did anything. In fact, they hardly ever left the office.

I had known Allen for the five years I'd survived in Dallas. He had sucked into a sergeant's slot with the Dallas Tactical Unit, an extremely volatile job for a wimp like him. He had, however, managed to remain an unproductive ass, staying out of range of both physical danger and controversial decisions that translate to danger.

I hadn't heard that he had made lieutenant. But I guess if you have a whole shift to hide and study for the lieutenant's exam-ination, you ought to at least write a passing score. Sergeant Samuel Allen, now Lieutenant, had been affectionately nick-named "Sammy Sheebang Allen" by a jury of his peers. The title only partially described the uselessness of the boy.

CHAPTER 18: THE LAW
OF UNAVOIDABLE POLICE PROCEDURE

Life is just one damn boring, routine day after another.

Westra strode out of the autopsy room, chin aloft, shucking gloves into a trash can. There was a tendency to salute Westra on sight.

"Come in a minute, gentlemen, please." We followed. I came last. Never go first in line to the morgue.

The cadaver of Shawnda Jackson had been surgically gutted, crotch to thorax, exposing her hollow carcass. The parts had been tossed into the ever-present metal tub nearby. Westra himself took a large pair of needle-nosed pliers, thrust them up Shawnda's well-used vagina, and pulled out a plastic ball point pen. He held it aloft for us to observe.

"Maybe she kept it there for signing customer's MasterCard receipts," said Hooper.

I said, "At least it's not a telephone."

"Ah," Westra peered over half glasses. "But as mutilators go, this ball point pen leans in the direction of matching the sadist who inserted the yellow telephone earlier this week."

Leans in the direction? "Does anything special make you think it's related to the fire death we had in here the other day..., Katherine Pritchard?" I asked.

"Well," Westra began, dropping the pen into a plastic bag, "most mutilators tend to mutilate in the same pattern. This guy bit the victim's breast area, also. That sort of pales in light of the 84-stab wounds, at least ten of which would have been fatal. This one died from trauma and loss of blood. As I recollect, the other girl had been bitten more, but not stabbed at all."

"So, does it appear related or not?" I asked.

"I'm saying that, while there are similarities, as is common in mutilation murders, there are also basic differences. It is not possible at this time, to connect the two murders directly." What he had said was basically nothing.

Jesus was stuffing parts back into the cadaver as we made our collective good-byes. Hooper called lieutenant Sheebang Allen at home, only to learn he was on the golf course with the mayor and the chief of police. Cops never plan or talk, they always confer. They never tell each other anything, they always advise. I advised Hooper that we needed to confer at some location away from the morgue.

He agreed. We retired to a coffee shop down the street to confer.

Over fresh coffee and a grease burger, Hooper made another observation." We have the place of death as a block from her apartment. Truth is, the apartment complex runs the entire block. She was killed just off the rear end of the premises where she lived."

We agreed that the oversized boyfriend was the best and only suspect. We needed to find him pronto. I faintly hoped his might be connected some way to Katherine.

Hooper said the DPD lab squints had already gone over the deceased's apartment and found nothing of great evidentiary value.

"Were any men's clothes there?"

"Yeah, a few, including a pair of size 14 yellow patent leather shoes," he smiled.

Hooper had left the restaurant telephone number with his office. The cashier paged him to the telephone.

He strolled back. "Lieutenant Sheebang says surveillance tonight...on Shawnda's apartment. The genius thinks the boyfriend will be there."

"If he did the murder, he'd be wise to be hitchhiking for Canada."

But we concluded that if the boyfriend had, in fact, been good for the murder, he would probably wait for darkness to fall before he would chance coming back to the apartment.

Hooper yawned. "I guess we should go home and try for some sleep. We're lookin' at a long night. And can you send a note home to my wife?" he smiled.

"Whatever it takes to complete this secret mission."

"Oh well," he said, matter-of-factly. "She knew what I did for a living when we married up."

We agreed to meet at Shawnda's apartment complex at 9:00 P. M. and Hooper left.

I finished my burger and drove around to the address Hooper had given for Shawnda Jackson. Not a mile from Katherine's address, it was a rear entry, lower unit. It faced an alley that separated the apartment complex from a row of business buildings that fronted out on Harry Hines. I drove around to inspect the front of the buildings.

The entire section that backed up to the area of the targeted apartment housed a firm operating as Sundown Music. The business was a successful retail outlet for all types of musical instruments, as well as records, tapes, and related items. I also knew that the store was owned by Chance McKittrick, a locally famous country and western singer.

Hooper and I surrounded the joint at 9:00 P. M. He'd dropped by the DPD motor pool and checked out a small Plymouth. He'd also brought a walkie-talkie, so I could communicate with the DPD radio in his Plymouth. Hooper parked the Plymouth about fifty feet south and I parked fifty feet north. Both of us could see the only entry to Shawnda's place. It was hotter than hell.

At 11:10 P. M., a working girl brought her trick to the alley and serviced him in the back of a pickup parked directly across from me. Hooper whispered into the radio he could see she was doing business, but he was too far away to enjoy the graphic particulars. He whispered a plea to me by radio to broadcast play-by-play action. I whispered back that I couldn't see because the action was blocked by the sides of the pickup.

I could, however, see both players clearly. I didn't count that as a lie, just obedience of radio rules. Hooper's heart couldn't have stood the stress.

At 12:50 A. M., two white males walked down the alley from Hooper's end arm-in-arm and fell into violent lovemaking on the hood of the car next to his. When they were finished, one urinated on the side of his Plymouth. At 2:05 A. M., a Dallas squad car cruised down the alley, but Hooper warned them off by radio.

By 3:00 A. M., it was becoming increasingly more difficult to stay awake. A phenomenon peculiar to all-night surveillances began to develop: rationalization. The mind begins to find reasons why the surveillance could be discontinued.

For instance, the suspect probably has been frightened off and won't show up here anyway. By 4:00 A. M., sleep became a hell of a lot more important than that apartment. Aside from the two above-mentioned diversions, we had only seen a half dozen people come and go, and all of them appeared to live in the apartment complex.

At 4:04 A. M., a very large man appeared against the distant street light at the far end of the alley. Hooper spoke softly into his walkie-talkie, announcing the stranger's presence. The man walked straight down the center of the alley until pausing to lean on a car within feet of Hooper. I assumed Hooper was, at the moment, attempting an action previously tried by many officers under similar circumstances—getting invisible or at least much smaller. The man relieved his bladder in front of Hooper's car and walked down the alley, past me, and out of sight.

"Bull," I whispered into the radio. "People who come through this alley perceive you the same way as everybody else."

"I'm being pissed on by half the people who come down this alley. A statistical fact," he whispered back into the radio. "That's ten percent less than you get from the general public."

By 4:25 A. M., the sky would soon hinted faint signs of sunrise. At 4:31 A. M., the husky man who had passed earlier walked back down the alley from my end. I whispered into my radio to warn Hooper.

He walked straight down the center of the alley and sat down on the step in front of the late Shawnda Jacksons apartment. He was carrying a small object in his hands that was not identifiable in the darkness. He got back to his feet and walked across the alley to within ten feet of where Hooper was sitting. I assumed that he was relieving himself again. An old timer like me shouldn't make assumptions loosely.

Suddenly the flame of a match illuminated his face. From my vantage point I could see dark hair and a scraggly beard. The small flame suddenly flared into a blaze that lit the entire alley as he threw a Molotov cocktail against the back of Sundown Music. The flaming liquid spread over an area of the rear door and wall but did not immediately penetrate the adjacent window. Flames instantly licked up the outside wall.

I bailed out of the Chevrolet and started the fifty feet to the man. I could see Hooper closing the shorter distance toward him in the light of the quickly spreading fire. The bulky man broke back across the alley and ran to the door of Shawnda Jackson's apartment, where he had been sitting moments before, and kicked open the door with one move.

Hooper and I each got a partial grip on his bulk in the doorway, but his momentum carried him into a heap on the dark apartment floor. Hooper threw several good punches, at least two of which caught me over the right ear.

In the darkness, the stranger began shrieking, "It's the goddamn devil. I'm in Satan's evil grip. Help! It's the devil personified."

I got my handcuffs out of my belt and began grappling for a wrist.

Hooper spat, "That's my wrist, Kobok, dammit!"

The suspect was shrieking, "Make the devil turn me loose." He was lying there, screaming at nine hundred decibels about being in the grip of human enemy Number One himself, the devil, if you would. The guy smelled like the city of Dallas sewage treatment plant.

In the darkness, I got both cuffs on the correct wrists, just as fire apparatus began arriving in numbers. As daylight grew, we could see the prisoner went about six-six and 300 pounds. We had the guy neighbors had reported living with Shawnda.

Dallas Fire saved the music store. Hooper and I waited until several DPD uniforms had gathered.

"Who y'all got there?" a tall cop asked.

"Damned if we know," said Hooper. Don't think he likes country music."

The suspect, who was having difficulty keeping both eyes pointed in the same direction, still leaned, handcuffed behind, on my Chevrolet, said, "I, to you dipshits, am Matthew Four."

"Well, "I said. "That clarifies a whole bunch."

CHAPTER 19: THE LAW OF MADNESS

Psychotic delusions always mentally seat the patient near the bottom step of the main stairway to hell. There is no exception.

We drove Fireball Five down to Dallas City Hall in my Chevrolet. We couldn't fold him into that little Plymouth. Hooper left it to be picked up later. By the time we got him printed in the Homicide office, his eyes had drifted more out of kilter.

The suspect continued to lapse into periodic diatribes about being in the clutches of the devil. I was beginning to suspect Hooper of being a spy for the dark underworld.

We placed the suspect in a small interrogation room, handcuffed to a metal table. Hooper, and I, squeezed in and began attempting to make heads or tails of the guy.

"What's your name again, jerkoffus?" Hooper began with some down-home diplomacy.

"Matthew Four," he answered, lucidly. This was going to be a long Sunday.

Hooper held up a Texas driver's license bearing the man's photograph the guy had been carrying in his pocket when we grabbed him. It showed him to be Robert B. Ball, age twenty-seven, with an address in Carrollton, Texas, a Dallas suburb. Via radio, Hooper had checked the local and national records and found the man to have a minor record of arrests for disorderly conduct and disturbing the peace. Two entries reflected temporary commitments to the Longview State Hospital.

We didn't know then, but the eventual file would be extensive.

Matthew Four had indeed been born Robert Blake Ball to

Marvin Lee and Lois Elaine Ball, twenty-seven years earlier in Fort Worth. The Ball family had a second son, James, who was two years older than Robert.

Dad, Marvin, a habitual, degenerate gambler, was employed in a large beef packing plant in the stockyards district, and Lois remained at home to raise the boys. By the time little Robert was seven, Marvin had gained fifty pounds, refused consistently to bathe or shave, and spent much of his spare time at Clyde's Cigar Store, a pool hall and gambling establishment located on South Colorado Avenue.

Lois, suffering the pangs of increasing loneliness and rejection, found the inevitable substitute. In fact, she found several. When Marvin's gambling forays reached weekend proportions, Lois found male friends who could fill the void left by the absence of her mate. She became increasingly open in her affairs. Frequently, after consuming too much gin, she made love on the living room floor with random strangers she had brought home.

Robert absorbed the horrible indiscretions of his mother as readily as a sponge absorbs water.

His mother was eventually murdered by one of her transients when Robert was seventeen, long after the Court had placed James and Robert in the home of an uncle. The death of his mother was long after Robert's effectiveness as a human being had been eroded. The damage was deep, permanent, and unfixable.

Robert held numerous menial jobs around Fort Worth. He often leaned for survival to the Salvation Army Mission, which fed him soup and religion. He consumed large portions of both. Neither was digested properly. He had several run-ins with Fort Worth police officers, who ordered him to move on from some location where he had chosen to loiter and reflect on the universe.

He landed in jail several times, twice resulting in thirty-day stays at the Longview State Hospital. The overworked hospital staff found him on each occasion to be "paranoid schizophrenic of long standing." That meant close supervision was necessary for any chance of Robert functioning anywhere near the behavior limits of what society had termed "sane."

The hospital had no room for a seemingly nonviolent type like Robert, and he was sentenced to return to the streets of Fort Worth. He began sleeping under a bridge near downtown by night and loitering on Taylor Street, under Interstate 30, by day. His loitering was less offensive than his ranting, which was becoming increasingly more frequent and obnoxious each week of his life. He began preaching eight hours daily on a downtown Ft. Worth street corner.

The neighborhood around Robert's chosen corner was patrolled by a Fort Worth police officer who had been assigned there for seventeen years. The officer had grown to consider the area his own turf. After many complaints from citizens in the area about Robert's preacher-ranting, the officer selected Robert for deportation. Deportation is a process wherein authorities of a given sovereignty ship certain undesirables to another jurisdiction. That is exactly what the Fort Worth officer did.

One summer morning the cop saw Robert standing on the usual corner, singing and babbling of things that only Robert seemed to comprehend. He slam-dunked Robert into the squad car, drove him to the Continental bus station, purchased a one-way ticket to Dallas on the morning express, and sent Robert on his way. In fifteen minutes, the officer was back on his turf, and in forty-three minutes, Robert was in downtown Dallas.

Robert found the Salvation Army Mission on Ervay Street. The Mission helped him obtain a janitor's job at Clancy's, Inc., of far off Carrollton and provided him with transportation to work for the three days that Robert worked there. On the third day of pushing the broom, Robert walked into the path of a forklift and managed to get thirty-two stitches in the front of his head. Clancy's reluctantly placed Robert on workman's compensation and forgot him. His compensation had expired on June 7th of the current year-about a month earlier than we'd arrested him.

"Why did you kill Shawnda Jackson, numb nuts?" Hooper growled.

"Say what?" replied Matthew Four, formerly Robert B. Ball.

"The chick you were staying with, asshole. Why did you kill her?" I asked.

"You don't have to use that kind of language, dammit!

"Mr. Matthew Four, the girl you were living with, Shawnda Jackson, has been murdered. Why did you kill her?" Hooper asked.

"I... I didn't."

We hammered him for about an hour. He progressed into more advanced nuttiness by the second.

"Come on, Robert," I said finally. "It's Sunday, the Lord's day. Tell us about Shawnda so we can get on with the day."

"Oh," he said meekly. "Well, I didn't kill her."

"Who did?" I asked.

"God," he replied calmly.

"Tell us how God did it," Hooper asked.

"Supreme Direction for final formation of the Divine Province of the Pentecost."

"Say again?" I asked.

"Supreme Direction for final formation of the Divine Province of the Pentecost."

Bull Hooper slapped his knee. "Hell, we've settled that. Let's turn Matthew Four here loose and go home."

"God happen to say why he directed you to kill Shawnda?" I asked.

"Sir, he directed me to make her co-director of my one-third of the universe. The only way I could get her to accept was to transform her into the spirit world."

"You killed her because you wanted to transmit her into the spirit world?" Hooper asked.

"Yes sir."

"Then why did you tear off her clothes first?" asked Hooper, rolling the cigar stub.

"Because she wore those awful whore's clothes, the bitch."

"Matthew, why did you firebomb the music store?" asked Hooper.

"Huh?"

"The music store, Sundown Music, the place you burned. Why did you do that?" I asked.

"Personification of Evil."

"Matthew," I said. "Around these parts, anybody that would

firebomb Chance McKittrick's music store is probably mean enough to murder the Easter Bunny."

"I didn't hurt no Easter Bunny, officer, did I? Who is that Chance guy?"

"Evil?" I asked.

"Voices told me to destroy all the evil around that place."

"Voices?" asked Hooper.

"Voices," repeated Matthew Four. "The spirit world always speaks in voices."

"Do they talk English?" asked Hooper.

"Oh no, officer, they only speak in tongues."

"Can you speak in tongues?" asked Hooper, leaning forward.

"Yes."

"What can you say?" I asked, genuinely curious.

"Abba dud rahh argh ofuff demious rabba, abba cvonceilien."

"What does that mean?" asked Hooper. He shouldn't have asked.

"Voices are saying that if these officers don't let me piss, I'm gonna have to piss on the floor in this little room."

"We'll let you piss after you tell us about transmitting the other girl to the spirit world," I said, probably violating at least three-quarters of the Fifth Amendment.

"Nope," was his reply.

"Nope what?" Hooper asked.

"Nope, I didn't transmit any other girls, only Shawnda."

We worked him for another twenty minutes and became convinced, collectively, that he knew nothing of Katherine Mae Pritchard. We discontinued the questioning temporarily when he pissed all over himself. I didn't think these spirit people had to go to the john.

We resumed questioning him after a short break, with his trousers and underwear hanging on a hook in the corner of the room. The huge, unstable man sat there, naked from the waist down, and continued to deny any connection with Katherine. At 10:30, a jail employee brought us some city jail white overalls, which Matthew pulled on.

"Matthew, if you piss on those, you have to go around buck

naked the rest of the damned day," said Hooper.

"What an asshole," said Matthew Four.

"We need to get this heinous criminal's confession on paper," said Hooper.

"I'll type it," I said, turning to the battered Royal in the room.

Matthew had uttered about twenty-five words when I realized that nobody would ever believe a word of what I was typing if I didn't get it in his own hand.

"Can you write, Matthew?" I asked.

"Well, hell yes," he answered.

I remained to be convinced. I located pencil and paper and handed them to him. "What should I say?" he asked.

"All of it. Everything. How you met Shawnda and transmitted her to the Spirit world. Just all of it."

We had a cup of stale machine coffee outside the room while he wrote.

After forty minutes, Matthew Four rapped on the door sharply. "He's pissin' his coveralls," shouted Hooper.

We rushed into the room and began trying to wrestle off the still dry coveralls. Like a wounded walrus, Matthew Four threw himself into a corner and cowered on the floor.

"Don't piss, you mindless blob!" shouted Hooper. "Hold his feet."

"Help. Heeeellllp. Rape," shrieked Matthew Four.

"If you piss, I'll kill you." In his fury, Hooper bit his cigar stub in half.

Matthew regained strength. "I don't have to piss."

"Then why the hell you startin' all this crap?" growled Hooper. He let go of Matthew's coverall, which he had partially ripped off.

"What crap, officer?" asked Matthew Four, still cowering in the corner on the floor.

"Rapping on the damn door glass," said Hooper.

"I was out of paper," said Matthew Four. "Christ, what a bunch of goofy mopes cops are."

I found some blank paper and gave it to Matthew. He resumed his seat and began writing. I'd heard that Moses took longer than one Sunday afternoon to do his work. I was hoping ol' Matthew Four would make a little better time. He did, but only because he had more modern writing materials.

After an hour, Matthew rapped on the door again. I opened the door, and he was cowering back in the corner of the floor again.

"Out of paper, Matthew?" I asked.

"No, sir, I've got to piss again."

I couldn't blame him for being a little edgy.

Hooper took him to the restroom, saying as he went out the office door, "You piss anywhere near me, you big hump, you're going out the third-floor window."

Matthew held his bladder. He had left his statement, completed and signed, on the desk in the small interrogation room. It was reasonably self-explanatory. But, it did not shed light on the murder of Katherine Mae Pritchard, however. The statement of Matthew Four said:

My name is Robert B. Ball, but I was reassigned as Matthew Four by the Director of the Spirit World on July 17. That date was significant because I had worked for Clancy, Inc., of Carrollton, Texas, until being hit in the head by a fork lift.

My workman's compensation ran out on July 17, which was the same day the Director of the Spirit World told me to come on over and fight Satan wherever I could.

The Director has told me that Satan works in evil magic divisions of three and one-third, and that when this evil bastard gets the universe divided into thirds, the goodness of fair mankind will be transformed to the dark side. I have been extremely careful to tear things into halves or fourths ever since receiving this information.

The Director has told me that I will inherit one-third of the universe, which I will rename Waxahachie II. The first Waxahachie down in Ellis County can remain as Waxahachie I. It took me two months to learn to spell the name of this new kingdom. I wish the Director had told me to rename my kingdom New York II, which is much easier to spell. I have wondered how we'll ever get all that on the new stationery.

I have been instructed to form a World Bank and appoint Harry S. Truman as Director. I have been instructed to open the World Trade Center and appoint Richard Nixon as Director. If they don't want the jobs, I don't know what the hell to do.

I was sent a spirit wife. She was a perfect person. She only visited me for love while I slept (or sometimes when I just kept my eyes closed) and told me to have sex with my hand. Her name was Rose Marie, and she was from Marfa, Texas, originally. I never did figure out where the hell that is.

I was searching the streets trying to find the outer boundaries of my one-third of the universe, when I met Shawnda, a Saint of the Flesh. She took me home and fed me some pancakes. Then she told me that she could show me a better way of sex than my hand. After she had showed me, she said that I shouldn't use my hand, because it would make me stutter and go blind.

Then voices in tongues told me to transmit her to the Spirit World so she could visit me while I used my hand and not talk so goddamn much. I cut her up some with a knife out behind the dumpster and then stuck a pen in her thing and then set her on fire. I hope she visits me in spirit soon because I need to use my hand.

While I was writing this, the Director told me in tongue to transmit that goofy, big-mouthed, red-headed sonofabitch of a cop to the spirit world as soon as I got the chance, because he is crazy as a fruit-orchard boar. What a low-class asshole.

I firebombed this building across the alley from Shawnda' s apartment because it was evil.

Written in the True Word of the Director, Matthew Robert B. Ball Four

I read the statement. Hooper brought Matthew back from the restroom, his pants as dry as August in Amarillo. I showed him Matthew's statement. He read it and said, "Lemme go on and choke this sumbitch some."

"Hooper, you're the case officer. You've got to witness this."

"Your ass sucks buttermilk if you think I'm gonna get my name on that thing," he said.

The police headquarters building was lightly populated because it was Sunday. We finally managed to get an elevator operator who couldn't read too well to witness Matthew's confession. I doubted that it would ever reach a courtroom.

We transferred Matthew Four to the Dallas County jail. We booked him in and showed the statement to the dozen or so employees on duty in the book-in area. They made copies for souvenirs and advised that they would put Matthew in a single cell under watch.

We cleared the jail at 3:10 P. M. I drove us out to Shawnda's apartment, so Hooper could pick up the Plymouth.

Tad was skating on the sidewalk when I swung into the apartment complex.

"Wanna play catch, Mr. Kobok?"

"Uhhh."

"What?"

"I said, how about the batting cage, Tad?"

We batted through eight dollars' worth of balls and seven dollars' worth of Coke and junk food. I have to admit that I helped eat the junk food. That night I had dinner at Tad's. I bit his mama's neck several times while she cooked, when Tad wasn't looking.

CHAPTER 20: THE LAW OF TRUTH

There are very few whole truths in cop-speak. Most truths are half-truths. Criminal investigation often goes in the toilet when we try to view the half-truths as whole truths.

I got up at 6:00 on Monday morning with an uncomfortable, but survivable, hangover. I know the Polish never die from hangovers. I accompanied the usual quarter of a million people toward downtown Dallas, arriving before most of the Agents had gotten to work.

I spread the Katherine Pritchard file on my desk vowing to re-read every word. I was still looking at ol' Charlie/Doris as a good suspect. However, we had no case. Higdon was an even better bet, but we didn't have one shred of evidence against him. But, by God, if the only thing between me and the pier at Miami was the Pritchard case, I wasn't through quite yet.

As a matter of fact, we had no evidence beyond mere speculation against anybody. Matthew had committed murder, but there was nothing to cause me to believe that Matthew had enough sophistication about him to get inside Katherine's apartment and do the number she had been subjected to.

I spent an hour on the Olivetti, drafting a report detailing the circus involving Slow Bill I had witnessed Friday night. I included a section explaining the arrest of Matthew Four Saturday night. I pointed out that although Matthew had confessed to one brutal murder, he apparently had nothing to do with the murder of Katherine Pritchard. I included a copy of his confession. It wasn't relevant, but it would keep the D. C. crowd busy reading rather than sleeping at a desk for a day or so.

I drafted a report on the Slow Bill confrontation, sort of. A few details like threats, I tailored to fit my needs.

At 8:15, the telephone on my desk rang.

"Kobok," I answered, trying to sound interested.

"Kobok?" asked the soft female voice.

"That's what I said." I wasn't into word games that morning.

"This is Maria Shelby," the voice said, "from the Garland Avenue Children's Home."

"Yes, Sister, I recognized your voice," I lied. I suppose lying to a nun counts double in hell. "How can I help you?"

"Well, I called because the Longview State Hospital just called and asked for copies of all of Sharon Jaco's records here at the Home."

"Damn," I said. "I mean, uh...excuse me, Sister. Is she a patient there?"

"Yes, I got them to admit that she was there. They didn't want to tell me; something about disclosure. I used our religious affiliation to pry. I thought you might want to know. My heavens, I dearly hope that I haven't misused my office."

"Sister," I said, "I could kiss you." Her giggle was absolutely schoolgirl.

"Sister, you have no idea how grateful we are. If there's ever anything I could do..." I once again allowed mouth to overload anus.

"Well, Mr. Kobok, in that case, I'll put you down as one of our regular guest speakers. I could place you just next month to speak to our class of senior high school girls. The curriculum will be: 'The Evils of Alcohol.'"

"Why, er."

"Good, it's a deal then. I'll call you later for a firm date." She hung up.

A class of senior girls. Evils of alcohol. Good grief.

As they say in Texas, I cut a trail for the Longview State Hospital. The facility was a large, state-supported mental hospital 120 miles east of Dallas on Interstate 20. The staff would be tight-lipped about inmates, a problem to be overcome. I walked into the administration building without any sort of firm plan.

A huge lady in white directed me to a hard-backed seat to

wait. I sat there for thirty minutes and studied my surroundings. The oversized lady in white at the desk was combination
receptionist, bouncer, head waiter, and analyst. I pondered
where she might have had to go to get that uniform—the Dallas
Tent and Awning Company, peerhap?. That one uniform must
have taken sixteen yards of material. I wondered if she would
give me a nude photograph of herself. Boy, I could frighten off
vampires with it! Or give it to Howdy.

"Mr. Kobok." She startled me. I must have been staring at
her. "Mr. Kobok, Dr. Teneris will see you now."

She ushered me into a plain office overlooking a manicured
lawn being tended by many white coveralled inmates. Were they
using sharp objects? I envisioned a hedge-trimmer massacre.

Behind the desk was Dr. Teneris. The doctor was a stunning
she, about a nine, perhaps, and better without those glasses.
She was wearing a white medical frock with a name tag on her
voluptuous left breast—I guess I mean over her left frock pocket.
It read: Dr. Kay Teneris.

"I'm Dr. Teneris," she said. She rose and extended her right
hand. I observed that the left bore no ring. She was tall, with
over the shoulder length strawberry blond hair combed straight
down her back. Her lovely, deep blue eyes appeared very cold.

I gave her my best pitch about international intrigue,
national security, and murder in North Dallas. I worked around
to telling her that it was gravely important that I learn all I could
about Sharon Jaco. I should have thought up another line.

"Hospital rules prohibit disclosure of patient information,
Mr. Kobok," she said, talking directly down to me. Things didn't
look too good-except her figure.

I then went into my top-of-the-line spiel. I waxed philosophic
and gave a poor-man's lecture on life in the Dallas lesbian community and the hard life of Katherine Pritchard. I used every
ounce of knowledge I had about the nuances of the gay bars, the
demands of the culture, and finalized by describing the horrible
burned remains of Katherine Mae Pritchard of Brown County,
Oklahoma. I tossed the high school cheerleader's photograph
onto her desk and then threw Westra's forensic work on top of
that.

She studied the photographs for several seconds. I searched the handsome face for a sign.

She leaned forward in her chair, surveying my general appearance over her polished wooden desk. "Do you sleep in your clothes, Mr. Kobok? You could pass for some sort of derelict."

I pondered the comment carefully. "No, actually, Doctor, I'm Catholic," I finally answered. I believe I saw a slight glimmer of a smile at the corner of her hard-set mouth. I felt a surge of hope of seeing Jaco's file.

"Kobok, has anyone ever told you you're full of shit?" she said finally.

"Yes, ma'am," I answered, truthfully. "Often."

"Okay," she said. She drew a file folder from her desk drawer. "I can arrange for you to see Jaco. I'll tell you in advance that she came in here badly beaten. Our preliminary diagnosis is permanent brain damage. She also appears to be suffering from pre-admittance, paranoid schizophrenia. She is partially bandaged and heavily sedated and is not going to be able to tell you much."

I thought about Morales. He'd indicated the Esperantos had slapped her around a bit and tossed her out, but the damage she was describing didn't fit. Had Sharon Jaco been beaten a second time in the few days between being ejected by Morales and the time she'd ended up half dead?

"How did she get here?" I asked.

"Transfer from Parkland," she turned through the file. "A passing motorist picked her up somewhere in Dallas County and drove her to the emergency room. Both cheekbones shattered, broken jaw, probable loss of sight in the left eye, one hundred percent probability of permanent impairment of mental facilities."

She looked at me coldly, waiting.

"I'd like to see her."

"Kobok, there is some information in this file that I feel is outside your inquiry."

"What do you mean?" I said.

"Psychological profile. I don't think it bears on your

investigation. And besides, state law just won't allow release of that data."

She crossed her slender arms, provocatively but defiantly. I'd better take what I could get.

"I understand," I said. "I appreciate your understanding in letting me see Jaco."

She looked at the carnage in the photos on the desk, then tapped a manicured finger on Jaco's file. "Understanding my ass. Somebody needs his nuts cut out."

She and I agreed on one definitive thought, assuming the killer was of the proper gender to have any.

Jaco was tied to a bed with Velcro straps. A tube protruded from her nose and over the side of the bed. Her fair hair was matted, and her scalp showed several areas that had been shaved in the process of treating her scalp wounds. Bandaged over the left third of her face, the rest of the face was swollen, purple, and scratched. She had taken a thorough beating. She looked directly at me with her uncovered right eye. The left two front teeth were missing. This didn't fit with Morales's comments. I concluded this beating transpired after Jaco had been tossed by the Esperantos.

"Sharon, this is Mr. Kobok," Dr. Teneris began. "Can you understand me?"

The eye looked up, terrified.

"Sharon, I'm Dr. Teneris. Do you remember talking to me during the last three days?"

"Yes," Sharon Jaco said from the bottom of a well. I would have wagered she did not remember. We spent thirty minutes in the room. Jaco could make an occasional lucid reply, but she couldn't climb from that bottom. She never really responded to questions about Katherine Mae Pritchard. Dr. Teneris led me back to the little office.

With her walk, she was easy to follow. I was too lost in thought to fully appreciate her liquid assets walking in front of me.

"Satisfied?" she said from her desk chair. "I told you she was out of it."

"Will she recover?" I asked.

"Some, possibly. Permanent brain and psychological damage. That's why she's here and still not at Parkland. Her face will clear up slightly, but she will be disfigured for life. And we can make another bridge."

"Bridge?"

"Yes."

"She had been fitted with a dental bridge at one time for those front teeth you see missing. It was apparently knocked out and lost when she was beaten. It is my opinion, Mr. Kobok, that she will be a guest here for a long, long time."

"Damn," I said, across the desk.

"I have another appointment," she said, rising to dismiss me. She looked across the desk, coldly. Her eyes shared an expression with some of Westra's guests.

"Thank you, Doctor." I shuffled out, wondering how long I could hold off Howdy's no potential marker.

CHAPTER 21: THE LAW OF FISH

The fish would never be caught if he kept his mouth shut. That line was really written as a warning to human who seldom heed the message.

I drove back to Dallas trying to formulate an opinion or theory. Higdon appeared to be a more likely suspect in the beating of Jaco than in the murder of Katherine. I had looked closely at Jaco's wrists and could see no sign of handcuff or other marks of bondage. Her condition had more in common with Higdon's kinky action than did the butchery of Katherine.

I found a payphone to call Tootie for messages. "Squad Supervisor James wants to talk to you." Then she whispered, "Better get lost. He's on the rag again." The girl had a penchant for the English language. Then she said, "A lawyer named Higdon called at two-thirty-five P. M., said it was confidential." She gave me a North Dallas number.

I dialed Higdon's number, figuring he wanted to compare handcuffs or sue.

"Lawyer's office," said the Playboy girl.

"My name is Kobok. I'm returning Mr. Higdon's call."

"He's in conference."

Do normal people know that lawyers spend more time in conference, out of town, ill, or in trouble with the IRS than the entire rest of the human population?

"Ma'am, I'm sorry, but he said it was gravely urgent. Can you chance temporarily interrupting the conference and asking if he could break free for a moment? Ma'am, tell him specifically that I asked if his hands were tied."

Gravely urgent loosely translates to confidential, especially if one is reminded of sexual aberrations.

"Kobok, that's not funny, dammit!" he said as he took the telephone.

"I know it," I smartassed, "particularly in such a confining matter, my dear fellow."

"Kobok, you can't keep pushing me."

I knew he wasn't recording the conversation, because he was using profanity and because he damn sure didn't want any recorded evidentiary testimony about the handcuffs. So I said, "I'm making reference to the handcuffs you have to 'cuff whores on the Line with, Mr. Higdon." That would kill the value of any tape recordings.

"Please, Kobok, I want to help."

"What do you have in mind?" I fought off the urge to add "double dating?"

"The girl who was killed, Katherine…"

"Murdered, you mean?"

"Yes, my whole life is on the line here."

"I believe hers was too." I guess that was turning the screw. I added, "What about the girl, Mr. Higdon?"

"I knew her."

"Yeah, I know."

"I didn't make it with her."

"Jesus, Higdon. Just stay right where you are, and now Santa Claus will bring you some new handcuffs."

"It's the truth, on my mother's eyes."

"You're some gambler with somebody else's assets."

"Well, that's a figure of speech."

"So is murder in the Texas Penal Code. And of course, there's always the old reliable, title 26, U. S. Code, prohibited tossing a firebomb on a victim wired to a bed. Both are mere figures of speech, Higdon."

"Kobok, I think we need to talk. Perhaps I could help."

"Then go ahead and talk."

"No, I mean in person. I know how you damn Feds are about recording things."

He was certainly right about that. I knew lawyers had the same habit. "Okay, where… when?"

"Can you come out to my office?"

"I'm on the way, Higdon."

I worked my way up the Central Parking Lot late afternoon traffic to his office. It was nearly 6:00 when I reached it. The building was unlocked, but nearly empty. I elevatored to his office, about half expecting to be ambushed by hit men in route. The Playboy girl was operating a computerized reader-printer at a startling rate of speed.

"There may be a speed limit on that thing, Miss," I said.

"Oh, Mr. Kobok. We've been very busy, and I'm behind."

"Yeah, I imagine working for Mr. Higdon could easily put you on your back."

She looked up at me from the machine, blue eyes invitingly inquisitive. I wondered if she would be turned on if I showed her my handcuffs.

Higdon had heard me and walked into the outer office. "Come in, Kobok," he said. I followed him into his office. It was even more luxurious than I recalled. I hadn't noticed all the fine detail on my first visit.

"Can Tonya get you a drink, Kobok?" he asked, raising a glass as he sat down behind his desk.

I could have used a couple of beers. "No, thank you, I'm on duty." Now I know that's not a real lie. "What do you want, Mr. Higdon?"

"Well, Kobok, I hope we can have a more civil conversation than during our last meeting."

I wanted to tell him that if we didn't, I might break his nose. I was still on guard, however, for hidden recorders. "I hope so, too, Mr. Higdon."

"Kobok, I never dated that hooker who was murdered. But I did know her friend, Sharon."

"Know her? Sharon Jaco?" I caught myself and tried not to act surprised.

"I think that might be her name. You know those street girls. Always using trick names and crap."

"Yeah, trick names while doing tricks," I answered.

"Yeah," he said, looking at me closely to see if I was still needling. I wasn't necessarily.

"Kobok," he sighed and hesitated. "You must know how hard this is for me."

"Hard, Mr. Higdon? A key subject with your girl friends on the Line."

He looked across the desk, shaking his head. "You aren't making this any easier."

"Sorry." I had abused him enough. "Tell me what's on your mind, please."

"Okay. I met Katherine, but she wouldn't make it with me. She was strange. She turned tricks all right, but she only dealt with a few customers. I saw her on the Line and called her over to the car. She was clean, I mean really a clean type. I talked to her in whore terms, and she answered me with 'yes, sir' and 'no, sir.' God, can you imagine the high? Getting some of that scrubbed farm girl and having her call you sir?"

"And?" I ignored his question.

"I saw her two or three times on the Line. And each time I tried to get her to trick with me, the goofy bitch wouldn't do it. Can you imagine a hooker who doesn't put out?"

I considered that Katherine might have more taste than I thought if she turned Higdon down. "No. What happened?"

"She introduced me to her friend, Sharon. I'm trying to tell you, Kobok, that I made it with Sharon, whatever you said her last name was, but not Katherine. Look, I paid Katherine two hundred dollars each time I dated Sharon, just to go along and be in the room. She gave me a major boner by just being there." His eyes took on a strange hue.

I wanted to kill him but considered throwing up instead. I couldn't stand not to ask the kinky question; "Did you use the handcuffs on Sharon with Katherine there?"

"Yes," he answered, eyes glazed. "Jesus, Kobok, you can't imagine what it was like."

"You got that right," I said impulsively.

"I couldn't help from premature ejaculation with Katherine in the room."

Man, talk about more information than I needed.

"But Kobok, I haven't seen either girl in over two weeks. That's the truth." He was re-entering earth's atmosphere.

"Then why call me?"

"I wanted to get it off my chest, unburden."

I wanted to blurt, "Damn, just call me Doc. Unburden yourself."

"Kobok, I swear, I knew Katherine, and I slept with Sharon. But Katherine would never let me touch her." Then a lawyer's hydrogen bomb. "I'll take a polygraph on that."

"Horseshit, Higdon. If lawyers took polygraphs, the Texas Department of Corrections would be full, and the bar association wouldn't have any members."

"I'll do it, I swear. I only request that we use an operator of my approval and that findings remain a secret. I'll have to have your word in writing on that. Results will be kept between us. I didn't kill Katherine, Kobok."

"A trumped-up polygraph by some jackleg operator? No way, Higdon. If I can get you indicted for murder, I don't want you cut loose because I was party to the test."

"You want to indict me for murder? Jesus Christ!"

"I'm saying that I don't want any part of a polygraph for you at this time because you would hire your own man and arrange to alter the results."

"We can agree on the operator."

"In that case, I'll pick Sergeant Bill Pool from Dallas homicide."

"No, no, not that vulture. Not anyone from the police. I... I meant an operator in private business. You could help choose. We could agree before I did it."

"No, thanks, Mr. Higdon." I got up to leave. "I play against enough loaded decks now." I walked out through the entry area where the Playboy girl was still burning up the word processor. "Good night, Mr. Kobok," she purred up at me beneath eyes partially closed, imitating young TV starlets.

"Good night." I looked back through bloodshot eyes, imitating a large share of the human race.

CHAPTER 22: THE LAW OF LOWER CASE OBSERVATION

Those working near the bottom of the well can sometime provide an unexpectedly broad view of things that would seem out of their line of sight.

I drove down to the Shouldn't Do and had two beers and a chat with Two Jumps. "Your old lady said Katherine tricked with a lawyer named Higdon, Jumps. Is she sure she's got the right girl?"

"Hell, Kobok, you know I wouldn't intentionally give you the wrong information. Let me call her out here. Martha, dammit, get out here," he called into the office behind the bar. Hortense whore-walked out. She had gained a little girth, but she retained the same practiced seductive sway of a meat-onthe hoof. She leaned over the bar, revealing considerable cleavage while parking her ample bosom on the polished surface. The tattoo of a mouse, rapidly being expanded to large sewer rat by age and weight gain, was centered in the cleavage. "Hortense, do you know Kobok?"

"Well, uh, by name, I guess." She assumed the reformed hooker's way of disavowing (especially to her incumbent bedmate) any prior knowledge with any man. I hadn't known her before she met Two Jumps, but she took no chances along these lines.

"Hello, Hortense," I helped her in the game. "I think I've seen you around here, but I don't know if Jumps has introduced us. My name is Kobok."

"Pleased to meet ya." She seemed relieved.

"Are you sure that the girl who got murdered and burned over off Lemmon was dating Higdon?"

"I got it from a dear friend who's still working." She shot a glance at Jumps, who discretely moved down the bar. He had no reason to hear trash talk between his wife and another man where the subject was sex and murder.

"Was there another girl involved in the dates? Maybe a threesome deal?"

"Hell, Kobok," she loosened up as Jumps moved away. "It could have been a foursome for all the hell I know. You know the sex business. If the dude has the cash, he can about name the floor show."

"But you don't know about the particulars of their deal?"

"Hell, boy," she laughed, "it's a kind of a secret business. People don't usually put what they do in the Morning Courier."

"Do you know anything about Katherine?"

"Who?"

"The girl who was burned to death."

"I heard she wasn't trashy like some of the girls. Like she picked and chose her tricks more than most. She also was said to have had some close attraction with older tricks. You know, the father thing. Some girls get off on balling older guys. Besides, they usually have more money to spend on a girl."

"Not trashy, huh?"

"From what I heard, she was country clean. Well-mannered and didn't swipe wallets from tricks and such crap."

"Was she gay?"

"You mean did she make it with other women?"

"Yeah, gay?"

"Hell fire, man!" Her laugh was loud enough to cause Jumps to look down the bar in our direction. She quickly lowered her volume. "When a girl takes in johns off the street, she's liable to learn to screw his dog if that's what pleases the bastard, and he has the money to pay for her time and services. Kobok, making it with other women in the whore business ain't got nothin' to do with being gay."

I knew all that but hadn't factored it in this case. I have already said that in the lesbian world of pitchers and catchers, the so called femes, the traditional catchers, retain enough feminine veneer to engage in heterosexual relations with men.

That's the foundation of the "go turn a trick" thing. Katherine was the inverse rule—a basically heterosexual female who could also engage in casual sex with other women. And that's not to say any female who considered herself a lesbian, couldn't and didn't have relationships with men.

Katherine's forays into the lesbian world were more a search for companionship than for sexual outlet. Had she been searching for company within a subculture where any closely interested parties couldn't make inquiry? But why would she do that? I thanked Martha and Two Jumps and left a five on the bar when Jumps insisted that the drinks were on the house.

I drove out to Spring Valley and closed my apartment door behind me against the last traces of the late summer sun.

Tad came to the door in minutes and told me that his mother had invited me over for dinner. I carried him piggyback the whole distance, hoping his mother had prudently kept at least one-well, maybe three-beers on ice. She had, and I whispered several secrets to her while she stirred spaghetti sauce in the kitchen. Tad didn't seem to notice, and soon he was zonked out on the sofa.

At 10:05, it occurred to me to call my answering service. My friend—the one I knew—purred into my ear. "Why, Mr. Kobok, how nice to talk to you." She sounded like she meant it. If she liked me, they would have her in the rubber room at Longview next.

"What do you say, kid?" I asked. I started thinking up an excuse to keep her from dropping by. I didn't need one.

"You just got a call from Sheriff Decker in Brown County, Oklahoma," she said. She gave me the number.

"Got another call," and she was gone. Was she playing "Love 'em and leave 'em?" Hell, that was supposed to be my game.

I dialed the number and got a matronly lady's voice. I had called the sheriff at home. He took the telephone immediately.

"Sheriff," I said, "Kobok here. You called?"

"Yeah, I did. Kobok, we got Willard Pritchard, Katherine's father, in custody up here. Thought you might want to know."

"In jail?" I said.

"Not exactly," he continued. "He's at Brown County Community Hospital. Been shot."

"Oh, oh," I said.

"He showed up this afternoon out at the old home place. Went apeshit again and apparently tried to kill Thelma, his ex-wife. She ended up shooting him with a twenty-two rifle."

"Bad?"

"No. Only a minor flesh wound in the left thigh. But enough to get him off his feet so she could call us. He had crawled off some, but we found him. Crazy as a damned loon."

I heard the matronly voice admonish him in the background about his language.

"Why?" I asked.

"Hell, who knows? He's just as damned spaced-out as he was the last day we ever had him in our jail. He don't make no sense and won't answer no questions."

"Sheriff, I'll drive up there first thing in the morning," I said. I had had too many beers to start the drive that night. "I'll leave at six and should be there by eight-thirty."

"Okay, boy, look forward to seeing you," he closed in the southern police phrase.

"Thank you, sheriff. See you in the morning."

When it came time to pay for my dinner, I had trouble concentrating upon the subject willingly at hand, Tad's mother, Anne. I kept trying to assimilate Willard Pritchard into my picture. After a sub-standard performance, I set her alarm for 5:00 and tried to put Willard out of my mind.

CHAPTER 23: THE LAW OF FAMILY LIFE

"It is not good that man should live alone." Genesis 2:18. "God setteth the solitary in families." Psalms 68:6. The practical application of these divine thoughts often becomes diluted by weaknesses of the flesh and a slew of other human shortcomings.

I wore a bath towel over to my apartment at 5:00 A. M., carrying my clothes under an arm. I showered and was on the road to Oklahoma, before 5:30. I put my foot to the old Chevrolet and made the drive north on Interstate 35 in just over two hours, arriving in Wilby, the County Seat before the town square had really gotten into full gear for the day.

I found the courthouse, traditional home of the sheriff and jail on the first floor. The lady on the front desk was expecting me, and she showed me into the sheriff's office immediately. He was dressed in a tan, informal uniform, with a Smith and Wesson, Model 10 with six-inch barrel, hanging from a simple belt arrangement on his right hip. He looked big and physical enough to be able to handle most of what needed to be done without the pistol. He rose, smiling broadly, politician style, and extended his hand.

"Good to meet you in person, Kobok," he said. "Did your trip go okay?"

"Yes," I answered routinely. "I burned up a little interstate."

He laughed. "The troopers will have some of the Fed's money if you aren't careful."

"You mean my money. How's the patient?" I asked, getting immediately to business.

"Well enough we transferred him to our jail this morning.

You can talk to him any time you want. How about coffee first?" he offered, again in the southern way. It would have been a serious social error to decline, so I walked with him over to the corner drugstore. I had coffee along with a huge plate of ham and eggs, prepared before me on a grill by a middle-aged, farm-type lady of whom there must be a hundred thousand in the Southwest. All seem to be able to cook delicious breakfasts.

Everyone who entered the drugstore greeted the sheriff cordially, and he returned each greeting, calling every person by a first name. Not unexpectedly, the sheriff insisted on picking up the tab. I left the lady a decent tip.

It was 10:00 A. M. before I sat down across a battered interview table with Willard Pritchard. He was limping but otherwise seemed none the worse for wear, considering that he'd been shot the day before. His knuckles were cut and scratched, apparently from beating on the side of his ex-wife's house.

He could have passed for a million other farmers turned truck driver gray hair, medium build, strong body of a man who supported himself by physical labor all of his life. I identified myself with credentials.

"Eat shit and die," he snarled over the table. He could cuss better than Higdon.

"Mr. Pritchard, you'd better hear what I ask before you show your ass," I said.

"I said, kiss my ass." Higdon couldn't have done better.

Sheriff Decker, who had sat quietly at the end of the small table, rose. With one very impressive swipe with his huge right hand, he bear-pawed Pritchard off his chair. Pritchard landed sitting more or less in the fetal position, in the corner of the room, eyes blinking in stunned surprise and pain. The sheriff had obviously studied interrogation techniques in some classroom other than Westfield College. He had successfully caught Pritchard's attention. Evidence of attitude adjustment was clear.

"Get back in your chair, Willard," the sheriff said, paternally.

Willard got. He tried to fix his blinking eyes on first the sheriff and then me.

"Do you know who I am, Mr. Pritchard?" I asked, after a few seconds.

"Yeah." His gaze fixed on the center of the small table.

The interview took over an hour. Pritchard freely answered questions pertaining to his past several years' employment and itinerary but dummied up totally when the subject drifted toward any member of his family. He never took his eyes off the center of the little table.

I finally got around to a line so old that I usually reserved it for illiterate types. "We know the whole story, Pritchard. You must know that the federal government keeps a file on everyone. You can lie and pout all you want, but we already know." I leaned across the table for emphasis of my b. s.

He never looked away from the tabletop. Tough guy.

"We know your whole story," I repeated, about ready to give up.

He looked up into my eyes. I saw something different. Not fright, not surrender, but perhaps a distant plea for understanding of some forbidden secret hidden in the recess of his mind. All of us have such a place in our thoughts. Thoughts that we carry to our grave. Secrets that only have to be disclosed when we get to hell. I saw both depth and resignation. I thought he was going to unload, but he just looked into my eyes for a long time. I saw him weaken and gave him another dose.

"We can't help you unless you help yourself." I leaned a little on a universal cop fabrication. We weren't trying to help him.

The eyes continued to burn into mine. There was a lot of violence in this simple-appearing farmer. But I could see he had believed me when I said I knew his story. I was instantly confident that a day or two in the Brown County jail would bring out his whole story. It didn't seem particularly important to our murder, but we needed to know what was behind the unstable man's twisted mind.

I stood and walked out, the sheriff following.

"What do you think?" he asked, back in his office.

"Two or three days, I think," I answered, confident. "He'll tell all he knows, which is probably damn little."

The sheriff and I had another cup of coffee in his office. Willard playing the Sphinx role was a problem. I needed a better handle on Katherine's background.

"Is there any way I can find someone around here who could give us more background on Katherine? I mean, school associates, boyfriends, somebody she might have worked with?"

He eyed the bottom of his cup thoughtfully. "Well, she worked at the bank across the street, as we know. Hell, I don't know right off who she might have dated or who her friends might have been."

I explained the alternative situation and that she seemed to be grouped with the lesbian community for some reason other than sexual preference.

"Damn, Kobok, we don't get much of that kind of thing in this neck of the woods. Fact is, I don't guess I've ever known of any kind of regular gay men, let alone women. What the hell do these lesbians do to one another?"

I explained as best I knew. His expression told me that he wasn't sure I knew what I was talking about. I was not the world's expert on such matters, but what I had explained was pretty basic. I didn't elaborate.

"Sheriff, I think I'll walk over to the bank and ask around."

"Feel free to ask questions wherever you think it'll do any good. If you'd like, I'll walk over with you. They'll talk to you quicker if I'm there."

"Glad to have you," I said. His presence in the small community opened doors.

"Jesus, are you gonna' bring up that lesbian business?" he asked as we walked across the street.

"Not directly." I intended to play it by ear.

The Farmer's State Bank of Wilby, Oklahoma was housed on the corner in the same row of buildings as the drugstore where I had earlier consumed mounds of breakfast. Two of the three tellers on duty greeted the sheriff by name.

"Mornin', Ms. Williams. How do, Ms. Branson. Is George in, ladies?"

A slender, balding man of forty walked out of an office adjacent to the bank lobby and greeted us.

"Morning, Sheriff," said the man. He was wearing a dark blue, western-cut suit and an open-necked shirt.

"Good morning, George. I'd like you to meet Mr. Kobok, a

federal officer from ATF, Dallas who needs some information. Kobok, meet George Sanborn. He owns this bank."

"Good to meet you, Mr. Kobok." He extended his hand.

"Mr. Sanborn," I returned the greeting, noting that he had more grip than the onlooker would have expected.

"C'mon into my office, gentlemen," he said, turning back into the doorway from where he had appeared. "Can I have one of the ladies bring you fellows some coffee?"

The sheriff and I both declined. I was full from the drug-store and the sheriff's office.

"Well, Kobok," began Sanborn, "is it a swindle, an embezzlement, or are the ghosts of Bonnie and Clyde coming to rob us?"

"No, Mr. Sanborn, I want to ask about a former employee of your bank who moved to Dallas three years ago."

"Has to be Katherine Pritchard," he said. "She is the only employee who left us to go to Dallas. A couple of other girls left, but they're still around these parts."

"That's right, Katherine Pritchard."

"Her funeral was Friday," he went on. "I didn't get to the funeral, but the wife and I dropped by the funeral home the day before to give Thelma our condolences."

"Can you tell me about her when she was here, Mr. Sanborn?"

"Good girl, as far as I knew. Played ball over at the school. Real popular and a fine worker while she was here."

"Did she have friends who might still be around?" I asked.

"Well, Millie Calkins back in bookkeeping here in the bank was in her class in school. I think they were friends."

"Anyone else?"

"Not that I know. Millie might can tell you."

"How about boyfriends?"

"Oh, well," he looked thoughtful. "I don't guess I know. Or if I do, I don't recall. Maybe Millie could tell you. Should I call her in?"

"Please do."

He dialed the old-type intercom on the telephone on his desk. "Millie, can you come into my office?"

A plain, but attractive young lady with light-reddish hair entered the office, tentatively.

The sheriff and I rose with Sanborn. "Millie, you know the sheriff. And this is Mr. Kobok, a Federal Agent from Dallas. He's asking for information about Katherine. I want you to help these men any way you can."

She looked at him, still standing. "Have a seat, Millie," I said.

She sat looking out the small window behind Sanborn, looking as if it wouldn't take much to make her cry. Her reddened eyes reflected that she had spent considerable time doing just that lately.

"I understand you and Katherine were friends, Millie," I said. "Is it okay if I call you Millie?"

"Sure," she answered, expectedly.

I wrote down her name, home address, home telephone number, and age. "Did you know Katherine all her life?"

"Only since seventh grade when we moved here. My father manages the grain elevator."

"Did you know her family?"

"Yes."

"Did you know the brother who was killed?"

"Yes, Jimmy was older, but I knew him. He was killed in Vietnam, you know."

"Yes, we know. What was he like?"

"Just an average guy. Played football, worked on his car, and chased the girls."

"Did you know the father?"

"Yes, but not well. Katherine never liked for us girls to come to her house. It had something to do with her father being sort of... well, strange."

"You mean, he seemed dangerous?" I interjected the charged word.

"Well," she looked across the desk at Sanborn, "it's a little personal."

Sanborn proved to be one of those rare people with insight. "I just remembered that Dalton Contract. Can y'all excuse me, please?" He closed the office door behind him, prudently.

"You were talking about Willard Pritchard," said the sheriff.

"Is there something about him that I should have known?"

"He was… er, inclined to put his hands on us girls. Katherine and her mother just always discouraged us from coming out there. But I was around him enough to know. And the word sort of got around among the girls. We always pitied Katherine, and she was always our friend. We just learned not to get around him. When they finally put him… I mean when you, Sheriff, put him in the Muskogee hospital, all of us girls weren't surprised at all. He was kind of creepy."

"How do you know Willard would put his hands on the girls?" I asked.

"He touched me once or twice when I drove out there to pick up Katherine. She made excuses, but we all knew."

"Did he come back after Muskogee?"

"No, but he wrote to Katherine. She showed me one of the letters where he wanted her to visit him in Kansas City. He said it would be okay to bring one of her girlfriends."

"Do you recall the address?"

"Oh, no, not after this long."

"Why did she leave here?"

"To go to Dallas to take a better job. She made good, too. It wasn't very many months after she left that she wrote and said she was making a good salary. She made enough to send her mother money regularly."

"What kind of job did she have?"

"You must know. She was some kind of executive with the telephone company."

"Did you hear from her?"

"Yes, she wrote often at first. But not in the last year, hardly at all."

"Did you ever visit her?"

"No," she said, crestfallen. "She said that her executive job caused her to work most evenings, and she would visit when she came home. Home here to Wilby. I figured she was living with a man."

"Did she mention her father or any friends in her letters?"

"No, and I don't see how her father could have known where she was. It's funny, Mr. Kobok, she was always close to her father. Kind of more than normal."

"What do you mean?"

"When she showed me the letter where her father asked her to come to Kansas City, she asked me if I would want to go with her. I knew she was thinking about going to see him. I made excuses."

"Did she go to visit him?"

"Not that I ever knew about. But she wanted to see him. I guess it was only a matter of her wanting to see a member of her family." Her face said she doubted what she was saying.

"Did she date boys here in Wilby, Millie?"

"She dated Larry Casey off and on for several years. He's the football coach down in Grainville."

"Where is that, please?"

"Just off the freeway, twenty miles back toward Dallas," the sheriff interjected. "It's in this county."

"Did she have any other friends or boys she dated?"

"No, none that are still around here. I could think about it and give any more names I come up with to the sheriff. Can he telephone you in Dallas?"

"Yes, that would be fine," I said, getting to my feet to terminate the interview.

She walked out without saying another word, still appearing capable of crying with little provocation.

"Do you think Larry Casey knows anything, Sheriff?"

"He's a good boy."

"Will he help us, you think?"

"Yeah, if he knows anything. He's married to a local girl here and probably hasn't seen Katherine in years." He drew me a map on the back of one of my business cards. "Take the State highway 236 exit, and don't miss the right turn at the red horse barn," he instructed in the rural way, pointing to the tiny map he had drawn with his big hands.

I made my thanks and goodbyes and headed south.

CHAPTER 24: THE LAW OF CONSEQUENCE

The conclusion of life is often only a consequence of the origin. To determine why the tree bore a bitter apple, forget the fruit. Examine what might have poisoned the roots.

I navigated the asphalt, then gravel toward Larry Casey's place, as the Sheriff's map directed. The horse barn was more pink than red, but prominent. I drove onto Casey's small spread without missing a turn.

A huge, white, shaggy dog blocked my way into the fenced yard with a combination of bark and display of many teeth. He turned out to be only the burglar alarm. When the husky young man in overalls rounded the frame house, the dog began smiling alternately at his master and then at me. He then came close for a sniff and a tail-wagging pat to show me that he hadn't really meant any harm. I wondered how he would have reacted if the boss hadn't been home.

"Mister Casey?" I inquired, still half expecting to be partially eaten at any moment.

"Yes?" He had blue eyes and short blond hair, cropped above his ears.

I showed him my credentials, which he examined longer than people normally do. "You after the whiskey still?" he grinned through Huck Finn-spaced teeth.

"Not this trip," I smiled back. "I'll need a squad to cage old Wolf here."

"He mostly only eats people at night," said Casey.

I knew the type. They weren't savage unless absolutely necessary. It was a rule that lots of society could profit by emulating. "I need to ask you some questions about Katherine Pritchard." I studied his face.

"Damn, I haven't seen Katherine in years," he said, looking at his boots. "Come in the house out of the sun."

The house was old but reflected considerable remodeling and strenuous broom work. A window air conditioner was doing battle with the rising afternoon temperature. It appeared the little machine would probably eventually finish second. We sat at a kitchen table.

"What about Katherine? Did she rob a bank?" He hadn't heard of her death.

"Murdered last week in Dallas," I answered, vowing to omit lurid details.

"Holy hell. What? How?"

"Apparently a sex crime. She either allowed someone into her apartment or someone broke in and murdered her," I said. I could see no need for the rest.

"Good God." He looked genuinely shaken. "She and I dated in high school and during my first year up at the university."

"Yeah, I know. That's why I dropped by."

"You don't think I? I mean, I didn't..."

It was an understandable reaction. "You're not a suspect, Mr. Casey. We're only trying to gather background information about her past." He appeared relieved that I hadn't brought out the handcuffs.

"How can I help?" He appeared genuinely stricken.

"Do you know why she moved to Dallas?"

"I don't know that she had any reason beyond making more money in the big city. You know, around here it's hard to earn much salary."

"Did she see her father after he was placed in the Muskogee Mental Hospital?"

"No, I don't think so."

"Was she close to him?" I got right to the question that had stuck in my craw.

Casey eyed me carefully, as if trying to read something else into the question. "You've already asked around, right?"

"Yes, some. But we need all the information we can get. We need to know all about Katherine. You know, her habits or anything that might tell us her background."

"Jesus," he said, rubbing his hands over his face as if weary.

"It's a long time, really. Yeah, I was close with her for several years. She always was a nice girl. I mean a decent, caring person, if you know what I mean. If you had a headache and she asked if you were sick, she genuinely wanted to know. She… oh, for instance, she would pet stray dogs and such like."

"I had asked about her father," I prodded.

"Yeah, I know. Her father, damn. I only barely knew him. When I went out to their place, he always kind of stayed out of sight. Jimmy was a good kid, but older than us."

"Katherine's brother?"

"Her older brother. He was killed at Da Nang."

"Yeah. Did his death change their lives? Any of them?"

"No, I don't think so. They were all broke up. At least Katherine and her mother, but I don't know about the old man, Willard. Jimmy had moved out a year or so before he joined the Marine Corps, and I'm not sure that he had been home since leaving."

"Why did he move?"

"Probably just sick of living in the same house with Willard. Willard was an obnoxious, overbearing asshole. When I came around, I could always tell if he was anywhere close, because Katherine acted different."

"How different?"

"Well, Willard drove a truck and wasn't around much. When he was on the place, Katherine just wasn't the same. It was always kind of like she was terrified of him but attracted at the same time. Kind of like insects to certain spiders. Damned weird, frankly. We never dated after… oh… about when I was twenty-one."

"When I was nineteen or so, I offered once to kick his ass for her. I was playing ball up at the university and thought I was mean as hell. He'd probably have shot me. Anyway, she nearly threw up when I suggested whipping his butt. In fact, we kind of drifted slowly apart after that. Well, I met Annie about that time, too."

"Annie?"

"My wife. A great lady. She works at the co-op in Wilby."

"Tell me, Mr. Casey, did you have sex with Katherine?"

"What the hell does that mean?"

"I was wondering about her habits. Who she might pick up or date."

"Oh. Well, we made it a few times, Mr. Kobok, but she was no mattress-back. It wasn't a sure thing that she would put out too often. She was always more into touching, hugging, and affection."

I nodded.

"She wouldn't have been the type to get too familiar with strangers, not even down there in the big city. She would have had to know a man pretty well before she would go to bed with him. At least that's the way she was when I went with her. I guess she could have changed."

"This is a delicate question." I had wanted to avoid maligning the dead girl among the home folks, and I tried to ask the question off-handedly. "She was living in an area where there were quite a few same sex relationships. Maybe her killer is connected to that someway. Can you think of anything in her makeup that would have made her... uh... sympathetic to gay women?"

Casey's Huck Finn countenance reflected disgust at such thoughts. "About the only exposure to lesbians I have ever had was in Oklahoma City one summer. I played softball on a diamond next to where women played. Some of the players were lesbian, and some didn't seem to be. Some of the lesbians would show up with really attractive, straight-looking girls. Jesus, what a waste. That's how us rednecks saw it."

"Would Katherine have been repulsed by them?"

"Hell, Katherine would not only pet stray dogs, like I said, but she would have been kind to snakes and alligators if she'd ever met any. Sounds like maybe she might have met some reptiles down there in Dallas. Yeah, she would have been nice to them. She was nice to everybody. But, man, as crazy as old Willard was, it would have been bad news if he ever found her within fifty feet of a lesbian."

"Well, I guess I've taken enough of your afternoon," I began the process of ending the conversation.

"Oh, hell, no, Kobok. I'm glad to try to help. I only wish you'd brought better news. I really liked her at one time. It just didn't work out. Something pulled her affections away from me in spite of all I could do."

"I need to get going south," I said, starting for the door.

He grimaced. "I'm gonna call Katherine's mother. Christ, I'm sorry I hadn't heard."

"She probably would appreciate that," I said.

"Yeah."

"What kind of football team are you going to have this fall?" I said as I started off the porch. A brown late-model Dodge pickup was parked against the white picket fence. I could see the word Cardinals and the outline of a red bird on a decal in the rear window.

His expression lightened. "We're single-A here in Grainville. We were second in the district last year, and I would figure about the same again this year. We're in a tough district."

"I'll watch the papers. Maybe I can drive up and watch your kids this fall."

He smiled at that, Huck Finn back in the saddle. "You can have a place on the sideline with us."

"Watch for me." I slammed the old Chevrolet door and headed toward Interstate 35. I thought as I watched his solid frame disappear in my rear-view mirror that I would probably be watching kids play in Alaska this fall or in hell. Do they play football in Alaska? I knew they didn't in the second choice.

CHAPTER 25: THE LAW OF DOGS

COPS, AND CROCODILES: It has been said that the dogs of ancient Egypt drank at the River Nile while at a run to avoid being seized by crocodiles. The police have a similar relationship with Internal Affairs.

I crossed the Red River at a high rate of speed at just past noon. I should have looked up Katherine's mother, but to ask or say what I knew of the heartbreak and now suspected a father-daughter relationship right out of a porn movie.

Forty minutes later, I was within radio range, and like a rookie, I called in for radio traffic. Howdy answered on his office console. "Kobok, call me at this office immediately." He sounded a little upset. He hadn't even used my official Buck Rogers secret radio number.

I drove another fifteen minutes, found a payphone, and called. That was fairly close to immediately.

"Where the goddamn hell have you been?" he opened the conversation.

"You sound upset, sir," I said, applying the usual needle.

"You goddamn right I'm upset. We been lookin' all over town for you."

Sounded to me like a classic case of not having enough sense to look in the right place, but I withheld that comment, too.

"Dallas Police Internal Affairs has got some business with you," he sounded triumphant. Lieutenant Samuel Allen of IAD wants to ask you about attempting to have a citizen murdered! Some goddamn pimp on Hines. I believe they're talking criminal charges. You're gonna have trouble double-talking your way out of this one."

"What did you say the IAD man's name was?"

"Lieutenant Robert C. Allen."

"Sammy Sheebang. Christ, James, last week he just made lieutenant, temporarily assigned to Homicide. How time flies when you have your nose up the right ass."

"What?" he said.

"I said, James, that all details are in my reports. Perhaps, sir, if you'd like some help in learning to read a little better, you would find that all of that crap is explained and witnessed."

"I don't have to put up with any more of your lip, Kobok. Have your ass down here by 2 P.M.. They're gonna have your buddy, Hooper down here, too. What do you say to that?"

"Like I've said before, Howdy, I'm too scared to talk."

"Don't call me Howdy, goddammit!" he screamed in my ear.

I hung up and drove toward downtown.

Howdy didn't have much of a case, or he would have requested our own IAD to enter the matter. He wanted to sit on the fence and see if the city could produce anything, and then tailgate to headquarters if they made a case. He figured that our own people would burn his fat ass if he made a bum report. He was right. They were somewhat smarter than he was.

From the cool interior of Denny's, I ran down Hooper on the telephone. He was eating Mexican food at a restaurant on Garland Road.

"What happened with IAD, big boy?" I asked.

"Slow apparently made a beef that we had arranged to have a whore attempt to murder him. Then Matthew Four decided that his rights of the universe had been violated. Also, Charlie apparently is feeling ignored in the county jail, so she decided me 'n you used unnecessary force in hauling her in. None of it has much merit. By the way, I'm gonna tell them you're the ringleader."

"Did Slow die?"

"No, in Parkland with some stitches to the stomach. Hell, a little stabbin' might make him sick for a while, but it sure won't kill him."

"What did you tell them in your report about Slow's incident?"

"The truth...sorta. We heard he wanted to talk to us. We

assumed he had some information for us. He was stoned when we got there and tried to start a disturbance. He struck a female acquaintance who fled—we thought safely. We attempted to assist the wounded Slow, but he fled, too. Seconds later we saw them at a distance with her chasing him. We called the Dallas police dispatcher to report the incident. We maintained security of Slow's car until he came back for it. And while we attempted to screen the attacking female off him, so he could drive away, he jumped into the trunk of his car in apparent fright.

"We tried to assist by opening the trunk by force after the woman had been moved away, but he refused our offer of help. I thought he mumbled something about a friend coming with another set of keys."

"Sounds like what happened to me," I said. "Matthew hasn't got a chance of making a complaint stick, because he's got no complaint coming."

"No, and he probably hasn't got any more chance of finding dry pants either," said Hooper.

"Did you see who the IAD officer was?"

"Yeah, Sergeant, now Lieutenant Sammy Sheebang."

"On the way to the top," I said.

I called the Central Patrol Station and asked the duty sergeant to find Patrolman Williams and have him call me on the Denny's payphone. I gave him the number. I knew the sergeant in passing. We had served a search warrant together several years earlier when he was an investigator in Vice. He promised to have Williams call me. I took a seat near the payphones.

I had just gotten a bite of my grease-burger when the telephone rang.

"You called?" Williams deep voice asked.

I explained the three complaints in detail, taking about twenty minutes to complete the story. He said immediately that he knew Matthew Four and that he had chased him off the Line about a week earlier for standing in the middle of the street while preaching the gospel in tongues.

"It's the whore that cut Slow that we need," I added.

"I heard Slow got cut right after we saw you Friday night. It won't kill him, though. Nobody much cared, and Slow would never testify anyway, so we haven't been looking."

"Do you know who the girl is?"

"By road name only. They call her Kitten. But I can have her in an hour or so if she's still alive."

I had just finished my cold burger when the payphone rang again.

"I got her here, Kobok," I could hear the traffic noise in the background.

"Does she say she cut Slow?"

"I haven't asked her. Waiting to see what you wanted to do."

"Ask her about it." I heard voices in the background.

Williams spoke into the receiver. "She says that Slow hit her, chased her into the alley, and tried to kill her with a knife. She grabbed the knife away and must have accidentally cut him."

"Does she recall Hooper and me?"

"She said that she vaguely recalls a white man or two standing there, but that she wouldn't have cut no pimp if she'd knowed you were the goddamn po-lice. That's a quote."

"I don't suppose you could have her in my office at 2 p. m. today?" I asked.

"Does a bear shit in the woods, bro?" he laughed. "Gimme the address."

I gave the address and hung up. I guess I owed him another beer.

I paid my tab and headed for the federal building. No way IAD had seen the statement from Matthew Four. Howdy hadn't read his in-basket.

CHAPTER 26: THE LAW OF RATS AND INTERNAL AFFAIRS

Every dork assigned to IAD volunteered for the duty. It's easy enough. Then they just sit around and wait to profit by a real cop's misfortune.

L ieutenant Sam "Sammy Sheebang" was sitting in Howdy's cubicle when I walked in. A second guy, who I could knock off as IAD from two hundred paces sat next to him. Hooper was riding a plastic chair in our tiny lobby.

It would be difficult to attempt to explain why Sheebang chose our office for a preliminary IAD interview. I suspected that this choice might have been at the suggestion of good old Howdy.

We assembled in a conference room. Sheebang and Howdy arrived at the chair at the head of the table at the same time. They exchanged possessive glances until I walked between them and sat in the chair. They sat down on either side of me, wearing facial expressions of children who had finished third in a two-kid race. Shebang started to open the affair but was interrupted mid-snivel by Howdy.

"Gentlemen," James opened the hypocrisy. "We are here to discuss a matter of extreme gravity. First, I want to introduce everyone here." He went around the room, naming Hooper, Sheebang, the second IAD rat, a stenographer, and me. He then introduced himself, completing the circus, as if everyone didn't already know everyone.

Sheebang jumped to his feet, interrupting. His weak face bore the trace of a smirk, reflecting contrived poise. It was going through my mind that a loud slap on the table might cause him to faint.

Sheebang spat officiously, "I'm here, gentlemen, to make inquiry about several serious complaints of conduct regarding an officer of the city of Dallas, as well as an agent of ATF. I have been assured by Squad Supervisor James that we will have complete cooperation from the federal government." He emphasized complete "Lawlessness" cannot abide among officers of the law. Hooper looked undecided whether to throttle Sheebang, or Howdy, or barf.

"And I can assure that the city of Dallas will guarantee the total assistance of our officers." He attempted to stare Bull Hooper down, a futile gesture. Hooper continued to look directly into Sheebang's eyes, unblinking.

Sheebang moved to more fertile ground. "Let's get directly to the charges. First, the matter of Robert B. Ball, white male, age twenty-seven, arrested during the morning hours this past Sunday. We have here copies of a sworn statement given by Mr. Ball to two of our IAD investigators in the Dallas County jail."

He withdrew several copies from a folder in front of him and passed them around to each man at the table.

"Mr. Ball has told us that Detective Hooper and Agent Kobok abducted him from a public street, handcuffed him, falsely arrested him for murder and arson, denied him access to religious writings, denied him the right to tell you of his religious views, and forcibly tore off his trousers in the interrogation room." He lowered his voice reverently at the trousers part, took off his half glasses, and looked pityingly around the room, slightly shaking his head.

"What are his religious views, sir?" asked Hooper, obvious to all in the room except Howdy and Sheebang that he was laying a trap.

"Well, naturally, officer, he didn't discuss them with us. We are forbidden from questioning a man about his religious preference."

"Oh," said Hooper. We, the accused, both looked at each other, unanimously realizing that Whizzbang had heard a different tale from Matthew Four than we had. We also now knew for certain that by some quirk of bureaucratic inefficiency, Sheebang's investigators had not obtained copies of the statement Matthew had given to us on Sunday. Howdy had them, they didn't.

I said, "Lieutenant, did you read the part of Matthew Four's statement where he confesses to murdering his roommate and firebombing a music store?"

Howdy said, paternally, "Let the Lieutenant speak, Kobock."

Sheebang went on. "The second allegation involves conspiracy to murder one Willie Harris, Junior, African American male, age thirty-one, on Harry Hines Boulevard, prior to midnight last Friday. You gentlemen had a busy weekend," he said snidely.

"Mr. Harris has said in a sworn statement to our officers that he was sitting in his vehicle on Hines when Kobok and Hooper dragged him from the car, threatened him with bodily harm, and then enlisted the services of an unknown female to attack him with a knife, thus inflicting a severe stab wound to his abdomen, which required eighteen stitches at Parkland.

"Mr. Harris has sworn that Kobok and Hooper thereupon forced him into the trunk of his car and left him locked inside in peril of his life." He looked around the room as if expecting some of us to make snap denials or run for the door. He then switched to past tense.

"We had a third complaint from a Ms. Doris Johnson, white female, age thirty-five, who alleged that Kobok attacked her while she was engaged in her occupation as a receptionist at the Club Twenty-Six on Maple Avenue. She further swore that on the following day, Kobok and Hooper used excessive force in handcuffing her and falsely arresting her. She also alleged that they threatened to bury her at Rosemont Cemetery after taking her to an open grave and repeatedly threatening her life." He slammed his leather folder shut. Boy, he was righteous.

He then continued, "We intend to get to the bottom of this whole business. We will not tolerate criminal activity."

"What kind of work does this fellow Harris do?" Hooper grinned.

Sheebang shuffled papers. "Promoter, it says in our report."

"What's he promote, sir?" I asked.

"How the hell do I know?" responded Sheebang, defensively.

Hooper belched loudly, the noise reverberating against the poor acoustics of the room. Sheebang twitched nervously but didn't faint.

Sheebang then ruled one-third of his evidence inadmissible. "However, we have found a limitation here. Unfortunately, Ms. Doris Johnson called the IAD office at eight-forty-one A. M. today and recanted her entire story. She had apparently been released on bond, and characteristic of these totally unreliable people we have to deal with, she had decided not to cooperate further. I would say, gentlemen, that you are collectively lucky as hell, or somebody has coerced our official witness. If we find the latter to be correct, some or all of you are going to be looking at criminal charges. I mean charges in addition to whatever develops from Mr. Ball and Mr. Harris."

Through the door, I heard voices in the squad room. "Excuse me for a moment," I said and walked out of the room over Howdy's surprise.

Williams was in his blue uniform, his bulk stuffed into one of the cheap chairs in the foyer.

The hooker was still in uniform also. She was in lavender hot pants and a brilliant yellow halter top with bright red spike heels and nothing else. Her perfume presented a four-foot barrier to anyone approaching. I wondered how Williams was going to explain to his wife about the smell on his uniform. He was grinning in his easy way. The girl appeared ready to bolt for the door at any moment.

"Afternoon," Williams said, rising to his feet. I came just about to his shoulder.

"Afternoon," I answered, shaking his big hand.

I called him aside and explained that Lieutenant Robert Allen of Dallas Internal Affairs was in the next room. I gave him a brief description of the charges.

"That little prick of misery, Sheebang," Williams said with narrow eyes. He was more man sitting than Whizzbang could have ever been even while standing on a chair and carrying a stick.

"What do you want me to do?"

"You don't have to go in there and get involved. I think we can handle it if the lady tells her story."

He rolled his eyes to the whore. "She can't wait to tell the truth. Ain't that right, Kitten?"

"Right on, Mr. Williams." Kitten got to her feet as if on command. Her droll expression freshened at Williams's attention to her.

"I want to go in, Kobok," said Williams, looking back through the office.

"Kitten, my name is Kobok. Do you recall me on Hines the other night when Slow hit you?"

She looked me over from forehead to crotch appraisingly, with the whore's equivalent of grading stock on the hoof. "No sir, I like 'em a little younger."

"Well, I need you to come with me into this room and tell exactly what happened out there. Tell the truth, and no harm will come of it."

"Don't tell the truth, Kitten," chipped in Williams, "and I'll be very disappointed."

She gave him a sidelong glance. "I just hope you see fit to give me somethin' else, Mr. Williams." She followed me into the room, Williams coming third with some trace of embarrassment at Kitten's comment.

"I have taken the liberty to produce the lady whom your snitch Mr. Harris has slandered. Gentlemen, this is Kitten." I had forgotten to ask her proper name.

"Goddammit, Kobok," said Howdy Doody James.

"This is out of order," said Sheebang. I guess he thought he had been elected to parliament.

Hooper got to his feet. "Are you saying, Sheebang, that this lady can't be allowed to tell her story?"

"Don't call me that," snorted Sheebang.

At the sound of the name "Sheebang," Kitten looked sharply at the bearer of the name. She continued to look at him, seemingly surprised, but made no comment.

"I suggest that if we let this lady talk, she may be able to shed considerable light on the incident with your citizen, Mr. Harris," I said.

"She has no place in this conference, Kobok, dammit," said Howdy stupidly.

"I think she might be what Mr. Slow Bill Harris promotes, Mr. Squad Supervisor, "said Hooper dryly. It appeared that he might be thinking of choking old Howdy some. I hoped to hang around and see the result. It never got to that.

"Well, for Christ's sake, let her talk then," said Sheebang. "Okay, whatever your name is. Tell whatever damn lie Kobok and Hooper have put you up to."

Kitten continued to look closely at him, her expression curious.

"Go on, lady, talk," said Howdy Doody James, perspiration showing on his ample brow.

"Go ahead, Kitten," said Williams from the doorway. Sheebang looked at the giant officer filling the doorway like the bad guys used to look at the Lone Ranger on TV—apprehensively. Sheebang's attention had been riveted on the prostitute, and he didn't appear to have seen Williams before the giant spoke.

At Williams's cue, Kitten spoke. She told it like it was. " Well, Slow told me to wait on him in front of the ABC Cafe. He wanted the money I had made already."

"Money?" asked Howdy, still the straight man. I don't guess his mother had explained whores and pimps to him.

"Yeah, dude, Slow is my pimp. He took up the money every two or three hours. Said you couldn't stiff him so easy."

"What money?" asked Howdy, further demonstrating his knowledge.

"Well goddamn, boy. The coins I took for turning tricks." She looked at Howdy like he might be a Russian spy. Howdy must have figured out that the girl was a whore, because he clammed up.

"What happened, Kitten?" I asked.

"He didn't show, and I had to walk ten blocks to find his ass. When I got there, he was standin' out talkin' to some white dudes. I thought they was customers, you know. Now I think they was cops. Them two cops right there." She pointed to Hooper and me.

She continued. "When I got to Slow, the sumbitch hit me. He say he's gonna kill me. I ran, and he got me in the alley, cornered me with a dirk."

"Dirk?" interrupted Sheebang.

"One of them knives with the gold handle, man. You sure you a cop?" She continued looking closely at Sheebang. "He tried to cut me in the alley, and when he tripped, I got the knife. He grabbed me again and I, uh musta cut him some in his guts. You know, on accident. I sure wouldn't be cutting nobody if I'd a knowed them was cops. Watchin'."

"What happened then?" asked Hooper.

"Slow run one way, I run another."

"Are you trying to tell us that these two cops didn't induce you to cut Slow?" charged Sheebang-on-white horse.

She leaned across the table to look again at Sheebang. "They was around the corner. The only sumbitch what seduced me 'round here is you, Sammy Sheebang," she said, throwing the white knight into the mud.

He tried to defend himself with indignation. "Now just a damn minute, lady, that's a big accusation."

"The only thing big about you, Whizzbang, was talk, boy. 'Cause your little old pecker was a junior-size three."

"That's bullshit," he said, perspiration beading on his chin. I wondered if he meant the story or the junior-size three allegation.

"You was a blue suit. You made me 'n Melinda give you freebies in the alley behind Big Lou's. You said you wouldn't bust us for vag if we done it good. Don't you deny it, Sheebang. I'll get Melinda. We did you three, maybe four, times."

Sheebang now looked once again as if he genuinely would faint at any moment. "Take her out," he ordered Williams, who complied immediately. "We need a recess." He looked ready to go to the floor momentarily.

"Well, before we do, I'd like you to read this statement," I said. I handed him a copy of Matthew Four's division of the universe—a duplicate of the copy I'd left in his in-box.

"After we break to get control of this situation," he said. "James, you read it," Hooper shot at Howdy.

I wasn't sure Howdy could read. It would be a live test.

Howdy accepted the statement, limply. He obviously hadn't read the reports. He obediently read aloud down through the one-third division of the universe and suddenly realized that he had been had. His whole expression changed. So, as a true bureaucrat, he also changed gears. He began the process of dumping Sheebang by hiding behind the bureaucracy.

"Now, Lieutenant," he began his break for freedom. "I can see that this witness may have some split-personality problem."

"I'm sick," said poor old Sheebang, starting for the door.

He staggered out, leaving his file folder behind.

Bull Hooper continued to look as if he might seize the opportunity to choke Howdy down. He eyed Howdy like a cat on a kill.

"Where would you hide the body?" I asked to get his attention.

He came back to earth."What?"

"Nothing, son," I said.

James got up and strode out of the room, leaving us flunkies alone. We filed out into the foyer where Williams and the hooker sat. Hooper shook Williams's hand.

"How long you been on?" he asked Williams.

"Six years," answered Williams.

"I know there's an opening in homicide. They need guys with some street sense. You interested?" said Hooper with policeman's gruff.

"Damn right, man. Damn straight." Williams's face filled with pleasure.

"Well, I don't do the hiring," said Hooper. "But our regular lieutenant is back. He's a good man. And he wants good men. I'll tell him he needs to look at your file."

Williams looked as if he would hug Hooper, which would have probably resulted in homicide and changed the hell out of the course of the day. Instead, he bear-shook Hooper's hand.

"Damn, Bull thanks."

"You ain't got the job yet, kid," gruffed Hooper. "Can we get the hell out of here? This here Federal Building gives me the creeps."

Williams exited, looking six inches taller. Kitten followed, hungrily. She couldn't touch a stud like Williams if she offered him the whole farm. She hadn't figured that out yet.

"Is the investigation suspended or what?" asked Hooper.

"Hellfire, Bull, it's your outfit in charge. I'll see what I can learn."

CHAPTER 27: THE LAW OF FRIENDS

Say it how you see it, but you gotta admit that friend's faces do often show up in the damnedest places.

We could see Howdy through his glass partition, talking stealthily into the telephone, probably to Washington, D.C., disavowing any complicity in the IAD conference. I walked into his office.

"Yes?" He covered the receiver with a quivering hand.

"What the hell's the deal, James?" I asked. "Is the dog and pony show over for the day or what?"

"I was only an observer, Kobok." He spun his chair to turn his back to me, and I walked back to join Hooper, standing at mid squad room.

Whizzbang crept back in from the hallway, apparently to retrieve his folder.

"Well, Lieutenant?" I asked.

"We'll have to re-evaluate these accusations and let you men know." He captured his folder and cleared the door at a half run, gaining speed at every step.

Hooper and I sat in the cramped foyer. We had collectively overestimated their strength of character. We had mistaken 0 for .000.

"I wonder what happened to Charlie-the-brawler." Hooper stuffed a fresh cigar in his mouth.

"Good question," I replied. "She's only charged with enough little cases to make her a probation. Maybe she just didn't want to rock the boat."

"Hooper, I figure that she figured you might haul her back to that graveyard."

He roared with laughter. "I gotta get back to my damned typewriter." He stood and walked out the door. I strolled back to my desk, still up the proverbial creek on why a farm fresh girl from Oklahoma would end up hiding amidst the Dallas alternative life style and prostitution culture and in some bizarre way, be butchered in her own bed.

My desk phone was ringing. It was Melvin Higdon.

"Kobok, I took a polygraph, and it looks okay."

"Well, Melvin, congratulations," I said, conscious of possibly being tape recorded although Texas Bar rules prohibited lawyers from doing just that. All lawyers weren't Higdon.

"Kobok, I'm serious, this clears me."

"Who did the test?"

"Bill Brantly out on Stemmons."

"Well, as I said, Mr. Higdon, congratulations."

"Is that all, Kobok? Just congratulations? I think you owe me an apology."

"Is that a fact?" I said and hung up.

I knew Brantly. He had been a Dallas police officer with a good record. He left the department about three years earlier, because he could make twice as much money in the private polygraph business. He did a sizable business with many people in society, including lawyers of all kinds. He was not, however, inclined to be unfriendly to his old associates.

I looked at my watch. It was 2:25 P. M. I looked up the number for Brantly's polygraph firm and dialed him. His secretary put him right on.

"Kobok here, Bill."

"Hey, Kobok, how's your love life?"

"Too good. If I told you the details, you wouldn't be able to work the rest of the day."

"Good God, then don't tell me."

"My sources tell me that you've gone over to the other side."

"The other side of what?"

"A little bird told me you ran a test on Melvin Higdon, famous lawyer."

"Yeah, first thing this morning. I was thinking of calling

you, Kobok. He was giving you a pretty good cussin' while he was here. He is not your friend."

I believed him. "Why?"

"He answered all questions relative to the murder of the Pritchard girl without deception."

That meant that Brantly accepted the results of his polygraph of Higdon as proof that Higdon hadn't murdered Katherine. And Brantly was no flake. Bad news.

"Rubbing a little salt in the gash, my boy?" I still wasn't ready to clear Higdon, no matter the polygraph results.

"No, Kobok, that's not why I was thinking about calling. I knew that little weasel would call and tell you that he had shown clean on Katherine. Kobok... uh, what's stickin' in my craw is a touchy situation."

"Why?"

"Well... uh," he stammered. "Higdon passed on Pritchard all right, but he flunked on another one. At least one other."

"Holy crap, who?"

"I don't know who. That's ya'll's business these days, not mine anymore. I only think that he murdered another girl, and I'll bet it was not long ago."

"What makes you think so?"

"His chart went nuts when I asked the question, "Did you murder the prostitute?' Strange, but he stopped the test and reminded me that I was only to test relative to the murder of Katherine Pritchard. Hell, I was talkin' about Katherine...who else? He also had some funny responses, you know. When I asked about how long he had dealt with street girls, the needle jumped off the chart and he reacted...uh, violently. I'm not wanting to get sued by Higdon, but I'll bet a beer he's good for another prostitute body somewhere."

"I don't believe it," I said dumbly.

"Will you keep this conversation confidential?"

"You can bet your license on it."

"I just did, Kobok."

I hung up. Unbelievable. Higdon and his handcuffs might be his ass after all. Then the desk phone delivered another chapter.

"Kobok here," I said.

"Goddam, boy," Chris Rochambeau gruffed. "I'm out here gettin' raped, and you don't come to the rescue. I'm a taxpayer, jackass."

"Who's the perpetrator, an escaped gorilla?"

She roared at that one. "Yeah, that's about what it would take, by God."

"What's up, Stud," I asked.

"I just called to tell you that I love you."

"Chris, you aren't turning into one of those funny girls that likes boys, are you?"

"No, by God! I've changed my mind, Kobok. I don't love you."

"Why did you call, Chris. Trouble?"

"No, I just wanted to say that old Charlie got out of jail and was up here running her head about puttin' some misery on you and a city cop...uh, Hooper. Somethin' about excessive force or brutality or some shit like that. She also said y'all took her to an open grave and threatened to put her in it."

"She made a statement to IAD to that effect, Chris. Then she backed out and wouldn't stay with the story. IAD said she would no longer cooperate."

"Kobok, maybe somebody made her an offer she couldn't refuse."

"Like what, Chris?"

"Like maybe telling her you was a friend of mine, and a statement against you was a statement against me."

"Jesus, Chris, we'll both end up in jail."

"For what, for Christ's sake? For telling a mug like Charlie that you was my friend? I didn't tell the bitch that she couldn't go against you. I only told her in the words I just said. And Kobok, I didn't tell her that directly. It got to her secondhand."

"Well, I'm grateful that you're my friend, Chris."

"Look, Kobok, I know you're an asshole some of the time, but for you to slap Charlie around, I know you had to. Besides, I don't like ol' Charlie for crap. She's a bully who's jumped a couple of my friends from behind. You know what I mean?"

"Yeah, Chris, I know what you mean."

"Now listen, Kobok, if you think Charlie might have

murdered that little Katherine chick -mutilated her for Christ's sake, just lemme know, and I'll guarantee that she'll be in Parkland with broken legs for the next six months. You can talk to her any time you want."

I was beginning to think everybody in town had been involved in Katherine's murder. "Chris, if I need her legs busted, I'll know just where to come."

"Listen, dammit, I'm serious."

"So am I, Chris. I'm not sure she's good for Katherine's murder. But again, she is a suspect."

"Okay, Kobok. If there's anything else I can do, name it."

"Well, Chris, there is one thing."

"What, son?"

"Can I see your secretary's tits?"

"You damn total pervert. The girl's a virgin as far as men go. She thinks men are dirty. She's got some sense, anyway. I'll just take a Polaroid and show it to you." At that she hung up, laughing.

I sat at my battered metal desk and contemplated the universe.

Chris had cancelled out Charlie/Doris's statement to IAD. Matthew Four had murdered Shawnda, but probably not Katherine. Higdon had murdered somebody, but probably not Katherine.

Somebody had certainly murdered Katherine. Who the hell was it? I was exactly nowhere in proving anything against any of them. Miami never loomed larger.

Looking for a stray hooker body? Go through Jane Doe murder victims with Dallas Homicide? That wouldn't cover the suburbs who had plenty of murders of their own. In Texas, the local Sheriff's Offices maintains a broader file of criminal records which would cover the suburbs. But the Southwest Institute of Forensic Sciences, which included the morgue, processed evidence, including autopsies of bodies for counties from miles around.

I phoned the records supervisor at the Institute, an all-business type lady who ruled with a big stick. She listened and agreed to accumulate the files of female murder victims who fit the general description of Katherine for the past year. She'd collect both Jane Does and those identified by name, but had no idea which, if any had been solved by the police agency involved. She estimated, that with the magic of a new computer system, she should have results in an hour.

I walked down the stairs to the eleventh-floor coffee shop, had coffee and a taco salad guaranteed to cause heartburn until midnight, and returned to my desk. The morgue lady called and said she's found four files which might fit my inquiry. I peddled the old Chevrolet out to Harry Hines Boulevard. The Hose Line was already partly filled with ladies of the night—in the blistering late afternoon heat.

CHAPTER 28: THE LAW OF ROUNDING OUT SQUARE CORNERS

If the answer to the immediate question cannot be determined, criminal investigation can often move forward by seeking the answer to a different, but related, question.

If I couldn't pin the tail on the donkey that murdered Katherine, I could damn sure pursue Higdon. A second murder? Tie it to Higdon and perhaps some fruit might fall from the tree after all.

The helpful clerk ushered me into an empty room where I was left alone with the four files of unfortunates. "It's nearly quittin' time, Kobock," she admonished sternly. "If you stay late, just leave the files on the table and make sure the door is locked when you leave. Copying machine is next door, and every file has extra photographs, so feel free to remove a photo from file if you need one or two. But," she added crustily, "don't take anything you don't need."

The first file was a fully clothed, unidentified white female found in a South Dallas field. I moved her to the bottom of the pile. No ID would make her nearly impossible to link to Higdon. A clothed victim didn't fit Higdon's profile. I'd try the others first.

Number two was a partially dressed, pure strangulation victim with limited additional trauma damage to the body. Strangulation didn't seem to be Higdon's bag. I threw the file on top of that of the unidentified female.

The third was a nude, sexually mutilated, heavily tattooed white female who had been identified from fingerprints as Paula Fletcher, 24, of Dallas. The morgue, of course, kept only forensic files. No previous criminal records would be available. I pulled a photo from the file and slid her folder aside for copying. I wondered if Westra had found her brain remarkable. Her case was assigned to Dallas P.D. Homicide.

Fourth, was Barbara Asbury, who had been twenty when found nude and mutilated in a dumpster in the City of Richardson five months before. Identified by fingerprints, she, as would number three, Paula Fletcher have a file with the Dallas County Sheriff's Office, assuming either had prior records. The file showed the case was assigned to Richardson detective J.E. Jones. Both identified, victims, in the carnage of death, appeared to be viable candidates for arrest records.

But with the luck it took to avoid Miami, I realized the photographer had spotted a clue worth recording. He or she had taken a closeup of her wrists, both bearing red rings consistent with restraints. Handcuffs, perhaps. On closer inspection, Asbury held what appeared to be a long ball point pen in her right hand.

I copied the files, and pocketed photos of the two victims who could be identified, including Asbury's wrists, locked the door, and drove through the diminishing evening rush traffic, to the Dallas County Jail. Both Paula Fletcher and Barbara Asbury had "jackets"—in house lingo for files of previous brushes with the law.

The clerk shoved files of both Fletcher and Asbury across the counter. Paula Fletcher had apparently been a topless dancer and a heroin addict and part time hooker. She had been arrested for prostitution, possession of narcotics, and evading arrest.

The photos I'd picked from morgue files were death scenes. Fletcher's mug photo, taken in life, did little to enhance her appearance. Her dull, hard eyes looked out of the mug photograph at me, trapped in eternity by the camera in her street-hardened gaze.

The second file revealed that Barbara J. Asbury also had a record. She had been arrested on seven occasions for prostitution and once for delivery of a controlled substance, to wit, cocaine, to an undercover Dallas narcotics officer. The chart also reflected an arrest for theft over fifty dollars, which appeared to be a matter of heisting the wallet of a customer. Her file-jacket showed that she had been sentenced to the Dallas County jail on two occasions for less than a week for the prostitution charges. She had received two years' probation for the wallet incident and was still on probation when she was hacked to death.

I requested copies of documents from the files for both girls and took the jail elevator to the basement sheriff's office, which housed the bonding desk. No bond could be posted to secure the release of an accused suspect from the Dallas County jail without being registered with the bond desk. The desk retained a record of each bond posted for each case for many years past. The entire section had been computerized several years earlier, allowing a near instant printout of all details of bonds posted for a given defendant.

I requested bonding records for Paula Fletcher and Barbara Asbury, and within minutes I was thumbing a sheath of printed matter. I took a seat on a hall bench and read the printouts. The answer I wanted leaped off the page, causing me to exclaim "sonofabitch" loud enough to be heard up and down the hallway.

Two days prior to being found butchered in Richardson, Barbara Asbury had bonded out of the Dallas County jail on one of the prostitution charges. Her lawyer of record, who also posted the $500 bond, was none other than Melvin Higdon. Method of bond: cash. How posted: person, lawyer. Double holy hell!

Higdon had been in firsthand contact with Barbara Asbury two days before her body had been found, and she had apparently been indebted to Higdon for securing her release. That translated to a trade of services.

I thumbed back through the copies from forensic. The medical examiner had ruled that she had been dead for approximately thirty-six hours before her body was discovered. Higdon, you have a problem, dude.

The Institute would have bagged and tagged the item in Asbury's hand, assuming the Richardson P.D. hadn't seized it for evidence. J.E. Jones's wife answered on the second ring.

"Hey, Kobock, how's things." He came on the line.

"You hadda twenty-year-old white female in a dumpster several months ago. Any leads?"

"Uh, Asbury was the kid's name. Had add on boobs. No leads and not a clue. Case is open, but I'm thinkin' hopeless."

"She had something clutched in her hand. Maybe a ball point pen. Did you take that or does the morgue...?"

"I got it from the morgue. It's in the evidence locker—piece of a car antenna."

"You make any inquiry on it?"

"All we woulda learned was what I just told you. A piece of antenna with nothing to tie it too."

"Reckon I could check it out of evidence?"

"Hell yeah. As I recall, you live out this way. Drive out here this evening and it's yours."

The western sky was nearly black when I walked out of the Richardson Police Department on Belt Line Rd, the antenna remnant in a plastic bag. It appeared no more remarkable than any other antenna busted off about a foot from the end. With a little luck, I might run that trinket up Higdon's ass.

A quick flip through the Katherine file and I re-located the lessor of Higdon's Mercedes: Bobby Dwyer Mercedes on Greenville Avenue. First on tomorrow, Bobby was going to have company.

I'd just made my apartment, popped a beer and was foraging in the fridge for a frozen delight when a tiny rap at the door interrupted. Tad stuck his tow head around the doorframe. "Mr. Kobock, mama says we got some beer and leftover spaghetti if you wanna...?"

I carried the kid across the courtyard on my shoulders. A couple of beers, a plate of re-heated spaghetti, and a night with Anne, went far in re-invigorating a tired, failed warrior.

CHAPTER 29: THE LAW OF JUNK

One man's junk is another's trip to death row.

It's surely no surprise that I arrived at Bobby Dwyer Mercedes an hour before they opened. Three cups of poor coffee and a plateful of grease at a joint across the street killed the wait.

The sales manager, a fit-appearing man of fifty or so with brown hair brushed over his ears, inspected my credentials.

"How can we help you, Mr. Kobock?"

I showed him a Polaroid of the antenna. I had checked to actual antenna remnant into the evidence locker.

"What is that, Mr. Kobok?"

"A photo of a portion of a radio antenna."

"And?"

"Can you tell me if it's from a Mercedes?"

"Hell, no, Kobok."

"Do you keep maintenance records for vehicles you have leased to customers?"

"Of course."

"Can you check to see if you replaced the antenna on the model 450 SL leased to Melvin Higdon, please?" I wrote Higdon's name on a slip of paper for his reference.

"Do you have a subpoena?" He'd watched too much TV.

"I get a subpoena, you get to bring every damned file in this place in an 18 wheeler and park behind the federal building a few days. Now we don't want that, do we?"

He moved away, not attempting to camouflage his aggravation, and returned in minutes with the file for the vehicle driven by Higdon. He flipped through the file and looked up. "Nope, Kobok, no record of replacing a radio antenna." He rose as if to dismiss me.

"Do you actually replace such items here in your shop?" Many specialty car dealers subcontract much of their repair business.

He reopened the file. "Well, it's possible that we could have sent the car out for replacement of the antenna."

"Did you in this case?"

"I really don't know, but here is a bill from Zimmerman's Stereo on Ross Avenue, for unspecified services." He tossed the bill over to me. He had apparently been going to withhold the information of this repair unless I asked the right question. I wrote down the address of Zimmerman Stereo, and left for Ross Avenue.

Zimmerman's was located in near East Dallas, just west of Henderson. A short, fat, bouncy man of fifty greeted me cheerfully. I explained the nature of my inquiry as I showed him my badge. He looked gravely interested. "How can I help, Mr. Kobok?"

I gave him the number and date of the invoice I had seen in the Mercedes dealership.

"It's in the basement, Kobok. I won't be able to find it for thirty minutes," he whined.

"I'll help," I said.

We collectively dug in cardboard boxes in a musty basement for nearly thirty minutes when he announced that he had found the correct box. He lugged the box back into the air-conditioned main level of the store and, in ten more minutes of digging, produced the duplicate of the invoice I had earlier examined at Dwyer Mercedes.

It bore the initials "MH", as in Melvin Higdon, near the bottom where the purchaser had indicated that he had accepted the merchandise on behalf of Dwyer Mercedes. Stapled to the invoice was a small card bearing the words, "ATLAS, NO. 21451."

"What was the merchandise?" I asked.

He opened a loose-leaf notebook and began turning pages rapidly, stopping near the middle. "Radio antenna," he announced solemnly, having no idea of the impact of his discovery on my blood pressure.

"What do you do with parts that are replaced?" I was hoping for a miracle.

"Take them to the dump."

I felt hope fading. "How?"

"Jesus Christ! We throw scrap parts in an old trailer out back and haul it to American Metals in West Dallas when it gets full."

"How often do you take the trailer to the metal company?"

"My, God, man, when it gets full."

"When was the last time it was emptied?"

"Hell, I don't have any idea."

"Who would?"

He sighed and shouted into the backroom workshop. Two dirty-looking white men in their mid-twenties appeared instantly.

"When the hell was the last time we emptied the junk trailer?" he asked exasperated.

"Boss," said one of the men, "We ain't in no violation by having that trailer out there."

"I never said anything about that. When, goddammit did we last empty the trailer?"

"Hell, boss, it's been nearly a year. It takes a while to fill that thing."

I looked at the file for Barbara Asbury. She had been dead less than six months. "Where can I look at the junk in that trailer?" All three men looked at me as if I had just grown a carrot out of my forehead.

"The thing has a ton of crap in it, Mister," said one of the two younger men.

"Good, I'm into junk," I said, starting through the rear door.

"Holy shit," said the fat man who had found the invoice, following me to the rear lot. He had lost his bounce. The trailer was only about five feet wide and six feet long and was piled about five feet deep in assorted discarded metallic refuse. I hung my sport coat on an eight-foot chain-link fence surrounding the back lot and started throwing parts out of the trailer into a pile on the ground.

"How long's this gonna take, Kobok?" asked the fat man.

"No time at all," I lied. Probably another one to count in hell. It was well before lunch. Plenty of time to sort junk.

"I gotta ask Mr. Zimmerman."

"Who?"

"Abe Zimmerman, the owner of this place. I'm only the manager."

"What are you going to ask him?" I inquired, throwing out handfuls of broken stereos.

"'Bout this shit man. Tossin' junk all over the damned place."

"Tell him what you need to," I said, continuing to add to the rapidly growing heap on the ground, as the fat man stood wringing his hands.

He walked hurriedly back inside, out of the late morning sun. I could overhear him between pieces of debris hitting the ground as I threw them out.

"Mr. Zimmerman, there's some pushy federal cop here throwing stuff out of our junk trailer. No...no, sir, we're not being accused of anything. He's looking for some broken car antenna part for a car we must have worked on. Oh no, Mr. Zimmerman, I don't mind helping the law at all, sir. No, no, no, sir, I only wanted to clear it with you."

"What? Oh, no, Abe, hell, you know I wasn't here after hours with no woman. No, no, no, hell, no! No, I ain't worried a bit about a little extra work to help the police."

He moved further inside away from my earshot.

"Sir, I didn't have no woman here last Tuesday night. I was working on the books. Sir, I don't use this place ... I mean, I would never use this place to bring some woman. You can count on me, Abe. I want to see the police get all the help we can give. Yes, sir, sorry to have bothered you."

It goes without saying that he came back out, but he was unaware that I could overhear his entire conversation with the lord and master of the house.

"Okay, Kobok," he said, "I told Zimmerman that I would help get to the bottom of whatever it is you're looking for. What the hell are you looking for?"

"That broken antenna I just showed you the picture of part of it." I tossed out a cardboard box of what appeared to be radio tubes.

"Yeah, but what for?"

I looked down from the trailer at him and calculated a

gamble on human nature. "Murder of a young woman. She was found raped and mutilated with a Mercedes antenna in her hand. It appears that she tore it off of a car as she was being murdered."

"Other cars besides Mercedes uses that same antenna." He rolled up his sleeves over pudgy arms and jumped up into the trailer to begin throwing out parts. It was already crowding a hundred at mid-day.

Within thirty minutes, we had three broken antenna parts that didn't fit the one in my photograph. Within an hour, we had five more, and I could see the bottom of the trailer coming up fast. I was beginning to see Higdon slip from the hook.

The fat man picked it up first. It was bent at the base. When it had been twisted off, it had been partially wrenched out of the car fender in the death agony of Barbara Asbury.

I could see from my photo that the parts fit perfectly. I was confident that the laboratory could successfully compare the initials on the invoice in the office of Zimmerman Stereo with the signature of Higdon. We could easily obtain his signature for comparison from records of the Texas Department of Public Safety where he had signed for a driver's license.

Higdon, the brain, had been one stupid ass. Even after murdering the Asbury girl, he was apparently too cheap to drive to some isolated repair shop and have the antenna replaced at his own expense. The invoice price for replacement had been $52.47. That was going to become a very, very expensive fifty-two bucks for Melvin Higdon, Attorney-at-Law. I put the antenna remnant in the pocket of my sport coat.

I obtained the fat man's correct name and telephone number and left him amid a pile of debris in the back of his boss's stereo shop, wringing his hands over reloading the trailer. Higdon's mistake would not clear the murder of Katherine Pritchard. I couldn't connect him in any way to Katherine, but I'd gain an attaboy, even if it wasn't our jurisdiction.

I found a payphone and dialed the Richardson Police Department. J.E. Jones came right on the line.

"How can I help save the federal government today, Kobok?"

"Send in an organization chart, for starters. We could use it."

"Consider it done. What else?"

"Well, then I need you to get all these damn uncleared murders cleared up."

"Workin' on it. I only have one."

"Boy, I hope you're sitting, because I'm about to give you an early Christmas bonus."

"Go ahead, Kobok. Suspense kills."

"Melvin Higdon, Attorney-at-Law."

"Never heard of him. Is he dead?"

"No, but he looks very good for your hooker murder. Barbara Asbury, remember?"

"Yeah, that's the one I just mentioned. You just picked up my best piece of evidence last night. That kid was probably murdered in Dallas and dumped in our city."

State law required that the investigative jurisdiction be assigned to the authority where the body was found. It made for some unusual investigations, but it was the system in use.

Translated, it meant that a killer could dump his victim in some remote area where the police were less well equipped to handle a complicated homicide investigation than within the more heavily populated areas where homicides were more common. The Richardson P.D. didn't have those limitations.

"Records of Dallas County forensic show that the girl was found with a car antenna in her hand," I said.

"Yeah, we figured she had torn it off the car somehow in her death struggle. Maybe tried to run. Perp and she fought outside the car. Like I said, not a way to trace it."

"Well, the big boys at the pool hall tell me that Higdon drives a rented Mercedes."

"Yeah."

"If you'll get a subpoena for records of Bobby Dwyer Mercedes for the Mercedes rented to Higdon, you'll find a repair invoice from Zimmerman Stereo on Ross. If you'll get another subpoena for Zimmerman's records, you'll find an invoice billed to Dwyer Mercedes for replacement of an antenna. If you'll compare the initials on the bottom of that invoice with the signature of Higdon's driver's license, I'll bet a year's pay that they match."

"Christ, Kobok, that's not enough evidence to support a homicide." He sounded as if he was writing frantically.

"Would it help if you had the lower half of the antenna? It would probably cause the indictment of your lawyer. I have it here in my pocket. Found it today in the junkpile at Zimmerman's. The busted end matches the piece I picked up from you yesterday."

"Outstanding," he exclaimed.

I explained Higdon's fascination with handcuffs. "Her body showed signs of wrist restraints. Higdon has a handcuff key hanging on the dash of his Mercedes. I have the name and address of a whore who has worn those 'cuffs, and I believe she'll testify."

"Damn, boy, you've been digging."

"Yeah, a grave for Higdon."

We concluded with the normal thanks, both wondering what the next act of the ongoing circus might bring.

CHAPTER 30: THE LAW OF PROTECTING THE REAR

Society invented rearview mirrors and back-door locks because of dangers that come up from behind. Use both and you'll still get ass-ended.

I dropped by the office to catch up on reports of progress on the Pritchard murder. Reluctantly, I included the Higdon interlude. It might provide a little diversion while I tried like hell to develop something solid on Katherine.

Needless to say, I was running out of time.

I had just tossed the report on Tootie's desk when Howdy sulked in. Probably coming from a session with his shrink. He ignored me. I waited for him to close his door behind him. When his cage door slammed, I seized the opportunity to disappear and walked out with the Pritchard master file under my arm.

I drove over to the Central Parking Lot and stopped at a dingy restaurant for some bad coffee and another greaseburger. I sat at a corner table drinking my third cup, thumbing the Pritchard file. I'd already read it so much that I was wearing out the print.

Sharon Jaco scowled steadily out of her mug photo at me, a relatively unknown quantity in the scheme of this investigation. Abandoned by parents, abandoned by foster parents, abandoned by society, abandoned by Juan Morales. She was not an unattractive girl, but her hard, cold eyes made her less than pretty. Looking at her was kind of like seeing high mileage on a new car—old before her time.

I paid the cashier, a fat lady in a baker's cap, and crept out Central toward Richardson. Daisy was at her desk on Bowser Street, doing her mummy impersonation.

"Weeelllll, my Gawd, it's Mister Kobok," she Marilyn Monro-ed. She had spent the large part of a century practicing to be the coquette. She flashed contrived petulance through ancient mascara-burdened eyes. While the equipment was worn to obsolescence, the methodology remained perfect. Her eyes were a rheumy, faded blue. As a matter of fact, so was the face.

"Good morning, miss," I opened with a lie.

"Did you apprehend that riffraff we had staying here? Those spies?"

"Well, unfortunately, not yet," I said, truthfully. The room was permeated with the odor of her cologne. It was the scent that I have associated with older women all my life an ominous combination of formaldehyde and orchids. It could probably be purchased at any cosmetic counter, but I have no idea what the hell it's called or why any woman would willingly bring that smell in contact with her body.

"What a terrible world it's getting to be, Mr. Kobok," she purred.

"Yeah," I answered.

"Have you had your morning coffee, Kobok? I believe we left our last meeting by making a coffee date."

"I'd like some coffee, yes."

"How do you take it?" She had a practiced way of casting her eyes downward and then slowly looking up through inch-long false eyelashes. I had seen Gloria Swanson do the same thing in an old movie not long ago. However, Daisy was considerably older than Ms. Swanson, and the effect wasn't quite the same.

"Black would be fine."

"It's fresh," she said, moving with remarkable spring toward a small kitchen in an alcove off the office. The space had been a small apartment at one time. Now it was a small office. Both were probably equally depressing.

She brought a cup of coffee in a china cup and saucer that were painted with tiny pink roses. I stared at the cup and saucer, marveling that anyone could put flowers on the cup, even by a mechanical process. The coffee was the only thing fresh that had been in this room for years. I sipped the hot coffee. It was slightly chicory flavored.

"Very good coffee, Daisy. May I call you Daisy?"

She looked at me with an expression that told me that she was thinking of echoing Williams's comment of "Does a bear shit in the woods?"

"Why, of course," she substituted.

"Good," I said, leaning forward. "Daisy, we need help in this investigation."

"Well, how can I help?" She would have disrobed in seven seconds and thrown herself into the clutches of a fifteen-member ravaging outlaw motorcycle gang on command, if her expression was any clue to what she was thinking.

"We need all the information possible about Sharon Jaco."

"I don't think I know anything about her. Spies, my good God."

"Can you think of any visitors she had? Anyone at all who might have inquired about her after she failed to return? Perhaps someone who came after I was here the first time?"

"She lived on the rear, Mr. Kobok. I couldn't see her visitors. There were some bill collectors who came around. Bill collectors are in here all the time."

"Do you recall who they were? Or what company they represented?"

"No...well, wait, I think I've got a card from one. He was such a nice young man, and a big boy, too, about six-foot, four. He had blond hair and wore tight pants. I kept his card."

"Could I see it?" I drained my cup.

"More coffee?"

"No thanks. But that was delicious, Daisy." I was thinking that at one time she'd been delicious, too.

"We have plenty."

"No, thanks. You were going to show me the card."

She dug around in her desk and came out with a business card. It read: American Associates Confidential Collections David Bayless, Agent 555-6778.

I copied down the number and Bayless's name. "Anyone else, Daisy?"

"Well, there was a private detective who asked about Sharon Jaco."

"Really?" I tried not to act surprised. Who would hire a PI to look for a social outcast like Jaco?

"Yes, he came about a day after you were here. Let's see you were here about a week or a little over ago. Yes, he was here about a day after you."

"His name?"

"Monroe. I remember, because that was my grandfather's name."

"First or last name?"

"Oh, it was his last. My mother was a Monroe. Native of Kentucky."

"No, Daisy, I mean the private detective. Was Monroe his first or last name?"

"Oh, it was his first, Mr. Kobok. It was such a professional name, Monroe."

"Did he leave a card?"

"No."

"Did he say where he was from?"

"He was from Chicago."

"How do you know?"

"I have—I had a cousin from Chicago. Monroe had the exact same accent."

"Did he indicate that he had come all the way to Dallas from Chicago to look for Jaco?"

"No, Mr. Kobok, I only said he talked like he was from Chicago. He said he lived in East Dallas. You know, I'm from Pittsburg, but I live in Richardson."

"Oh. What did he ask you, Daisy?"

"About the same as you. He asked to look at my apartment records. Then he looked in her room. I had let you in. I supposed it would be okay. It was okay, wasn't it?"

"No problem," I said. It wasn't okay.

"I thought he was from an insurance company, actually," she continued.

"Why?"

"He asked me, after he had looked in her apartment, if

anyone else had been around asking questions. I told him about you. I didn't think you'd mind. I thought he would get in touch with you."

"Why did you think insurance?"

"Because when he was looking through the apartment, he asked all about records of Sharon Jaco's date of birth, where she was from, did I know her relatives, I mean stuff like that."

"Why didn't you get his business card?"

"He just walked away without giving me one. I even asked him for a card, so I could call him if I heard from you. That's when he left… when I told him that I wanted to give you his name. He said for me not to contact you. He said he'd call you himself."

"What kind of car did he drive?"

"A little blue car. I think it might have been a Volkswagen."

"What did he look like, Daisy?"

"Big as you, didn't wear a necktie or coat. He had a little mustache and was a little bald in the front."

"How old?"

"God, real young. About forty."

"By bald, do you mean a receding hairline?"

"Yes, with black hair."

"Daisy, if he contacts you again, call me at this number right away." I jotted my home telephone number on my own business card and gave it to her.

"Mr. Kobok, did I screw up by letting that man look in Sharon's room?"

"No, no, of course not," I assured her. "But call if he contacts you again."

"Okay, Kobok."

"Daisy, did anyone claim Jaco's belongings?"

"No, they're out back in the storeroom. Do you want them?"

"No, I just wondered who was interested in Sharon. I thought someone might have claimed her things."

"Nobody asked, but I'll call you if someone does."

"Well, thank you again, Daisy," I said as I rose to leave.

"Come back anytime, Mr. Kobok," she said seductively. If you couldn't see her, she would have fooled you by forty years.

I drove over to the Richardson Police Department to borrow a telephone. I needed to locate a private detective whose first name was Monroe and who drove a Volkswagen. That could prove very difficult.

Although Texas law requires that private investigators be licensed with the state board, an identity problem is always a factor. Some of the large national firms of which there are many, operate under a single license. They might, for instance, employ part time investigators.

They might also hire people who are not actually licensed as investigators, but records searchers. Finding this Monroe could be a full load.

I had a hunch that old Monroe was not connected to a national firm. Private investigators in Texas are not allowed to carry firearms. And, contrary to the television conception, they seldom solve large murder cases, as in Katherine Pritchard. Somebody had hired this bird to ask about me, not Sharon. What the hell was that about? I drove to the Richardson Police Department.

I sat at a vacant desk and studied the yellow pages. I went through every name listed under private investigators and, as I expected, drew a blank.

J.E. Jones walked in out of the heat. "Hey Kobock, what' up?"

"Some P.I. has been asking about a chick mixed up in the Katherine Pritchard murder, Sharon Jaco. Wonder how they knew about her."

"Katherine's murder isn't a secret," he said. "It's been in the papers and on the late news."

"Nothing was in those stories about Jaco, J.E."

"Yeah, that's true."

If the Monroe guy had found Daisy, he could find other sources. I headed through the simmering heat toward East Dallas and the Garland Avenue Children's Home.

CHAPTER 31: THE LAW OF PURSUIT

If pursued, don't circle the wagons-circle the pursuer.

I had learned of Sister Maria and the Garland Avenue Children's Home from Daisy's apartment records. Monroe had either learned the same thing and contacted Sister Maria, or he had known about the Home from the beginning. If he had known to go to the Home before locating Daisy, somebody else knew about Jaco being there in her younger years. Somebody who had known her correct identity.

But, hell, that didn't seem to be a valid motive for murder not anywhere, except in English murder mystery novels.

I found the Sister supervising the mass feeding of sloppy joe sandwiches and milk to a hundred children in the well-worn school cafeteria. The gentle eyes twinkled amiably as she invited me to her office. She appeared relieved to escape the kitchen.

"How can I help you today, Mr. Kobok?"

"Has a private investigator been here lately asking questions?"

She looked puzzled. "Private investigator, Mr. Kobok? Investigators come here fairly often."

"Not the police, Sister. I'm asking about a white man, about forty, black hair with receding hairline and a small mustache. He would not be a policeman, but he would refer to himself as an investigator."

"There was such a man, Mr. Kobok."

"When?"

"Two or three days ago." She rose, walked to her file cabinet, and returned with the folder for Jaco. "This is Wednesday He was here Monday."

"What did he want?" I had hoped that Monroe had inquired at the Garland Avenue location before he had visited Jaco's apartment. He had found the Garland Ave Children's home the same way I had. He had not known Jaco's early history, and like me, was only fishing.

"About the same things you asked, Mr. Kobok. But I didn't give him any information."

"Because he wasn't a police officer?"

"Well, partly because he didn't have police identification. But mostly because he was sort of dirty, smarmy, unsavory type, and I didn't think he needed to be looking in our files."

"Why didn't you call me?"

"It just never occurred to me. People come here often to ask about some of our scattered flock, and I just never thought to call you. I'm sorry if I've withheld valuable information, Mr. Kobok." The gentle eyes displayed alarm.

"It's not serious, Sister. I wasn't scolding you. Do you remember his name?"

"I wrote it on the file folder, Mr. Kobok." She opened the folder to the inside flap. "Monroe C. Lee," she announced proudly.

"Did he give you a telephone number?"

"Why, no."

"Did he show you any form of identification?"

"No, I don't think so. At least I don't recall seeing anything."

"What was he driving?"

"A blue Volkswagen."

"Did you happen to get the license number?"

"Oh, no. I guess I should have."

I scribbled the info in my notebook. "May I please use your telephone, Sister?"

"Of course."

"Could I look at your telephone book—the yellow pages, please?"

She produced the yellow pages from behind her desk as I dialed the office. Tootie answered on the first ring.

"Do you have anything for me, kid?" I asked.

"Um... lemme see ... some nasty-sounding character named

Chris called. He, or maybe she, said you had the number." She didn't ask me any particulars about Chris Rochambeau, and I didn't volunteer any.

I dialed the number for Chris's bar on Hines. It was early afternoon, and I got Frankie, the same bartender I had talked with the week before at the club.

"Is Chris there, please?" I asked.

"She's busy."

"Tell her Kobok is returning her call, please."

"She said not to bother her. She's in her office."

I took that to mean Chris was dictating to her secretary. "Tell her that I'm going to drop by in about thirty minutes."

"Okay," said the linebacker as she hung up.

I thumbed the yellow pages for private investigators. There was only one listing for the name "Lee," a man named Ronald Lee, with offices on LBJ Freeway, near Farmers Branch. I dialed the number and asked for Monroe Lee. The girl who had answered told me, through her nose, that there was no such person associated with that office. I thanked her and started toward Boobs on Harry Hines.

When I drove up Hines from the downtown end, a handful of girls from the early shift were working the Hose Line. God, maybe the early bird catches the worm?

Frankie was on duty behind the bar at Boobs, and three women with man-cut hair were sitting around a table near the door. Two of them had their chairs turned backwards, so they were sitting facing the backrest but still facing the table. I had seen John Wayne do the same thing in Rio Bravo. They gave me the eye, man-style, as I walked in. I ignored them. I had whipped enough females for this month.

"Frankie," I opened the sparring, "I need to see if Chris is finished with her business yet."

"Jesus Christ!" she exclaimed, but she picked up the telephone and appeared to push a button behind the bar.

"Look, Chris, I'm sorry to disturb you, but your friend Kobok is out here." She looked sidelong at me over the receiver. "Okay, Chris, I'll tell him."

She turned full toward me. "She says for you to have a beer, and she'll be out in a minute. She said to tell you that she's right in the middle of something and can't quit." She slid a draught beer across the bar toward me.

I sipped the beer. "Frankie, have you had any strange men in here asking questions about any of your patrons lately?"

"Christ, Kobok, all men are strange." I had asked for that. She was partly smiling a sort of evil leer. I think it was intended to be friendly. It appeared to be an overture of friendship or truce. I accepted.

"Yeah, I guess you got that right," I laughed outright. The patrons at the table were too far away to overhear, but they scowled in my direction anyway.

"I mean, have you had any other police-types in here asking about Katherine Pritchard?"

"Yeah, as a matter of fact, there was. Yesterday. Straight lookin' guy, about half-bald, dark hair."

"Did you get his name or find out what he wanted?"

"No, hell, no. I send all cops to talk to Chris."

Chris sauntered out, fully dressed. "Goddamn, Kobok," she roared, "I was going over some important work." Even though much of her conversation tended to end in infectious laughter, she appeared formidable, standing there in the center of the bar area.

"You called me, Chris."

"Yeah," she laughed. "But you damn cops are never around when needed. I half-assed expected you to take two days calling me back. Come on into my office," she ordered.

I followed, lustfully envisioning Shelly putting on her cut-offs. She already had them and a T-shirt pulled on, but she was flushed with slightly disheveled hair. Secretarial work often causes considerable stress, I've heard.

"Excuse us, Shelly," Chris dismissed the girl. Then she added, "Shelly, this is Kobok, a friend of mine."

She looked at me with large blue eyes. "Nice to meet you, Shelly," I said.

"Nice to meet you, sir," she returned.

Her eyes reduced my lustful thoughts. They conveyed a strange mood of remote indifference. It was much like reaching to pet a dog and finding it to be a tame wolf. What a uniquely beautiful creature.

I looked into the wolf eyes for signs of narcotics or a sign of anything at all and saw nothing but distance. Could this have been Katherine Pritchard or Sharon Jaco? Distant eyes that had somehow missed the so called American dream, had found love in an alternative lifestyle. She walked out demurely.

"Nice boobs, Chris. Does your regular old lady know about her?"

For the only time in our acquaintance, Chris looked somber. "No, and I don't think she'll find out. God, I hope not. That's why I installed the buzzer for the bartender to warn me to clean up my act." She looked at the door Shelly had just closed behind her. I sensed a tragic, love triangle that, in the end, could end in violence that would interest very few.

"Have you had somebody asking about Katherine's murder, Chris?"

"Yeah, that's what I called you about. Some asshole was in here just a while ago, asking all kinds of questions."

"About Katherine, you mean?"

"Katherine, Sharon Jaco, the whore business, people in this neighborhood. And get this, Kobok, he asked about you. Did you ball any of these hookers? Would you take a bribe? All kinds of crap like that."

"What did you tell him?"

"Hell, Kobok, I told him you were too old to screw anybody and weren't smart enough to ask for a bribe," she laughed, deep in her chest and throat.

"Well, thanks, but I guess I was asking if you ran him off."

"Damn sure did. Called you as the door hit him in the ass."

"I don't suppose you asked for some identification?"

"Hell, yes, boy. That's how I jiggered that he wasn't right. He hem-hawed and horse-assed around and tried to tell me he had left his ID in his car. I told him to get his ass out of here while he could still do it standing upright."

"Did he do or say anything else?"

"He didn't say shit. Just turned tail and split."

"Did you see his car?"

"Yeah, Sherlock, and I got the goddamn license number."

She handed me a slip of paper with a current Texas passenger vehicle license number written across it.

I used Chris's desk telephone, called the office, and asked Tootie to run me a 10-28, which is cop-speak for asking for a vehicle license registration check. Tootie put me on hold while she queried her machine.

"How the hell did that guy find Boobs, Kobok?"

"I don't think it would have been difficult to find out on the street that Katherine and her friend Sharon Jaco hung around here from time to time, Chris."

Tootie read back the name and address of the person to whom the license was registered. I wrote it in my notebook: 1976 Volkswagen, two door, LEROY MORGAN, 4666 Gaston Avenue, Dallas.

I flipped open Chris' yellow pages to Private Investigators, and found the door prize, Morgan, Leroy, 4666 Gaston Avenue, 555-2255.

I dialed the number, and Leroy answered on the second ring, only he was on tape. The machine told me that I could leave a short message at the sound of the tone.

I did: "My name is James, H. D. James, Mr. Morgan. I need a… an investigator. It's my wife… there's another man." I gave the private number on Chris's desk telephone. I hadn't realized she had a private line until then, or I might have interrupted her in the middle of something a few minutes earlier.

I sat with my feet on Chris's desk and sipped my beer. I had a feeling that Morgan might be near the telephone but had an aversion to direct contact. The telephone rang in less than two minutes.

"Talk nice, Chris," I said.

"Hello," she said in nice-talk. She sounded strangely feminine. "Yes, Mr. James is right here. Hold on, please."

She even clicked the receiver button as she handed me the telephone, simulating secretarial procedure.

"Yes," I said.

"Mr. James, my name is Leroy Morgan, private investigator. You telephoned my office, I believe."

"Why, yes, sir, I did. My, you certainly act quickly."

"Yes," he said. "Instant response to us in this business is often a matter of life or death. How can I help you?"

"My wife. Can you follow her? My God, she's seeing a younger man. It's a guy she works with. A damn stock boy!"

"Of course, Mr. James. We can get together and work out details. How about first thing in the morning?"

"But I had hoped you could start today."

"Well, I'm in the middle of cracking a major murder involving corruption by officers of the law. My investigation will be finished by tonight, and I'll work all night completing my report. I can start on your investigation by nine A. M. tomorrow."

"A major murder-corruption case. My God! Maybe I can wait. Should I call you at this number in the morning?"

"Yes."

"How much will it cost?"

"Well, er... my fee is two hundred dollars a day with the first three days in advance. However, if that's too steep, we can work out a payment plan."

"No, I have the money."

"Great, call me first thing in the morning." He didn't sound overly prosperous.

"Mr. Morgan?"

"Yeah?"

"Can we arrange to fix that kid so he won't bother my wife?"

"Like how, James?"

"Beat the little bastard. Kick in his nuts. Break his pretty face."

"Well- let's talk about that in the morning. I'm sure we can take care of him any way you want. Of course, the fee will run more."

"I'll call you in the morning, Mr. Morgan."

"Okay, Mr. James." He hung up.

"Damn, Chris, I wish I'd had my tape recorder on that telephone."

"Sounded like he talked dirty. If I'd known he was a badass, I woulda' hid behind the bar when he was in here." She looked across the desk, eyes dead serious. "Hey, dude, I oughta tell you.

When he was in here, Frankie out there said when he pulled out his wallet to pay for a beer, she could see the outline of a pistol in his right front pants pocket."

"Look, Chris, I thank you, and I have to run. In fact, I'm thinking about kissing you."

"Now forget a bunch of that shit," she laughed with sufficient volume to be heard at the top of Reunion Tower.

CHAPTER 32: THE LAW OF FINESSE

The distance between nipping a problem in the bud and choking it to death before it starts can be very slight.

Before ol' Leroy had a chance to get behind me, I figured a little early reconnaissance would be in order. A surprise might be just what Leroy needed.

I herded the Chevrolet through gathering afternoon traffic to Gaston Avenue. The building at 4666 was dingy, two-story, and squeezed in with several other complexes of the same general description. The area was heavy with similar apartment buildings that were built over thirty years ago and designed to last only the length of the twenty-year mortgage in effect at the time.

I found the blue Volkswagen parked beside the rear stairs. The entire building was in need of a coat of paint. If some of that paint had dripped on the Volkswagen, it wouldn't have hurt anything either. The car was losing its struggle with rust. I waited a block down, where I could see the car.

A functioning payphone in a gas station was only a few feet away. I called Tootie and asked her to call the state P.I. licensing people and double check the status of Leroy Morgan. I held and in four minutes she came back. Leroy Morgan, former P.I., had allowed his license to elapse a year earlier. The big boy, packing a pistol in a licensed liquor joint was chancing five years in the joint.

In about an hour, a guy matching the description I had for Morgan came out and drove away in the blue Volkswagen, heading east on Gaston. He stopped at a sleazy topless bar near the intersection of Gaston and Garland Road. I gave him time to get inside the door, then I parked and followed him inside.

He was wearing double-knit blue jeans, popular at the time, blue rattlesnake boots, expensive at the time, and a macho-western shirt unbuttoned down to about the navel, stupid at the time. I could see a cluster of gold chains at his neck, like old Slow Bill. His stomach hung well over the front of the double-knits. He appeared to go about 225, mostly flab.

The place was scarcely occupied that early in the topless club day. Leroy was sitting at a low bar that extended into the center of the room, upon which was dancing a skinny, embarrassingly small breasted, valiantly topless girl. She had a tattoo on her right forearm, and she appeared to have been driven over a hundred thousand miles already. It was possible that she was no virgin.

Leroy was transfixed, his neck crooked back to compensate for the odd angle of the girl standing immediately above him. Near the conclusion of her number, he produced a dollar bill, which he waved for her. Without missing a beat of her listless dance, she stooped to allow him to slip the bill under the leg band of her G-string.

She finished her routine and walked around the far end of the bar, where she stepped down onto a chair and then to the floor. She picked up a black T-shirt that she had apparently been wearing to begin her performance and walked semi-nude to the side of Leroy Morgan, unlicensed private investigator.

She gave him a peck on the cheek and slipped onto the adjacent barstool. They shared his beer for about ten minutes over intimate conversation.

A second girl slouched her way up and down the bar before and after she removed a leather vest under which she was bare breasted. Working to a country and western tune, and she wore low-cut, fringed, cowboy boots that clomped each time she changed directions. Cigarette was so thick she was mostly invisible anyway.

Leroy slid backwards off the stool, with a show of masculine swagger. The skinny dancer walked him to the door, still without her T-shirt. Nobody seemed to notice—a mater of not having enough TO notice. She gave him a lingering hug, her small breasts pointing upward as she strained to reach his neck. He whispered into her ear and left. She pulled on the black T-shirt and walked back to the lady's room. I sauntered outside to my Chevrolet in time to see Leroy pull away from the parking lot.

Leroy headed toward downtown in the Volkswagen, weaving in and out of the now heavy evening Gaston Avenue traffic. He made a sudden right turn at Carroll Avenue, moving north with the Volkswagen at maximum acceleration. The car in front of me was filled with at least twenty Mexicans, and the driver cautiously slowed to a stop at the yellow light, even though he could have been in the middle of the next block before it turned red. I could see Leroy disappearing up Carroll, and I drove the Chevrolet diagonally across the curb and sidewalk of Gaston, causing immediate evacuation of a bus stop that the city of Dallas had unwisely placed in my path. No one was injured as far as I could see. But when I cleared the opposite curb after running down some small shrubs, what I couldn't see was Leroy.

I hurried up Carroll to the point where I thought I had last seen Leroy's Volkswagen. I looked up and down the side streets. The Volkswagen was not visible in any direction.

I assumed that he had pulled into one of the numerous small apartment buildings strewn throughout the neighborhood. I guessed that he had probably gone to the apartment of the dancer I had just seen him with. Leroy the lover.

I drove back toward Gaston, but I detoured two blocks around the bus stop I had just used as a short-cut. You never can tell. Some of the evacuees may have been armed and might open fire as I drove by.

When I arrived back at the topless place where Leroy had just shared a beer with the skinny girl, the parking lot had picked up several cars. It was past 7:00, but still fully July hot daylight. The blue-collar crowd was filtering in to invest some of its hard-earned dollars on the bottom of worn G-strings. I ordered a beer at the bar and sat at a small table about halfway to the front door. The skinny girl was not in sight, although a girl I hadn't seen before was gyrating around the stage.

Presently, Monroe's girl reappeared from the rear of the place and walked near my table, toward the jukebox. Girls in these establishments not only were expected to take off most of their clothes and go through some semblance of a dance routine in front of a house full of drunks, but they were also expected to panhandle that crowd for jukebox money and watered drinks. A large, nationally operated vending company with alleged organized crime connections owned this particular joint, which naturally included the jukebox. This double dipping increased the lucrative profit ratio. Bare-chested girls were fanned out among the customers, hustling loose change.

When Skinny walked near enough, I called her over. "What's your name, sugar?" I asked in the accepted topless bar language.

"Carla, baby, what's yours?" she answered in dialect.

"Sebastian Kobok. Can I buy you a drink?"

"Sure." She heeled and walked to the waitress station at the rear of the liquor bar, which was across the room from the dance bar upon which the present girl was moving about. She returned shortly with a glass of clear liquid, which I knew to be a soft drink.

"Ten bucks, hon," she smiled.

I gave her twenty. "Will that cover a second beer, Carla?"

"Sure, baby." She pranced back to the bar and returned shortly with another lukewarm beer. She was still wearing the black T-shirt that came down to just above the waist. Her barelegged G-string and high heels completed the outfit.

"Can you sit down a while?" I asked.

Of course, she could. It was part of the routine. She and the bartender split the price of whatever amount she could squeeze out of the customer for ginger ale drinks for herself.

Up close, she appeared about twenty. Up on the stage, with all the makeup, she looked several years older. She had bleached blonde hair that she combed straight down in the back, dark color was visible at the roots. She sipped her five-dollar soft drink.

"How long you been in this club, Carla?"

"Couple months. I love to dance."

I had just seen her act. She needed to practice the focal point of her affection. She was not going to push Mitzi Gaynor off the podium.

"You're a beautiful dancer," I lied, reflecting for a second if that was a real lie.

"Thank you."

"When do you go on next?"

"Oh, damned Freddie, that's the bartender, says I gotta go on after the next girl. Not this bitch," She gestured toward the tired blonde currently occupying the bar stage. "The next one."

"Too bad. I like your company."

"Thank you."

"I come in here every once in a while, to watch you."

"Really?"

"Yeah. You're really my favorite," I lied again. What a poor way to get to hell.

"Thank you."

"I see you with some dude all the time. Must be your old man. That's why I never talked to you."

"I talk to a lot of guys in here. Which one do you mean?"

"Big guy, older, with receding hairline." I pointed to my forehead.

"Oh, man, you mean Leroy. He's a cop. Works out of the Narcotics Division. He uses me for cover. You know, man, like blending in with the scene."

"Yeah, I guess, Carla." Now Leroy was flirting with five to do for impersonating a police officer.

"He's not really my old man. I just help him out, you know."

"Damn, you mean, he's got a gun when he comes in here?"

"Sometimes. He carries it in his boot in a holster… sometimes in his pocket."

"Boy, I'm glad I didn't talk to you with him here." I feigned a worried expression and shot a glance over my shoulder toward the door.

"Aw chill, man, he's a teddy bear. It's cool."

"Well, he looked tough to me. That kind of work must be dangerous."

"Wow, man, if you won't tell anybody, he's meeting some guy at the Centurion tonight. Some big super-undercover contact. He's gonna meet the guy and be here in time for my ten o'clock show."

Leroy had lost me in route to paradise. The Centurion was an "in" disco bar operated by a former major-league baseball player on Greenville Avenue near University. It was a popular gathering place for the young singles crowd for furtherance of the beautiful-people syndrome. In that place, thirty was dirty, and Leroy was ten years beyond that. I wondered where that put me.

I labored through my warm beer and abruptly excused myself, telling Carla that I had forgotten an appointment. As I walked away, she waived indifferently and moved listlessly toward another table surrounded by men whose clothes were flecked with paint-stains.

I found a bar where I had a grease-burger with mushrooms and cheese and another beer. I pulled into the parking lot of the Centurion at 9:10 P. M. I got out on foot and in two minutes had found the blue Volkswagen parked near the rear door. The sky was dark and the lighting poor. I knelt and let enough air out of the right rear tire of the Volkswagen. Leroy could now run, but not rapidly.

The cover charge was two dollars to a leggy brunette with a painted smile. She had stopped the two youths ahead of me in line and closely checked their identification for proof of age. She didn't question my proof of age. I had plenty clearly written on my face.

The place was only partly filled at that hour. The decor was early weird with flashing strobe lights and music so loud that communication with the next person was only possible by shouting directly into an ear. The air conditioning kept the temperature below the fatality point, but the air was steamy with smoke and close proximity of human bodies in a small area. This was the personification of the false sub culture that drew many young people to the Dallas area.

Leroy Monroe was sitting at a table near the dance floor with three other people. Two were attractive young blondes about half Leroy's age who were listening raptly to the conversation of the fourth person seated tableside. He was cultured and suave, a master at talking a good game. He gestured with his hands with the practiced air of the self-assured. He was talking animatedly, the center of attention. The two blonde girls listened to every word as he shouted above the din.

I found an empty chair and drug it over to the table. The cultured man looked astonished as I sat down at the table to make an unwelcome fifth hand.

"Why, Mr. Higdon, how nice to see you," I shouted. "Got your handcuffs on you?"

"Leroy!" shouted Higdon.

Leroy rose and stepped around his blonde toward me. I stood and drove a right fist into his fat stomach to the point that I was sure I could feel backbone, of which I doubted that he had much.

He crumbled, like a burning kite as he sat back on his chair, bent forward, holding his whale belly. His face reflected the look of a constipated sailor as he gasped for air. He wasn't going to be much of a conversationalist for the next hour or so. The two blondes sat, frozen.

"Go on with your story, Mr. Higdon," I shouted, sitting back down in my chair.

"What the hell are you doing, Kobok?"

"Socializing with the people. How about yourself?"

"You followed me," he shouted.

"No, actually, my man, I believe that it's you that's been having old Leroy over there trying to follow me."

"I am entitled as an officer of the court to obtain investigative assistance in the pursuit of criminal activity," he bellowed.

"Does that include conspiring with your boy there to impersonate a police officer. Or interfere in an official investigation, or operate as a P.I. with an expired license?"

The waitress approached, having seen the extra chair at a table in her area.

"What will you have, sir?" she screamed. She was wearing shorts that disappeared into her crotch. That looked unhealthy.

"Beer, please," I answered. "Just put it on his tab." I pointed to Leroy, who was slowly sinking to head level with the table top.

"Is he ill?" the waitress asked.

"He has stomach trouble," I explained over the noise. "Happens every time he eats fried oysters. He was gut-shot in the war."

She shrugged knowingly and disappeared toward the bar.

"Kobok, you can't push me this way," screamed Higdon.

Neither blonde had moved or said a word. Leroy's head was down on his knees, but he remained sitting on the chair, bent double.

"Damn man, that's not a very nice way to talk to a guest."

I turned to the blonde on my left. "It certainly is nice of your father here to bring you girls out on the town."

She smiled through a mouth-worth of straightened teeth. She appeared capable of smiling at will and holding the pattern indefinitely. The smile blended to a soft laugh, which I could only recognize by sight in the deafening noise.

Higdon jumped to his feet. "I'll settle your shit for this, Kobok."

I eyed him up and down. "If you walk the tab, Higdon, I'll settle with you at the county jail."

He stormed away. I saw him throw a handful of currency at the waitress as he passed the bar, bills landing on and behind the bar. She picked them up with the help of the bartender and two drunken patrons before she brought my beer. Leroy was still doubled over and sitting.

I drank part of my beer while carrying on a high-volume conversation with the two abandoned blondes. The chit-chat made little sense, but as well as I could gather, both were from McKinney, Texas, and Higdon had told them that his law firm owned a modeling agency that could offer great tomorrows to both girls. Of course, they would have to come over to his office for some preliminary photographs first. By the time I had finished my beer, Leroy was back to half-mast.

I leaned over the table and shouted in his ear. "I want to talk to you outside you big dumb sonofabitch. If we have to wrestle to get out of here, I'll see that you spend the night in the Parkland. Or maybe two nights. Understand?"

He nodded through clenched teeth. I excused the two of us and helped Leroy to the parking lot. We reached the blue Volkswagen, and I leaned Leroy against the rear deck. He was still holding his middle.

"Leroy, you know the rules. You can ask all the questions

you want. You can go anywhere, talk to anyone. Nobody gives a damn. You can even ask my friends if I'm on the arm. But you can't tell anyone you're a Dallas police officer. You cannot, repeat, cannot carry a pistol. If you get caught in a beer joint with a pistol, Leroy, you get five years in the Texas Department of Corrections chopping cotton. Understand? Practicing with no P.I. license, same damned thing?"

"Ughhhhhugh. Didn't play like no cop. Ain't got no pistol."

"Well, Leroy, someone I know says different. I'm confident that if I shake that little car down…or go through your pockets, I'd find a pistol. Or maybe it's in your boot. I don't want your pistol or to see your ass in the joint. I only want you to understand what I just said. No playing police, no carrying a pistol. And no making nasty comments about Kobok taking bribes."

He nodded. I think he understood.

"Did Higdon hire you to get involved in the Pritchard murder?"

He nodded, gasping.

"Why?" I asked the impossible question.

"Don't know," he gasped. I believed him. Only Higdon and I could provide the answer.

Leroy vomited on the Volkswagen. I wondered if he had figured out yet it was me with whom he had made tomorrow's 9:00 A. M. appointment. He also would have to limp the Volkswagen somewhere to blow up a tire.

I walked over to my old Chevrolet and drove out toward Spring Valley. Tad was at the door in about 47 seconds. I didn't ask why he was up so late. I spent the night with Anne, four beers, and a plateful of pasta. All in all, not a bad way to end a pretty satisfying day. Now all I had to do was catch who the hell ever murdered Katherine Mae Pritchard of Logan County, Oklahoma.

Being a good boy, I called the switchboard and left Anne's telephone number in case the world needed me.

CHAPTER 33: THE LAW OF BAYONETS

How's that adage go: A man who builds a fine throne of bayonets will have a hell of a time finding a seat. Bayonets?

Anne's telephone rang at 6:00, and I awoke to find their TV had been left on and some skinny little man was staging an exercise program on the TV. He was on his back, frantically demonstrating the female half of the standard missionary position of intercourse. I wondered how he had learned that position. I answered the telephone guardedly, expecting the worst. It was only J. E. Jones.

"Are you asleep?" he asked.

"No, I was just sitting here hoping you'd call."

"What are you doing today?" he continued.

"Later on, I'll go out and get a tattoo, maybe take a yodeling lesson. What the hell do you want?"

"I have an arrest warrant for Higdon here in front of me. Just thought you might want to help serve it."

I was awake enough to fill him in on the contact with Higdon the night before. "What time did you have in mind?"

"Whenever he gets out and about. I figured you knew his schedule."

"I'll bet a case of Coors that if we can pop him in his Mercedes, he'll have his handcuffs in the glovebox."

"Does that mean you want to go?"

"Yeah. Where are you?"

"Christ, Kobok, I'm at home. It's six o'clock in the morning."

"I thought you were on nights."

"Doubled back in this morning for this Higdon warrant."

"I could meet you at your office in thirty minutes or so. We could sit on his house and stop him on route to his office. I've been there. He won't leave until past eight. See you in a half hour or so."

"Okay," he said and hung up.

I showered and pulled the Chevrolet into the Richardson Police Department parking lot at 6:35 A. M. It was nearly vacant. Jones rolled in three minutes later, driving his blue Ford pickup. He let himself inside the Criminal Investigations Division for car keys, and we left the parking lot in a new four-door Fairmont, the interior smelling of newness. We stopped at a 7-Eleven for large coffees and Danishes and had edged through the Central Expressway traffic to north Dallas by 7:25.

Higdon's house appeared to be still settled into the night mode, and we drove around the corner to Snider Plaza for another cup of 7-Eleven's wake up elixir. We parked a block down and finished the coffee.

At 8:40, Higdon came zipping out of the driveway and was through the gears by the time he passed us on the street. Jones U-turned the Fairmont and accelerated as fast as the under-powered vehicle would proceed. Higdon stopped at a signal at Mockingbird, allowing us to pull behind him.

"Better let him get some distance from the house," I said. "No sense in his wife coming along and making a scene."

"Okay."

Higdon eyed us in the rear-view mirror. I was surprised that he didn't seem to recognize me. He probably didn't expect to see me so soon after the evening before.

We followed him east, where he missed another light. He turned north on Greenville, and Jones hit his red grill lights as soon as we fell behind him. Higdon pulled immediately to the curb and got out of the Mercedes to walk back toward the Fairmont, smiling and confident that he could charm his way out of any scrape involving a routine traffic stop.

Jones got out of the driver's side, his great bulk squeezing out of the opening built for normal-sized men and met Higdon half way. I had gotten out on the passenger side, and when Higdon saw me, his smile blended to rage.

"Goddamn you, Kobok."

"I'm glad to see you too, Higdon," I answered.

"By God, this is it, Kobok. I'm going straight downtown toand file a complaint on your ass for harassment." He started back to the Mercedes.

"Are you Melvin Higdon?" asked Jones.

"None of your damned business," replied Higdon without breaking stride toward the Mercedes.

"Wrong, Mr. Higdon," Jones grinned.

Higdon turned back to him with hands on hips. "I'll have a piece of your ass too, King Kong."

"Mr. Higdon, I'm Detective J. E. Jones of the Richardson Police Department. I have here a warrant for your arrest." Jones waved the warrant under Higdon's nose. He held out his badge case with the other hand.

Higdon retreated, his face now showing fear. "What...what for?"

"Murder, Mr. Higdon, of one Barbara Asbury, violation of Section one nine-zero-two of the Texas Penal Code. Put your hands on the side of the car. Now!"

Higdon complied meekly. He stood with his manicured hands on the top of the $50,000 automobile. Near collapse, his eyes welled with tears. He knew he was screwed.

"Who...who is this you think I murdered?"

"Like I just said, a prostitute named Barbara Asbury. Her body was found in the city of Richardson in February."

Jones began the routine body search necessary to a lawful arrest. Vehicle traffic was forced to slow before swinging into the next lane to pass us. Higdon looked as if he would go to his knees at any moment.

"I want a lawyer," he said weakly.

Jones read Higdon his Miranda warning from a small card, placed handcuffs on his wrists, and assisted him into the rear seat of the Fairmont. Jones called the Dallas Police Department's channel two dispatcher on "intercity" and asked that a supervisor come to the scene.

In a few minutes, a white Plymouth rolled up to the scene, bearing the Dallas police logo on the door but lacking the overhead visi-bar, signifying that the car belonged to a supervisor of sergeant or higher rank. A thirtyish sergeant, slightly built with gold-rimmed glasses, got out to greet us guardedly.

In less than a minute, a second marked squad, this one bearing the visi-bar of a patrol officer, arrived. The officer was young, fleshy, with black hair. When we explained that Higdon was a prominent attorney whom we had just arrested for murder of a prostitute, both officers became professionally interested. Neither knew Higdon nor had they heard of the murder of Barbara Asbury.

We then explained that since we could not leave Higdon's Mercedes abandoned on Greenville Avenue, we needed their assistance in towing the car to a safe place. The patrolman immediately summoned a wrecker that would tow the car to the Dallas police auto pound on South Good Latimer Expressway. Its contents would be inventoried completely before it was accepted by the pound.

We did not search the interior of the car to avoid creating an evidentiary problem in the event that something incriminating to Higdon would be found. We didn't tell the Dallas officers of the possibility of handcuffs in the car. The inventory required by the Dallas Police Department would eliminate any search problems. They would conduct our search as a routine vehicle inventory. But from outside, the handcuff key was clearly visible hanging on a radio button on the dash. I would have bet a hundred the cuffs themselves were in the glove box. Higdon was screwed.

We left the Mercedes in the hands of the Dallas Police Department and started toward the Richardson Police Department. Higdon would be booked, fingerprinted, photographed, allowed a phone call, and then arraigned before a city magistrate—a duplication of Jones already having read him his Miranda rights. The system always trusted judges more than they did cops.

None-the-less, Jones had already "Mirandized" Higdon and we could question him at length. I slid into the back seat beside the prisoner who Jones had only handcuffed in front in deference to his "non-dangerous status."

"Higdon," I began. "You're in deep shit."

He took a Winston from his shirt pocket and lit it with a gold lighter. He was wearing an expensive, dark blue, hand tailored suit of what appeared to be a wool and silk combination. He wore a light blue silk shirt and a blue and white striped silk tie. He would make a nice figure in front of the city judge, who probably earned one-tenth as much as Higdon in a year.

"You, too, Kobok," he spat back. The boy was recovering his composure.

No investigator with enough sense to find a post office will tell the accused all the facts known against him. Regardless of the outcry of that element of society who would turn all criminals loose, the accused does not have access to the evidence against him at the arrest stage, only the charges. He had no clue that we had the broken antenna remnant, taken from Barbara Asbury's dead hand.

"Do you know Barbara Asbury?" I asked.

"I want a lawyer, goddammit."

"Why don't you hire yourself, Higdon?" I asked.

Why would he hire a lawyer? He could tell himself to refuse to answer questions.

We rode in silence the rest of the way to the Richardson Police Department. When we drove into the book-in area, Jones parked the Fairmont, got out, and came back to open Higdon's door. Higdon got out, again arrogant. He needed kicking in the nuts. I did so, by throwing him a hot piece of evidence.

"Higdon, did you think to get rid of the handcuffs that were in the glovebox of the Mercedes? It sure will be tough if the laboratory can match some mark they make to Barbara's wrists."

At the sound of handcuffs and Mercedes, he reacted as if he had been actually kicked in his own genital area. He looked certain to go down, but he held his feet, although shakily.

I knew then the handcuffs were still in the Mercedes and that he had used them on Barbara Asbury. Whether or not the laboratory could tie them to Asbury was another story. But at this point, Higdon thought he was a dead man, and I had no intention of easing his pain. I did not mention the broken antenna remnant.

CHAPTER 34: THE LAW OF RELATIVE INNOCENCE

The innocence of any person is relative, because it is diluted by their guilty deeds. The innocence of a child is absolute.

It was nearly one o'clock when I fired up the old Chevrolet and started down Central Parking Lot to the Federal Building. Traffic was moving at a high rate of speed-about fifteen miles per hour. I made the office in forty-seven minutes.

Chadsey and his crew were busy feeding the incinerator the ton or so of paper that bureaucrats had discarded during the past twenty-four hours. He waved and grinned from the door to hell as I cut a wide swath around his position to avoid the searing heat.

I walked by Tootie's desk and down the corridor past Howdy's hole. He wasn't in. I forgot to ask where he was. I had several telephone messages, most of which I laid aside with good intentions of returning them later. One, I answered right away.

"Hooper," answered the distinctive, growl.

"Returning your call, sir."

"Makin' any headway on the Pritchard case?"

"Nope. Fixin' to go home, have a beer, read that damned file another time."

"Call me if I can help."

"Will do." I hung up. Thanks to pre-rush hour traffic, I made Spring Valley by three, played catch with Tim for a half hour, and soon had the thick Prichard file spread on my kitchen table. I was no stranger to failure, and that was the prognosis.

I re-read every word of every note. I opened my third beer and studied the burned photos of Pritchard. Her crotch gaped at me, violated by the meat cleaver of Jesus. The shots of the top of her head were particularly revolting. The facial shots revealed a horrible mess. Her gaping mouth, even teeth glinting starkly white against the blackened flesh, defied description. A huge chunk of logic is missing? What's not here?

I answered a timid rap on the door. "Come in, Tad." I had just spent an exhausting half hour in the heat with the kid. I had really grown fond of him. Hopefully he felt the same. I knew one day his mama would find a better deal and Tad would evaporate from my life like nearly anything I'd ever held dear. He was just paying a social call.

He had blond hair, bleached white by exposure to the hot Dallas summer sun. His suntan from afternoons at the apartment pool was good enough for a TV suntan lotion advertisement. He was such a nice little kid. Too bad, I thought, that he'd grow up to be an adult.

"Want a Coke, Tad?" I offered.

"Aw… I don't care."

I popped the top of a canned soda and handed it to him. I was good at popping those tops.

"Thank you," he said, shyly.

I looked at his suntan, his hair. My mind flashed back to a case I had worked on two years ago. I had responded to a fire-bombing on Northwest Highway. Witnesses had seen a white male with shoulder length hair toss a Molotov into a dumpster behind a sporting goods store. The fire had caused considerable damage to an outside corner of the building next to the dumpster. Experienced firefighters had reported what they thought to be the odor of burnt flesh inside the dumpster.

Dallas homicide had sent a couple of guys, but they didn't have proper gear to climb into a dumpster which firefighters, in suppressing the fire, had filled to the side door with water. Water was slowly running out a partially clogged bottom drain. I pulled on my boots and coveralls, climbed over the top, and began groping in the waste deep goop.

In a half hour, I came up with a small, burned human cadaver about the size Tad was as he stood in my kitchen, nursing a coke. The remains were cooked until entrails oozed out the abdomen.

Normal people fortunately never have to endure exposure to burn victims. All clothes are usually burned off, with the occasional exception of a leather belt or shoes. The flesh beneath is invariably burned dirt black, making recognition impossible.

The small body in that dumpster was in that condition. It was face down. When I turned it over, his right hand was drawn up against the side of his head, probably in an involuntary gesture of defense as he was being beaten to death. When I pulled the body away from the side of the dumpster, the little hand slipped away slightly, revealing a patch of unburned yellow hair.

"Mr. Kobok, are you all right? Why are you looking at me so funny?"

"Oh, sorry, Tad," I woke up. "You just remind me of somebody I knew once."

"What's all this stuff and these pictures?"

I had hidden the burn and autopsy photos in an envelope. "It's a case I'm working on."

"Did somebody hurt this lady?" He was looking at the high school photo of Katherine.

"No," I lied again, calculating the weight of it in hell. "She is going to work for us, and I am doing an investigation on her. We have to make certain that she is not a bad person before she can start work."

He was looking at the dental chart. "Do you have to see if she has good teeth?"

"Yeah, sort of, I guess," I said.

The little body was charred and leaking. When I turned it over there were no genitals. The field agent from the medical examiner's office jumped down into the dumpster with me. "This is a girl, Doc," I had said, letting my guard down.'

"Hell, Kobok, it's a boy all right. Perp bit off his nuts."

"Mom says to invite you over for dinner when you get hungry. Mr. Kobok, have you had too much beer? You look funny. ."

"Oh, uh, Tad, uh, all the heat today must have upset my stomach a little bit," I stammered. "Why don't you watch TV while I look at this file?"

"Okay." He turned on the television.

A TV cameraman had pulled his car alongside the dumpster. He was standing on top. His camera had caught the action of turning the kid over, with the falling hand, the patch of yellow hair, the jagged tear in the crotch.

"I want that film," I said, in violation of a large chunk of the U.S. Constitution.

"Hey, Kobok, no need to get pushy," he said down to me.

"What you just saw is nobody's business."

By the time he had climbed down from the car top to run for cover in his news van, I had jumped over the other side and cut him off. I stood between him and his anchor newsman, who had hidden the back of the van.

"If you want a shot of me on the evening news breaking your arm, just hold tight to that camera."

He looked around, furtive, rat-like, trapped. I got the film, and a lawsuit, and ten days off. The film didn't belong on TV. The lawsuit was dismissed when the judge took one look at the film. Two women on the jury fainted. Several men on the jury looked as if they might lynch the camera operator off the roof of the courthouse. I never got my ten days' pay back. Hell, I didn't need the money anyway.

"How come you got so many pictures of her teeth?" Tad had come back to the table to help me some more.

"There are pictures there for two different ladies."

He was looking at the dental chart of Katherine that Texas Bell Telephone had given us along with the machine copy of Jaco's chart that I'd pinched from the apartment on Bowser Street.

"What does 'XX' mean?" he asked in his child's voice. "Does she got vampire teeth?"

"No, Tad, I think that means a tooth is missing. Ms. Jaco probably had to have some teeth replaced." I thought about herpes and fell back to reading. Had I forgotten to ask Dr. Teneris if Jaco had herpes?

"Mr. Kobok, how do you spell Jaco?" He was still studying the charts. He had probably realized that the road to owning your own Learjet lay in learning how to make these little charts.

"J-A-C-O," I answered without looking up. "What does P-R-I-T-C..."

"Pritchard," I preempted. "That's the name of the lady who is going to work for us that I told you about. The lady in that picture there."

"Oh," he continued to study the charts, face serious. I continued to read.

"Mr. Kobok?"

"Yes, sir."

He grinned at that. Then he threw a bomb into the whole works. "This picture here with the X teeth says P-R-I-T-C-H-A-R-D."

I turned the chart around. "No, Tad, let me look at these." I looked again at the dental charts. Sharon Jaco's chart reflected thirty-two teeth with no fillings. Clearly indicated on the Pritchard chart were two Xs, indicating extraction of numbers seven and eight. The two upper-left front teeth had been removed.

Pritchard was missing two front teeth. Dr. Teneris had said Sharon Jaco was missing front teeth in the Longview Hospital and needed a new dental bridge. I visualized the rows of perfect, white teeth when Westra was doing the autopsy on Katherine. Had he said the teeth were remarkable?

The cadaver in the morgue had a full set of glinting white teeth that leered out in even, uninterrupted rows! Uninterrupted! I pulled out the facial shot from Forensic recording the burned and mutilated face of "Katherine," showing an unblemished mouthful of ivory. I laid it beside the dental chart of Pritchard from Texas Bell. Numbers seven and eight had been extracted from Katherine's chart, Jaco's chart showed a full set of teeth.

The body in the morgue wasn't Katherine. But who was it? Mother of God, what had happened?

Fingerprints came to mind. The body autopsied as Katherine had no fingerprints, only burned off stubs.

Why no dental chart comparison? Then, I recalled, I had never sent the chart from Texas Bell to the medical examiner's office. I had just assumed that Bruce McClain had given them a copy. Just assumed. Holy double hell, Texas Bell had also assumed that I had forwarded Katherine's chart to Westra and company.

With nauseating finality, the unthinkable disaster was obvious. The tormented, shattered body I'd witnessed being autopsied in the morgue was not Katherine Mae Pritchard, and I couldn't be certain who it was. But in sinking horror, I had a fairly good hunch.

I found Sheriff Decker's telephone number in the file spread on my table. I dialed the number and got his wife. He came to the telephone immediately.

"Good evening, Sheriff. Kobok here," I said.

"How are you, boy," he replied. "Good to hear from you."

"Did I interrupt your supper, Sheriff?"

"Just gettin' up. No problem. What can I do for you?"

"I forgot to ask when I was up there the other day," I said, "They did have the funeral without any unusual problems, didn't they?"

"Yeah. Let's see. It was the Friday after she was murdered. Funeral at Parker Brothers Mortuary, and they buried her out in Brown County Cemetery. No problem."

"I suppose they kept the coffin closed?" I asked a dumb question.

"Oh, hell, yes. Had to from what I heard from you about her condition. Why do you ask?"

"Oh, I was just sitting here going over her file and got to wondering if her mother had claimed her body." I felt another small churn in my gut.

"Yeah," he said. "Her mother buried her. Town took up a collection to help her out. Funny, you ask. Damn strange that her father Willard hadn't been seen around for several years, and then he showed up right after the funeral, crazy as hell."

"Yeah," I said.

"I kind of figured that hearing about his little girl's death and him missing the funeral and all might have had something to do with him goin' off the deep end again. We still got him locked up."

"Well, Sheriff, that's all I needed. Just trying to tie up loose ends," I lied. "Thanks, and good evening."

"Come see us," he said in the standard southern way, hanging up.

CHAPTER 35: THE LAW OF IMPOSSIBLE TRUTHS

When all is eliminated that is impossible, then look to what remains as at least partial truth, no matter how unbelievable.

Dr. Teneris had said Sharon Jaco had been transferred to Longview from Parkland because of brain damage. She had also remarked that the devastated patient needed a new dental bridge. Jaco records showed perfect teeth—no denture needed. Armageddon had just crashed the front door.

I sent Tad home as politely as I could and drove down to Parkland Hospital. It was still daylight at 6:00 on a Thursday evening, and I knew records would be closed. But it was worth a try. I crossed the asphalt parking lot in the blistering heat of late afternoon and found the Dallas police officer on duty. In five minutes of explanation that I needed to see the admitting records for the previous week, I saw he knew more about the system than some of the regular employees.

His passkeys helped find the file on Jaco, Sharon, in less time than I could have filled out the request form during regular hours. She received emergency treatment a week before Katherine had been murdered and released. That would be a result of Morales admission he'd beat her up.

She'd had been readmitted in critical at 4:35 A.M. last Tuesday morning- the same morning that Hooper had summoned me to the apartment of Katherine Mae Pritchard. Under the blank marked "Person Admitting Patient," the notation "John Jones, no address known."

The admitting nurse was Wanda Melbourne. I asked the officer if he knew Wanda Melbourne, and he replied that she was working at the present time.

Wanda was a tall, slender, fortyish lady in a white uniform with half-glasses hanging on a retainer in front of her. I asked her if she recalled admitting a battered young female under the name Sharon Jaco in the predawn hours of last week. She recalled immediately. "She was semi-conscious, Mr. Kobok," she said, "and bleeding from several areas of trauma. I ordered Ringer's lactated solution before she ever saw a doctor."

"Ms. Melbourne, the man who admitted her was John Jones. Can you tell me about him?"

"A little." She looked thoughtful. "I didn't really think that was his correct name."

"Why?"

"He just didn't act right... nervous, agitated, or such like."

"Can you describe him, please?" I thought of the "older" trick Katherine had reportedly dated.

"Just an average gray-haired, middle-aged man. Medium length hair, not bald, but not a lot of hair either."

"Tall or short?"

"A little taller than you, maybe, but mostly about average size, but more than average seedy. He left his coat."

"What?"

"The coat she was wearing was his. In fact, it was all she was wearing. He left in a rush and never got it back. I assumed that he had given it to her. He said he had found her that way. Naked."

"How did you learn her name?"

"He told me as I filled out the admission form."

"Where is his coat, now?"

"I'm certain that they sent it with her to Longview when she was transferred."

I thanked her and headed the Chevrolet east on I 20 toward Longview. I drove in the sinking realization that in some perverse, bizarre way, a still alive Katherine Mae Pritchard had been warehoused in the Longview institution as Sharon Jaco.

I rolled up to the front gate of the institution at just past 9:30 P.M. I guess I had intended to ram the gate and storm the administration office. I asked the attendant at the gate how I could reach Dr. Teneris.

He looked at me like I might have to be admitted to the rubber-room ward. He told me that I would have to come back in the morning during regular hours and make an appointment. I thanked him and drove off to regroup. In the rearview mirror, I saw him writing down my Texas license tag number. When he ran it, he would find no record existed.

I located the Longview Police Department on high ground near downtown, next to a blinking red transmitting antenna. I badged the desk sergeant, who greeted me cordially. I explained that I was trying to get into contact with Dr. Kay Teneris of the state hospital staff. I went through the local telephone directory, while he thumbed through a large revolving file system. I found no listing. The information operator advised Teneris had an unlisted telephone number.

The chunky desk sergeant came back to his counter with a three-by-five-inch file card, which he handed to me. Dr. Teneris had called police to complain of a neighbor's barking dog several months ago. She had given the dispatcher a home address of 1419 Adams Court, Longview.

"That's one of those condos out on the south end of town. Full of Yankees," he explained.

He wrote out directions, complete with a homemade minimap, and I found the address in ten minutes. She answered my ring through a door-chain security lock, talking through the small crack afforded by the chain. She recognized me but did not seem enthused. She was wearing cut-off blue jeans and a half T-shirt that gave a tantalizing view through the slit in the door.

"Doctor, I'm sorry to bother you," I lied once again. "I need to talk to you about Sharon Jaco. There have been some new developments. Horrible developments I fear."

"It's a little late," she said. "Perhaps tomorrow...?"

"It's very important... urgent really."

She closed the door sufficiently to disconnect her chain lock and opened it completely. She had a lot of nice legs. As a matter of fact, she had a lot of nice other things, too. She motioned me in with her head, wordlessly, with a look of disgust and resignation.

"Would you like a drink, Mr. Kobok?" I noticed for the first time that she was holding a mixed drink in her left hand. It was also the first civil comment she had sent in my general direction.

"Do you have a beer, please?" I answered.

She directed me to a chair in her den and glided out of the room on those long legs. She returned with the beer and a glass and took a seat on a sofa across from me. "What is it?" she said, the eyes still cold.

I spent nearly an hour and two more of her beers re-explaining the details of the investigation to date. I omitted some unpleasant detail.

I couldn't see a need. I didn't mention that I suspected, with increasing horror, that the battered female under her care and bearing Sharon Jaco's name was Katherine Mae Pritchard, who was officially dead and buried in Brown County, Oklahoma.

She listened without comment, my story diverted only when she walked into the kitchen twice to bring back my two beers and another drink for herself. When I had concluded, she stared at me silently for several seconds.

"What do you want from me?" she said.

"How did you get the vital statistics for Jaco?" I began. "I know that Parkland sent out her name and some clothing, but how did you know to call the Garland Avenue Children's Home?"

"Her uncle called with the information. I think it was an uncle. At least a relative."

"How do you know it was a relative?" I tried to act nonchalant and confident. I was fumbling.

"Because, Mr. Kobok," she said patiently, "he asked to talk to her attending psychiatrist, and I asked him for her background on the telephone."

"Was it a local call?"

"No. He called twice, and both times the long-distance operator placed the call to me in person. He didn't know Jaco's exact date of birth or other facts, but he knew to refer us to the Garland Avenue Home."

"Would you know the voice if you hear it again?" I asked a stock police question for want of a better comment.

"No. Well, probably no."

"Did he have an accent?"

"Not that I remember. He was concerned with learning details of the extent of damage that would be permanent. I told him the prognosis was probable brain damage, that's why Longview had her. He never called back."

"Naturally, he didn't identify himself or leave a number or address?"

"No, he only said he was her relative. He knew enough about her to convince me. And we needed all the info we could get."

I was considering as many possibilities as my simple mind would grasp.

"What kind of boots are you wearing, Kobok?"

"Justin, lizard."

"How did you get that scar under your eye?" She had leaned forward and was studying my face.

"Fell off a church pew."

"You really have a nice face, Kobok. Ugly, but sexy at the same time. You do have sort of a rumpled appearance, you know, rough and ready, but tough."

"Yeah, I know."

She might have needed an ophthalmologist if she saw my face as nice.

Her expression had softened. She was gorgeous. As she leaned forward her half-shirt pulled up on the side, revealing tan skin.

"Thank you, Doctor," I said trying to keep my voice from scratching. "There is something that I've wanted to say to you from the first moment in your office." Of course, I didn't tell her what I had been thinking since I first met her. It's probably illegal to say that sort of thing to a professional person.

"I wanted to say how impressive it is to meet an attractive, professional lady who has accomplished so much at such a young age. I mean you're an M.D. and much younger than me. Very impressive, actually." I struggled for a grip. I needed to focus here and ignore carnal thoughts.

Focus went to hell in a wheelbarrow when she got up and

moved to my chair. She straddled me, facing me with knees jammed into the corners of the soft chair. It is truthful to say that this was the last thing on my mind. But as I've said before: "A man does what he has to do, regardless of the sacrifice." With her up close, straying from the mission was not difficult.

"I'm warning you, I don't usually put out on the first date," I said as she smothered me.

"This is the second," she said, softly. "The other day can count as the first."

My specialty was low-class broads. I was a little out of my league with this lady. However, it only took less than an hour to realize that professional ladies have the same needs and general inclinations of answering-service queens.

CHAPTER 36: THE LAW OF PROPER TIMING

A problem that should have been nipped in the bud can often result in having to bludgeon it to death later, when the constable fails to comprehend the problem.

She pulled back on the shorts and half shirt, leaving her bra on the floor. "Are you hungry?" she asked, prompting me to wonder if they trained psychiatrists to read minds. I was ravenous.

"Yes," I answered. "Let's find an all-night restaurant."

She ignored my comment and glided back into the kitchen.

In moments she was rattling dishes and pans. We had eggs, ham, and the works right in her little kitchen. God, this lady is marrying bait, I thought. Then I regained my senses after a few seconds of that kind of thinking.

She poured me another cup of coffee. "Kobok, I'm going to take a chance with you."

Jesus, I wondered what she had in mind to climax the past hour. I waited.

She brought a small portable tape player and a cassette into the kitchen and inserted the cassette into the machine. Her cultured voice drifted out of the machine.

"Dr. Kay Teneris, Longview State Hospital." She gave the date. "It's Friday morning, nine A.M., and I am conducting my second of two preliminary interviews with Sharon Jaco, patient number J75014, Ms. Jaco has been with us for a few days and has suffered some physical and cognitive injury from being beaten. Sharon, can you hear me?"

The voice I had heard emitting from the patient velcroed to the bed days earlier answered, "Yes."

The first fifteen minutes or so of the tape was occupied with

Kay probing into the background of the patient. She eventually progressed to the question,

"Sharon, you told me yesterday about Katherine. Can you remember that?"

"Yes."

"Have you seen Katherine lately?"

"Katherine's dead."

"What happened to her?

"I…I can't…"

"How did she die? Was she sick?"

"He killed her. He killed her."

"Who killed her, Sharon?"

"If I tell, he'll kill me, too."

The voice dissolved into sobbing. There was a long pause and a click, as if the recorder had been turned off while the patient regained some control. Kay studied me across the table. She said nothing. Again, I waited.

Another click. Then, "Can you talk to me now, Sharon?"

"Yes … I think so."

"You were going to tell me who killed Katherine."

"I can't."

"How did he kill her?"

"Beat her. Hit her with his fists. Hit her on the head, hard."

It was a tortured answer. Pain dripped from the horrible undertone in the girl's voice. I was now certain that we were actually listening to the voice of Katherine Pritchard, not Sharon Jaco. But something beyond normal understanding was being said.

"Where did it happen?"

"In my apartment."

And then my lightning bolt of revelation belatedly fell when the voice painfully said,

"He killed us both. He killed us all. He made me do it."

She fell again into uncontrolled sobbing.

A series of clicks followed, indicating that Kay had again turned off the recorder. I was hearing the implications, but I wasn't sure I understood what the voice was saying. Kay's voice came sharply:

"How many others did he kill, Sharon?"

"I don't know."

I was now considering that the girl in the apartment might not have been either Katherine or Sharon. How many others? Holy hell. The voice immediately clarified the situation.

"He killed Sharon. He tied her to my bed and did...his awful thing things. He never did it to the rest. He burned her. Said she'd given him a disease."

More sobbing ensued. Kay reached across her kitchen table and flipped off the machine.

"Merry Christmas, Kobok," she said, eyes again cold. I read from her expression that it hadn't occurred to her that the body I had described in Katherine's room was not Katherine Pritchard. I think she assumed that the Sharon the voice had just described as being murdered was only a confusion of names. Someone with a powerful domination of Katherine had used her to lure Sharon to her death. A death that Katherine must have witnessed, or even participated in. A shiver worked from my belt line up my back.

"Did the tape make you sick, Kobok? You don't look so good."

"No, no, I'm fine," I said. "Just too many short nights."

"I'll bet," she said defiantly.

"Kay, did your staff run tests on Sharon Jaco?"

"Tests?"

"I mean, does she have any venereal disease?"

"No."

That was because Sharon Jaco, with herpes, was buried in Katherine's grave, and Katherine, without herpes, was in a ward in Longview tied to the damn bed under Jaco's name. I was the only person who knew, except the murderer.

The killer had to know she was in the Longview hospital, because it had to be him who referred Kay Teneris to the Garland Avenue Home. And the only way he could have known Jaco... or Pritchard passing for Jaco, was in Longview was to have known that she had first been in Parkland in Dallas.

"Kay, did Jaco bring along any personal effects?"

"I don't know. I know she didn't have any identification,

because when the guy called me, I checked. No purse or anything."

"Where could I check to see what she brought in with her?" I smelled blood.

"The admitting unit keeps a record. They have a storage facility in the building where they keep personal effects of patients." She looked at me strangely, between cold and warm, if that's possible.

"Take me there," I probably said a little too authoritatively. "I mean, can you take me there, please?"

"It's one A.M. in the morning, for Christ's sake." She was smiling. A first.

"It's important," I said. It wasn't important, it was catastrophic.

"Kobok, has anybody ever told you that you're nuts?"

"Frequently, thank you. But I'd like to see her personal property, now, if possible," I said.

"Well, I can try," she sighed, and got up to walk toward the front door.

She sat in the driver's side of the seat as we rode downtown. Without warning, she leaned across and gave me a lingering, wet kiss on the lips, which didn't improve my driving capability. I swerved and nearly wiped out a section of downtown Longview. Man, think of how the accident report would have read on that one. We rolled up to the hospital gate, unscathed. The attendant was a different man than I had encountered earlier.

Kay got out and talked to the attendant, who took one look at her scanty outfit and would have plunged straight through the gates of hell at her request. He probably hadn't realized that the good doctor had that much skin.

The gate attendant had called the night admitting clerk, who greeted us with a look of skepticism. He brought out a small cardboard box and handed Kay a clipboard, bearing a sheet of paper that she was required to initial before he would relinquish the box. He left us, shuffling back to his chair in the next room.

"Kobok, you're probably getting me fired this very moment,

even as we stand here in this ridiculous situation," she said, giving me another little peck on the cheek.

I pulled off the tape binding the box and opened it to its sole content: A hip-length man's raincoat. It was one of those canvass-type garments that sell for about six dollars at any discount store and that usually can be relied upon to turn away at least ten percent of any precipitation falling about the wearer. It was the cheap kind of garment that might be issued to workers in mass.

"Damn, she wasn't wearing much more than I am," she giggled, girlishly unprofessional.

I went over the coat. It didn't take long. The pockets were empty. I looked for markings. Under the collar, in laundry marking ink: initials "W. P."

Holy mother of Jesus!! Was it possible? Could W. P. be Willard Pritchard, locked up in the Brown County Jail? I returned the coat to the box to the attendant, poker-faced as I could be.

"Well, Sherlock, enlighten me," she said finally as we drove away in the early morning darkness.

"I'll go back and try to assimilate this into what we already know," I said, struggling to withhold emotion, and information. We drove back to her condo in silence. I made my good-bye after a protracted necking scene in front of her place.

"Well, Tarzan" she said sincerely, "you've loved me, and now you're leaving me. Will I ever have occasion to see you again?"

"Look, I need a shrink about thirteen times a week," I said. "I'll call you until you're tired of my action. It's only a short hop over here." I didn't tell her chances were good that hop might have to start from a distant location.

She gave me another meaningful kiss before slipping back into her silent act, popping out of the car, and slinking away. It was 2:15 A.M.

I gassed up the Chevrolet at the first entrance to Interstate 20 and bought a road map to determine if I could cut across country to Brown County, Oklahoma. I could and I did, at speed.

I drove through the coming dawn. The moon was full, large, and red. I had heard my mother comment many times that when the moon took on that hue, it was known as "blood on the moon." How appropriate.

The trick Charlie had spoken of: gray hair, a regular from way back. Christ, he'd been a regular from childhood. The men's clothes in Katherine's closet. That must be Willard Pritchard.

"John Jones" brought her to Parkland and left his coat bearing the initials W. P. Only John Jones would have known that she had been transferred to Longview. The appearance of Willard Pritchard at his old residence after years of absence came too soon after the funeral. Too close for coincidence. Damn, I should have seen it much sooner. Stupid, stupid, stupid.

Willard Pritchard, in some perverse way, had known enough about Sharon Jaco to use the knowledge to try to hide his hideous crime by calling the Longview hospital with false leads to her identity. He had probably checked Katherine into Parkland in desperation after beating her. He probably used Sharon Jaco's name on the spur of the moment. The idea to call Longview must have come later.

Willard Pritchard and the Katherine case were the end of me. I could partly atone by choking that pervert bastard to death in a jail cell.

CHAPTER 37: THE LAW OF THE PERCEPTION OF TRUTH

The truth is often right there in the shadows, visible, if you'd only take time to look closely.

With the help of truck-stop coffee and wanton disregard for the traffic laws of 145 miles of highway, I arrived in Wilby at just past 7:00 A.M. The town was still sleepily calm, but the sheriff's car was already parked in his reserved spot. Two other marked Brown County cars were parked in front of the court-house along with an ambulance, red lights flashing.

I hurried through the door of the sheriff's office, expecting a jail-break. The news was worse. I encountered Sheriff Decker in the outer hallway, his face ashen.

"Kobok, how the hell did you get here so quick, fly?" he asked.

"More or less," I answered.

"He used the mattress. Goddammit, I've fought with the commissioners for years over those things. I kept saying that some body was going to hang himself with one of those damn things. Too fragile and easy to tear into strips."

"Hanged?" I said.

"Yes," he looked at me, surprised at my apparent ignorance in view of my presence there. "Night jailer found him at six thirty this morning as he was making his final check. He tore up his mattress, made a rope, tied it to the bars, and jumped off the damn bunk. It didn't break his neck though, just choked him to death. If we had found him a few minutes earlier, we'd have saved him. I ain't surprised. Willard always was crazy as hell."

"Did he leave a note or tell anybody anything?"

"Nothing. I guess I'll drive out and tell Thelma. I doubt she's gonna miss him much."

I asked him for directions to the Pritchard farm, explaining that it was routine. He wrote them out, and I promised him that I'd have breakfast and give him the chance to break the news to her before I drove out.

I walked back over to the drugstore and watched the effervescent lady prepare heaps of food. My appetite was dulled by the night's activities, as well as by the middle-of-the-night snack I had enjoyed earlier in Kay's apartment. I dawdled in the drugstore over coffee for over an hour.

As I sat at the drugstore counter, I considered what I was going to say to Katherine's mother. I didn't have a brainstorm, so I decided to play it by ear. Following the sheriff's directions, I herded the Chevrolet out to the Pritchard farm. The sheriff's car was gone when I got there.

White frame house faded to the color of ashes. Brush creeping close to the house and out-buildings. Fences on a lean, gates down. The place appeared about as I would have predicted. It struck me as even more forlorn because of the tragic circumstances that had devastated the occupants.

She had opened the front door as I turned into the drive and was waiting for me behind the screen door. The sheriff had told her I was coming. The wind across the loft of a decaying barn behind the house greeted me with an Oklahoma moan, the sound muted, like the distant lowing of a lonely calf.

I showed her my credentials. "My name is Kobok, Mrs. Pritchard," I tried to say gently.

"I know. The sheriff said you were coming by." She looked worse than many I had seen stretched out in Westra's stainless steel parlor. She invited me in and offered coffee. I accepted, although I had ingested about a quart while loitering at the Wilby drugstore. The interior of the house was shabby, worn, old, and musky but spotless. Her face and her surroundings were classic despair.

I took my second cup of coffee before I could really force myself to ask any questions that touched her family.

I spent two hours probing. I heard the story of her life unfold from the date Katherine's older brother started first grade until Katherine quit the Farmer's State Bank and moved to Dallas. She spoke of early years with her husband, of Katherine's high school basketball career, of her son's enlistment in the United States Marine Corps. At length, I concluded that Katherine's demise at the hands of a friend was no worse than she had expected. This lady died the traditional separated parent's thousand deaths each night since her daughter had moved to the city to take an "executive" job. She had always lived in horror that the city held only the promise of a violent end for Katherine. I'm not really certain that she was surprised the morning Sheriff Decker had driven out to deliver the final message. Mortally wounded, perhaps, but not really surprised.

"Was Katherine missing any teeth, Ms. Pritchard?"

"Yes, got her two left front teeth knocked out in a basketball game in her junior year."

The appearance of Willard after so long should have been unexpected, but her manner hinted that she knew more about Willard's years of absence than she was saying. It was something in her manner of speaking of him. Perhaps it was her way of referring to him too easily in the present tense.

When she discussed Willard, which she did surprisingly freely, a strange expression of hatred and longing framed her face.

Whatever Willard had done, it ran deeper than breaking down the front door.

I mulled the idea of telling her Katherine wasn't dead. But Katherine was dead. At least dead for all intents and purposes. Brain damage, psychiatric disorder, facial disfigurement, a vegetable. All her mother would get from the knowledge that she was in Longview would be a large bill from the state. I looked around. She couldn't handle any more bills.

Morning would soon pass to midday. I couldn't bring myself to tell her. I rationalized that telling her could wait. I unloaded in an area where she seemed more likely to bend but not break. "Mrs. Pritchard, we have reliable information that Willard may have been involved in crimes of violence since leaving here."

She looked at me, hesitant.

"Is it possible, Mrs. Pritchard, that he could have been a sex offender?"

I expected a volatile reaction. I got agreement. The Pritchard's were a never-ending source of surprise. She faded to coffin white anguish, eroding her kitchen face.

"Yes, Mr. Kobok, he was a disturbed man," she began. Then she evolved a story of incest and horror that even a low rate loser like me would have had trouble believing if I hadn't already known the conclusion.

She sat there in her shabby kitchen and told me that Willard had molested Katherine repeatedly for years before he was confined to the Muskogee Mental Hospital. Thelma had threatened him with the sheriff for his abuse of her daughter, and the weeklong squabble had culminated in the sniping incident that had caused him to be sent to the mental hospital.

Although he had lived away from the residence afterwards, the years of abuse had caused a deep psychological attraction by the girl for her father. She told me that the records didn't reflect that Katherine had run away from home several times. She said that she always suspected, but never knew, that Katherine had fled to her incestuous father. A mother's horror of horrors.

After the move to Dallas, Katherine had told her once, during a visit, that she had seen her father. Katherine had hinted of an instance where her father had used her to bring other younger women to him.

Mrs. Pritchard didn't seem to remotely suspect the real horrible truth beyond Katherine's partial confession to her mother. The aberrations of Willard and the victimized Katherine had progressed beyond group sex to a grisly mutilation murder. More than either of them could apparently handle. I didn't think Thelma Pritchard could handle it either.

"He won't bother you again, Mrs. Pritchard," I said, borrowing a Clint Eastwood imitation.

"No, I suppose not, Mr. Kobok," she stared out the window.

CHAPTER 38: THE LAW OF THE ZOOKEEPER'S SURVIVAL

Civilized men who are appointed as zookeepers must, of course, be constantly vigilant to avoid being destroyed by the animals. They must be even more vigilant to avoid allowing their behavior to degenerate to the level of those jungle creatures, thus destroying themselves.

I made my good-byes and fled south on Interstate 35 in midday Friday traffic—Fled in headlong haste. What the hell could I have said to Thelma Pritchard? Could I have salved the wounds? No. I drove toward the Red River in the rising heat.

I could clear the investigation by "exceptional circumstances." That meant that although the investigation was solved, the circumstances did not allow prosecution. The death of the defendant by suicide was certainly cause for no prosecution. I could avoid another no potential rating by this classification—a last gasp of a desperate man.

I had suspected Charlie/Doris, Jaco, and Higdon. Each was guilty of something- perhaps helping to destroy Katherine. Under the law, none was accountable for Katherine's death because she still lived.

The interstate sped smoothly past. "Exceptional circumstances" would include a full narrative of events leading up to the suicide of Willard Pritchard. In all probability, there would be an inquiry to determine if I was in some way responsible for forcing Willard Pritchard to hang himself. I wished I had, but I hadn't.

They would retrace my steps as only IAD rats could and would undoubtedly find a patient in Longview under the name of Sharon Jaco. Could they piece together that Jaco was dead and buried in Brown County Cemetery and that Katherine was the brain damaged patient in Longview? There was no reason to assume that I was smarter than the follow-up team from Internal Affairs. When they figured it out they would proceed directly to Wilby to tell Thelma Pritchard of the next and probably final chapter in her lingering horror story.

Jaco was a homeless, wretched, largely unwanted misfit with incurable herpes and only God knew what else. Her tombstone in Brown County was superior to anything Dallas County would have given her as a pauper. Nobody missed her, and nobody would inquire unless I told them by filing an exceptional circumstances clearance. Willard Pritchard had been in Dallas all along. The man's clothes in Katherine's apartment were his. He was the gray-haired trick who had been Katherine's "regular." Now he was dead, dead, dead.

Had I managed to reach a courtroom with a case against him, even if he had given full confession, it would have been difficult to get a conviction in view of the condition of the only witness against him: Katherine. I hoped that he was receiving his trial at the moment in a court where the rules were more absolute. Surely, when he got to hell, he'd be confined in a different chamber than liars, adulterers, and fallen doves. It had to be different some way. It had to be.

Katherine was receiving professional care superior to anything she would be exposed to if she were not a ward of the state. Blow the whistle and the State of Texas would ship what continued to live as Katherine to Brown County Oklahoma.

All three had wasted away their lives in the ugly, unforgiving cycle of the street. Live for today, because there is no tomorrow. All of them were out of tomorrows. Thelma was close to the same.

Howdy Doody James would be laying in the gap for me on this one. I pulled into the garage at 3:30 P.M. The air inside had been re-used again and again until little oxygen was left. I walked through the basement and found Chadsey supervising his crew as they fed paper lunch to the incinerator. The heat of hell kept them in front of the small opening for only seconds at a time.

Chadsey greeted me good-naturedly, as usual. He and his entire crew were soaked wet with perspiration.

"Get your ass over here, Kobok, and hang around while I take my gin break," he called.

I strolled over, held at some distance by the wall of heat radiating from the opening of the incinerator. I studied the opening. Anything that went through that hole was gone in vapor in seconds.

I looked at the fat file folder in my hands, concealing the horror of the Pritchard family. In another violation of ATF rules, I had taken the master file from records. It contained the morgue photos, the dental charts, records of Jaco's unpaid bills, and the end of Katherine May Pritchard. Wait until the news media gets a smell of that. Katherine, Willard, Sharon- would become household words. I pictured the news trucks in Thelma's yard, swarms of news people in Sheriff Decker's office. But without this master file, they had nothing.

"Screw you, Howdy," I said, as I threw the file into the incinerator.

"What?" said Chadsey, startled.

"I wasn't talking to you," I said. "Just getting rid of some trash."

"Right on," he laughed.

I stopped in the first-floor restroom. Having not shaved or changed the night before heightened my haggardness. I walked into the office to be greeted by Howdy Doody James, whose very presence meant a village somewhere was being denied an idiot.

"Well, where in the hell have you been this time?"

"Out," I replied as calmly as I could.

"What the hell kind of comment is that?"

"English declarative. Check your grammar textbook." I said, trying to brush by him.

Again, he retreated. "What's the status of your crispy critter deal?" he asked.

I sighed. "It's not going to make, James. I'm going to have to no potential it." I walked back to my desk.

He could barely conceal himself. He was so happy to see

another of my cases fail that he actually smiled.

I began looking through my desk to see what I would need when transferred. Most of that stuff I could throw away. I would get the notice in a week or two. I had always liked the Dolphins anyway. Maybe the trip from Miami to hell took longer than from Dallas. I got out an old road map of the Eastern United States and folded it out on my desk.

I could see James through the glass partition in his office stealthily talking into the telephone, calling an ally in headquarters to report his good fortune. He'd managed to stab somebody.

The telephone on my desk buzzed. It was Tootie. She told me to call Bull Hooper. I assumed he wanted to borrow money.

Hooper was not around the office. The Homicide desk man said that he could find him and have him return the call. I hung up and resumed studying my road map.

The telephone buzzed in a few minutes. It was Bull Hooper.

"Reverend Kobok here," I said.

"Where the hell you been?"

Everybody was concerned for me when I was out of sight. "Nut house and jail," I said, "and points between. Oh yeah, I seduced this good-looking female psychiatrist and went to a hanging. And I read a road map of the East Coast."

"Boy, you tell a hell of a story," he said. "But did you do anything exciting?" If he had believed a word of what I'd said, he would have hung up immediately. It was just as well.

"Listen, damn it," he got down to the commercial, "when TAC ran in on that Morales biker, Asshole, we caught him with enough assorted dope to start a drugstore. He's lookin' at three felonies and/or fifty years. He ain't wantin' to go back to the joint any longer than he has to. He's willing to give up his dope connection in return for some assistance with the district attorney and the court on these dope cases."

"Son, you want the dope cops," I answered.

"Just listen. His connection is the head of the East Texas chapter of the Spiders motorcycle gang. Morales can't say for sure when the guy'll be holding dope, but he says there was a whole case of M-16 fully auto machine guns under his bed two days ago. Asshole says he's willing to put on the wire and go inside. If we'll help him cut a deal with the prosecution in this case, he'll testify."

"Oh, my," I said.

"Yeah, Kobok, and I'll tell you something else. This guy used to snitch to the DPS. They verified that he was reliable. We can certify him as reliable for search warrant probable cause today."

"Oh, my," I said, Miami fading from view. "We gotta go to East Texas. I'll pick him and you up in a half-hour."

I folded up the East Coast map and walked into the supply room. I picked up forms for authorization to place the wire or listening device on the informant, a form for submitting the informant's name to headquarters, search warrant forms, and other necessary food for the paper mill of the criminal justice system.

I walked past Howdy's office without looking in. He swaggered to the door and glared at me. "Where you gonna hide now?" he shouted, his voice carrying the knife edge of triumph.

"I haven't got time for you right now, Howdy," I threw back over my shoulder. "I've got to get over to Longview to get a search warrant together for the residence of the president of the Spiders biker gang. I'm coordinating a major investigation in that area by us and several other agencies. I may be gone for a week or two. I'll call Tootie with a telephone number." I walked out.

It occurred to me that I'd fed Kay's numbers to Chadsey's incinerator. She wouldn't be hard to find.

I'd drive out to Spring Valley to pick up some clothes and to tell Tad that I'd be gone for a few days. My deal with his mama, Anne, was loose and transient at best—a sort of a catch as catch can, temporary gig. No "true love" deal was involved. I'd work my way back soon enough but would not have been surprised if she'd found other friends. I'd find a way to stay close with Tad, no matter what mama did.

I wondered if Longview was ready for Bull Hooper and me at the same time. Maybe Kay had a great big girlfriend who had trouble getting dates her size. In fact, maybe she had two great big girl friends for Hooper.

"Oh, for Christ's sake," Howdy said weakly as the door closed behind him. As I reached the elevator, I could hear him shouting the same epithet over and over. I think he was upset. I certainly hoped that his strange behavior wouldn't get him transferred to Miami.

The heat in the parking garage was too hot and putrid to fully breathe. Outside, traffic was just north of stationary. As I squeezed into traffic, a delivery truck driver laid on his horn and shot me the finger. It was another beautiful day in north Texas.

.

ABOUT THE AUTHOR

Gary Clifton, forty years a cop, including a twenty-five-year career as an ATF Agent, has spent a lifetime squarely in a free front row seat to the damnedest show on Earth. Having been shot at, shot, stabbed, sued, lied to and about, and frequently misunderstood, there is no violent crime, vicious situation, nor clever criminal subterfuge he hasn't seen. Of the many tales he's written, each is based in some actual crime he's handled, with names changed only to protect the guilty. He has a master's in psychology, an invaluable tool in trying to unravel the violence human beings can inflict upon each other.

Clifton published a novel, Burn Sugar Burn in national paperback in 1987. Since, he's found more fertile ground in short fiction pieces. The Toronto based magazine, Bewildering Stories, has published more than fifty of Clifton's stories. He has published upwards of sixty more in various venues, including Broadkill Review, The Simone Press, Beat to a Pulp, Yellow Mama, Rusty Nail, Crack the Spine, and numerous others.

Currently, he's retired to a dusty North Texas ranch where he doesn't much give a damn if school keeps or not.

A selection of Clifton's work is available on his blog at:

http://www.bareknucklethoughts.org.

Curious about other Crossroad Press books?
Stop by our site:
http://www.crossroadpress.com
We offer quality writing
in digital, audio, and print formats.